THE
CALCULUS
OF
MURDER

THE
CALCULUS
OF
MURDER

Erik Rosenthal

A Thomas Dunne Book

St. Martin's Press
New York

Excerpts from "I was a Prisoner at Santa Rita" by Tim Findley
© San Francisco Chronicle, 1969. Reprinted by permission.

Design by Amy Bernstein

Typeset by Fisher Composition, Inc.

Library of Congress Cataloging-in-Publication Data

Rosenthal, Erik.
    The calculus of murder.

    I. Title.
PS3568.08374C3   1986   813'.54   86-11374
ISBN 0-312-11412-5

First Edition

10 9 8 7 6 5 4 3 2 1

In memory of Esther S. Rosenthal:
mother, friend, always there when needed.

THE
CALCULUS
OF
MURDER

$\int 1$

GREGORY LANGLEY

Well, I've solved the case.

It was on the plane ride home from Portland. I was depressed. It was raining in Portland, and the pilot said it would be raining in San Francisco, too. I sat there thinking about how I had blown the interview at Reed. They wanted someone who knew computer science, and I insisted that mathematics was much more interesting. I explained to them that I did know computing, but it was mathematics that really turned me on. They said that they felt the same, and that that was why they needed a genuine computer scientist. So much for Reed. At least I wouldn't have to leave the Bay Area.

I wondered how a week could start out so well (what with the Raiders winning the Super Bowl and me finally catching up with Herbert Delkin), and end so poorly, feeling that there was no future.

I thought about the Melton case. I looked through my notes, not expecting to find anything, when the solution came to me suddenly—there was only one possible explanation. But before I reveal the identity of the killer, let's review the case from the beginning.

My involvement began on Monday, November 10, 1980. I was awakened early in the morning by a telephone call. A wrong number. I made coffee and read the Sunday paper. The coffee was good; the paper was not. That's probably why I was reading the Sunday paper on

1

Monday morning. (I never could understand why San Francisco didn't have a decent newspaper.) A front page headline read, "Clothing Magnate Slain." The story said that fashion manufacturer Bradford Melton had been poisoned at his fifty-fifth birthday party Saturday evening. I was interested because a friend of mine at Berkeley had written a magazine article exposing the sweatshop conditions in Melton's Chinatown plant. The Sunday story did not say much, but Monday's *Chronicle* had more information. Melton's daughter, Susan, had been arrested, and the police claimed to have conclusive evidence: She and her father had been fighting for years because of her involvement with SDS (in case you've forgotten, *SDS* was *Students for a Democratic Society*, the leading radical student organization of the sixties); she was engaged to a former "Berkeley activist"; she stood to inherit; she had access to the poison. Inspector John Ashe, who was in charge of the case, refused to give further details.

I turned to the sports page. The Raiders had won their fifth in a row. Plunkett was playing well, and the defense was getting stronger every week.

I tried the crossword puzzle—anything to avoid the inevitable phone call to Greg Langley. Calling meant telling him that I had failed to serve the subpoena on Herbert Delkin.

Serving subpoenas is what started me in this business. I came to Berkeley in 1967 with two friends, Greg and Jim Berkowitz. Greg wanted to be a lawyer, Jim was planning to study economics, and I was a budding mathematician. We had been friends at Brooklyn College and drove to California together in my '52 Studebaker Champion, which blew a piston in Fresno. It cost $280 to have the engine rebuilt, and we spent two trying days there.

By 1972, Greg had become an attorney with Halloran and Mackey, a left-wing law firm in Oakland. Greg and I

2

had been active in SDS, and we knew (which is to say, I was defended by) Halloran and Mackey. (Jim was a staunch Democrat, but we loved him anyway.) Jim had taken a position in the Department of Economics at Stanford University, and I was still working on my dissertation.

The Department of Mathematics at Berkeley rarely supported a graduate student for more than four years, and the $5,000 that I had borrowed from my parents was running out; lack of funds might have prevented me from continuing my studies. Fortunately, the Fates were on my side. Greg asked me to serve a subpoena for one of his clients, paying me $20 for what turned out to be less than an hour's work. I suggested he call on me again. He eventually gave my name to other attorneys, and before long I was serving ten subpoenas a week. After a while I got pretty good at it, and I began specializing in finding people who could not be found. I can remember one case in which a key witness had not been seen for several months. . . . But that's another story.

I finally finished my Ph.D. in 1976, the primary significance of which was that I knew a lot about bounded linear operators on a separable infinite-dimensional Hilbert space, but little that was useful to anyone outside a university. This left few choices besides teaching, which was fine with me because I wanted an academic job. The problem was my unwillingness to leave the Bay Area. There are not that many colleges and universities in or around San Francisco, and none wanted me. Serving subpoenas remained, and I applied for a private investigator's license. It was three years before the application was finally approved because of a couple of arrests (no convictions) during peace demonstrations at Berkeley. The license did not guarantee clients, however, and I was still tracking down witnesses long after it came through.

A few days before the Melton murder, Greg had hired me to serve the subpoena on Herbert Delkin. Greg's client was PURE (People United to Restore the Environment). Its goal was to save redwood trees in northern California. One member of "The Delkin Industries family of fine companies dedicated to serving people" was a lumber company logging redwoods. PURE was not arguing that all redwoods should be left standing, but rather that they should not be logged so indiscriminately. Since Delkin Industries tried to picture itself as an enlightened conglomerate "set up to meet the needs of a changing population," PURE seemed to think that getting Delkin himself on the stand would put him in an awkward position, and somehow that would change the world. It didn't seem to me to be a very good idea, but I was willing to serve the subpoena as long as they were willing to pay my fee.

That brings us back to that Monday morning and to Susan Melton. I thought that I might have known her at Berkeley, but I could not remember her from SDS. I finally decided it was time to call Greg when the phone rang. I picked it up and said, "Hello Gregory."

Pause. A voice with a phony foreign accent said, "Run! Zee F.B.I. eez comink for you."

"Greg, I can always recognize your ring. I suppose you want to know about Delkin."

"Later, Dan. Heard about the Melton murder?"

"I was just reading the *Chron.* I think I may have known Susan Melton from the good ol' days. The story said she was in SDS, but I can't remember . . ."

"She was in RSU. She didn't get to Berkeley until 1970 and was active for only a couple of years. She's my client, and we're trying to bail her out now. Danny, it's time you had a real case."

"We could talk before the game tonight. Get here by seven. I'm making one of my curries."

4

"Hot and spicy, or for general consumption?"

"Hot and spicy."

"You're on. But we better meet for lunch. I'd like you to talk to Susan. The bail's high, but her mother's getting it together. She should be out by noon. The Café Bancroft."

"If it doesn't rain, I'm playing tennis with Jim at eleven, so make it one. Here."

"Make it the Café Bancroft. I'll pay for lunch."

"And then bill it to your client. See you later."

It didn't rain, but it was cloudy and cool, and I never fully warmed up. Jim won both sets.

I arrived at the Café Bancroft at 1:30. Greg was not there, which didn't surprise me since he's always late. The Café Bancroft is on Bancroft Way, a half block east of Telegraph Avenue. Telegraph is the main drag in South Campus, a twenty square block area south (naturally) of the Berkeley Campus. (Yes, there is a North Campus, but I have never heard anyone speak of a "West" or "East" Campus.) On and near Telegraph there is an amazing variety of small shops, bookstores, and street vendors, and a larger variety of eateries. South Campus is crowded with all sorts of people from early in the morning until midnight, seven days a week. In the late sixties, it became a haven for dropouts who wanted to turn on. "The South Campus Circus" was a common description. There was major reconstruction along Telegraph in 1971, and since then as many tourists as natives can be found.

The South Campus scene is especially interesting on a Sunday afternoon. If you stroll down Telegraph Avenue, the most striking feature is the sundry street vendors, reading books or newspapers behind tables displaying their wares. Many sell clothing or leather goods, pottery or jewelry. You expect the prices to be low but are in for a shock when you ask. As you saunter along, you are struck by the assortment of people. On one corner you see a barefoot musician wearing ragged jeans and a torn T-shirt playing a bass fiddle. He is accompanied by a well-dressed violinist, and they are surrounded by fifteen listeners. The violin case is open, and you notice a few coins and a dollar bill in it. Across the street you glimpse a man in a business suit praising the ways of Jesus. On the next block you observe six men in pink and white robes with partly shaven heads chanting "Hari Krishna."

You continue walking and a young woman says to you, "Can you spare fifty cents?" (It was a quarter when I was a student.) Then you see a man who has not shaved or cut his hair in three years and appears to have been wearing the same jeans and shirt since he last had his hair cut. He is sitting on the windowsill of a delicatessen and explaining to the world that it is time to abandon materialism. Nobody is listening. And throughout your stroll you observe crowds of spectators intermingling with the participants.

The Café Bancroft is on the second floor of a modern building. Most of the tables are on an outside terrace, overlooking Bancroft Way. They serve an assortment of coffees and pastries and have a limited but quite good luncheon menu. I had a capuccino while waiting for Greg, who finally showed up a little before two. He was alone.

Gregory Langley is five-feet-eight-inches tall with wavy black hair. He is a bit on the pudgy side and looks rather awkward. We've been good friends since our freshman year at Brooklyn College.

He pulled up a chair and said, "Sorry I'm late. We're still trying to get Susan out. She and her mother should be here soon. I'll tell you what I know while we're waiting. But first, what's the problem with Delkin?"

"What makes you think there's a problem?"

"Danny, if there were no problem, you'd have called me this morning. I had to call you."

6

"There's really no problem, but I haven't served him yet. I went to the Delkin Tower on Friday and got as far as his personal secretary. She was a woman in her fifties and looked like a pushover. I told her that I was acting as an officer of the court and had to see Mr. Delkin on official business."

"Go on. Go on," he said. "This one I've gotta hear."

"Well, she asked the nature of my business, and I said I had a subpoena. She said, 'Is that the same as a warrant?' and I said, 'Just about.' 'But is it something I can handle?' 'No,' I said, 'I must give it to Mr. Delkin himself.' She said, 'Then I'm afraid you'll have to wait a couple of weeks because he's in Houston.'"

"So you blew another one," he said.

"I don't blow that many, Greg. And I do have a lead."

"What's your lead?"

I smiled and said, "I followed one of the secretaries home. Got her name and address. If I turn on the ol' charm . . ."

"The last time you did that, you billed me for a $70 dinner. Don't count on PURE paying that kind of expense."

"Greg, you have a short memory. That particular dinner led to my serving a subpoena two days before you went to trial. And that witness saved your client's ass."

"Okay, okay. But try to keep the time and expenses down. PURE doesn't have that much money."

"Greg, forget it. You'll pay my bill in the end anyway. Tell me about the Melton case."

"I don't really know very much. I spoke to Susan yesterday and this morning, but I'll let you question her. It would be better for you to hear her story directly from her. I also spoke to the assistant D.A. in charge of the case. A man named Arwyn Feldnor."

"And what did you get from him?"

"Not much. He doesn't want to reveal his case."

"Sure," I said. "But he would give you the highlights."

"He did. And I'm convinced that Susan's innocent."

"You, of course, have to think she's innocent."

"Perhaps, Dan. But that's not relevant. Your job will be to find out what really happened."

"Suppose I find out she's guilty?"

He stared at me for a few seconds and said, "Don't!"

I returned his stare and then nodded. "Tell me about the circumstantial evidence."

"Bradford Melton was fifty-five years old on Saturday. His family gave him a party at Le Petit Chateau. Before the dinner was served he collapsed. He was rushed to a hospital and died shortly thereafter. The autopsy revealed that he'd been poisoned with arsenic. Susan had been sitting near her father. Traces of arsenic were found in his wine, which she had poured."

"Is that all? Sounds pretty thin."

"There's more. Susan and her fiancé, Billy Raskin . . ."

"Raskin?"

"The one and only."

"Go on," I said.

"Susan and Raskin bought rat poison that afternoon. Something called Rat Ravager. Feldnor said the police found an open box in their apartment. And a receipt for it dated that afternoon."

"And of course Rat Ravager contains arsenic?"

He frowned. "Yeah. Arsenic trioxide. The poison that killed Melton."

"They couldn't establish that the arsenic came from Susan's box?"

"No, certainly not. But Feldnor claims they can prove Rat Ravager was the source of the arsenic. Because of other ingredients."

I sat back and said, "That's not so thin. What did Susan say about the rat poison?"

"I haven't talked to her since meeting with Feldnor."

"One thing's bothering me . . ."

"Only one thing?"

"One thing in particular. The police acted very quickly. Melton was killed Saturday. By Sunday evening an autopsy had been performed and enough evidence gathered to arrest Susan."

"That is strange. I guess they pumped his stomach in the hospital on Saturday, found arsenic, and got right to work."

"Maybe, Greg. I guess we'll have to . . ."

I was interrupted by a female voice behind me calling, "Greg!" I turned and saw two women. One was perhaps twenty-seven, five-feet-four-inches tall with long brown hair. I recognized her from my student days. I did not remember much about her, but I did know that I had not been very fond of her.

The other woman was in her fifties, thinner and taller than the first, with gray streaks in her hair. She looked rather stern and walked with authority; she was used to giving orders.

Greg and I stood, and he introduced us. "Mrs. Melton, Susan, this is Dan Brodsky. Dan, Alice and Susan Melton."

∫2 SUSAN MELTON

Greg said softly to Susan, "Are you all right?"

Mrs. Melton answered. "She's fine. I'm sure we'll have everything straightened out shortly. I've called our attorney, Jason Bealer, and he's talking to the district attorney. I don't know why we're talking to you today."

Susan spoke up, quite sharply. "We're meeting with Greg because he's a good lawyer. He defended Billy and got him off when he was arrested last year during the strike. *I* trust him. Besides, Mr. Bealer is a witness and certainly can't be my attorney."

"And what is *he* doing here?" Mrs. Melton said, pointing at me.

"I asked him to join us," Greg said. "He's a private investigator and can do a lot of the legwork for me. We need him."

"Well, I'm sure there will be no trial," Mrs. Melton said. "Once Jason talks to the district attorney, they'll drop the charges."

I suggested we order lunch, and the conversation changed to the menu. I ordered quiche and coffee (the Café Bancroft makes a potable cup of coffee). Greg ordered a chef's salad (he's always on a diet). Mrs. Melton also had the quiche; Susan said she couldn't eat anything. I mentioned how well the Raiders were doing, but when Mrs. Melton said, "*What* are the Raiders?" I said nothing. The food was served, and we ate in silence.

When we finished I said to Susan, "I'll want to go over the dinner party in detail, but first tell us about . . ."

"Why is *he* asking the questions?" Mrs. Melton said.

"I've already spoken with Susan," Greg explained. "Dan needs the same information. If he asks the questions, we may find out something new."

Mrs. Melton seemed to accept that explanation. I thought Greg was being much more patient with her than necessary. He didn't need clients that badly. Of course, I did, and I began questioning Susan again.

"Tell us about Saturday afternoon."

"Saturday afternoon? What's to tell?"

I said, "There's a report that you and your fiancé

bought some rat poison, and that it was that rat poison that killed your father."

Susan seemed stunned. Was she acting for our benefit, or was she genuinely innocent?

"We did buy rat poison, but only because we have a rat problem in our apartment."

She began to cry. Greg put his arm around her and said, "Don't worry, Susan, we'll take care of everything. Dan's a good investigator, and he'll find the real killer."

I remembered why I had not liked her when I was a student at Berkeley. She was the "poor little rich girl," misunderstood because of her wealth. She could turn the tears on and off at will; she was used to getting her way; she was a spoiled brat. I was convinced that she was also capable of killing her father, but there were two unfortunate consequences of proving her guilty. First, there would be little chance of getting the Meltons to pay my bill. Secondly, perhaps more important, it would not do much for my then nonexistent reputation as a private investigator. After all, I was being hired to help, not convict her. I concluded that Susan Melton must be innocent.

"You don't have to prove your innocence to us, but we do need to know what we're up against," I said. "Now, Susan, what was the rat poison you purchased?"

She looked at Greg as if to ask, "Must I answer?" and he nodded. "Rat Ravager," she said.

"Why did you buy the rat poison on that particular Saturday afternoon?"

"Billy and I live in an old house in Albany. We have part of the first floor and the basement. There are rats in the basement. I can't stand rats." She screwed up her eyes and contorted her face to show how much she detested rats.

"But why did you buy the poison that day?"

"We didn't make a special trip. We were driving along

Grove and saw the Berkeley House and Garden Shop. I asked Billy to stop."

"So you didn't go out with the intention of buying the poison?"

"No."

I stared at her, trying to give her the impression that while I was considering what she said, she would not be able to lie to me. Greg gave me a dirty look. I sipped my coffee and said, "Okay. Tell us about the dinner party."

"Gregory," Mrs. Melton said, "who's the attorney here?" She didn't like me very much. The feeling was mutual.

"Dan may be rude," Greg said, glaring at me, "but we can trust him. I've already discussed what happened with Susan, but it's important for Dan to question her himself. Answer his questions, Susan." He gave me another dirty look. I smiled to myself but managed to keep a straight face.

"Let's start at the beginning," I said. "When did you get to the restaurant?"

"We arrived at 6:45. We'd told everyone to get there at seven, but Mother thought we should be early. So Mother, Father, Billy, and I were there at a quarter of. Ralph, of course, came with us."

"Ralph?"

"Ralph Cordova," Mrs. Melton said. "He was Bradford's bodyguard."

"Was a bodyguard necessary?"

"Certainly. After the strike last year, with all those student radicals." She looked at her daughter with obvious disapproval. "Bradford thought it best."

"So he's worked for you for only six or eight months?"

"Actually for several years. Bradford occasionally had trouble."

"What kind of trouble?"

"Well, just some trouble."

I wondered what she meant but didn't push the point. "What can you tell me about Cordova?"

"He had been a policeman before working for us. I don't know much about his personal life, but he's been a perfect bodyguard. Quiet and unobtrusive but there when you need him."

"Have you ever needed him? Any incidents requiring his services?"

Mrs. Melton paused and then said, "Bradford felt safer with him around, especially since the strike."

"Who else was there that night? Try to name them in the order they arrived."

Susan answered. "It must have been close to seven before anybody else came. Roger Mayfield arrived first. He's Dad's accountant."

"Personal or business?"

"Both," Mrs. Melton said. "He does our personal income taxes, but he's also the comptroller of Fabricon. Bradford, of course, is, uh, was president and chairman of the board."

"Who came next?"

"Uncle Henry and Aunt Margaret, I think," Susan said. She looked at her mother, who nodded agreement. Susan anticipated my next question. "Uncle Henry is my father's older brother. He's executive vice president of Fabricon and also a member of the board."

"He's the older brother, but your father was the boss?"

"That's correct," Mrs. Melton said. "The business was started by Susan's grandfather, Elias Melton. It was originally a small, one-man operation, producing women's fashions. Henry began working for Elias in 1943, Bradford in 1946. Elias died in 1950, and Bradford and Henry inherited the business. It had grown quickly in the postwar boom, mostly because of Bradford."

"When was the company incorporated?"

"In nineteen fifty-one or fifty-two. They merged with

another firm and incorporated. The name was then changed to Fabricon, Inc. Bradford naturally assumed command because it was his shrewd business sense that was responsible for the company's rapid growth."

"I see," I said. "Do you think Henry might have resented having his younger brother as his boss?"

"I shouldn't think so," Mrs. Melton said. Her tone left no room for discussion.

"Who else was at the dinner?" I asked.

"My brother, Joseph, and his wife, Doris," Susan said. "Joe also works for Fabricon."

"What does he do there?"

"He's in sales. He deals with big department stores."

"Does Doris work for Fabricon too?"

"No," Susan said. "She's a high school teacher."

"What does she teach?"

"Chemistry."

Chemistry? Poisons are chemicals. Keep that in mind. I said, "Was anyone else there?"

"Yes," Susan said. "Jason Bealer and his wife, Sarah. Bealer, Martin, and Wood. They're Fabricon's law firm. And, of course, Mr. Bealer does all the family's legal work."

"He's a close personal friend," Mrs. Melton added. "He and Bradford went to school together. Stanford."

"They were the last to arrive," Susan said.

"What time was that?" I asked.

"Maybe a quarter after seven."

"Then what happened?"

"We had drinks and sat talking for a while. Then we ordered our dinners. Wine was served, and so were the appetizers. Father collapsed before the entrées arrived." Susan began crying again. Greg gave me a look that said, "Keep your mouth shut!" before I could say anything.

Susan calmed down. I sat back and said, "How were you seated around the table?"

Mrs. Melton answered. "Bradford was at the head of the table, and I was at the opposite end. Billy Raskin was on his right, with Susan next to him. My son was on Susan's right, with his wife next to him. Roger Mayfield sat next to Doris on my left. On Bradford's left were Jason, his wife, Ralph, Margaret, and Henry."

I took note of the seating arrangement and said, "Did anyone get up after you were all seated?"

Mrs. Melton answered, "We toasted Bradford with our drinks, and then everyone congratulated him."

"Was that before or after the wine was served?"

"It was after," Susan said. "I remember Father tasting the wine and saying, 'satisfactory,' just before Roger stood up and said, 'I'd like to propose a toast.'"

Greg, who had been quiet during my questions, leaned forward and asked, "Did anyone come near the table other than the waiter?"

"There was a waiter and a waitress," Susan said. "I can't remember anyone else at the table."

"The maître d' did come back to congratulate Bradford," Mrs. Melton said.

"Come *back*?" I said.

"We had the room behind the bar."

"A private room?"

"More like semiprivate," Susan said. "The way the restaurant is set up, the bar is toward the back. There's a small room behind the bar. The restrooms are near there, and the room is not closed off."

"That makes every patron a possible suspect."

"Was your father seated near the restrooms?" Greg asked.

"Not really. The restrooms are along the wall opposite the table."

"Did you see anyone near your table?"

Susan said, "No," and her mother agreed.

"One last question," I said. "Who will profit, financially or otherwise, from your father's death?"

Mrs. Melton answered, "No one. You see, while several people are in Bradford's will, Fabricon's success is due largely to his leadership. Without him, profits will fall. The stock went down eight points this morning. Everybody would be better off if he had lived."

It was after three by then. I found that I liked Mrs. Melton even less than Susan. I said, "Well, that should be enough to get started. I'm late for a seminar, and I have exams to grade by tomorrow morning. I'll call if I need more information."

Mrs. Melton said, rather haughtily I thought, "Are you a teacher or a private investigator?"

"A private investigator," I answered, admittedly in a somewhat condescending voice. "But I do teach a calculus course at Berkeley and attend a seminar on Monday afternoons."

Greg told them not to worry, several times in several different ways, and he and I left together. Once out of earshot of the Meltons, Greg said, "What's the matter with you?"

"Susan Melton is a pain in the ass, and her mother is worse. Look, Greg. You know me. I'll do the best job I can. But I don't have to like them."

"What have you got against Susan?"

"Everything. She's a spoiled brat. In any case, I'll expect you by seven tonight. Jim and Anne are coming, but we can still talk during dinner. I do have to get going—the seminar does start at three."

∫3
HYPATIA

Monday night is poker night unless the Raiders are playing. There are five regulars in the game in addition to Greg and myself: Jim Berkowitz, who drove to California from New York with Greg and me in 1967 and is now a professor of economics at Stanford; Paul Hobart, my dissertation adviser when I did my graduate work at Berkeley and still in the math department there; Marilyn Greene, a CPA with Smith, Whalen & White, short and plump and one of the sweetest people I know; Joel Carpenter, a mathematician who perished at Berkeley because of insufficient publications, and who now runs a successful computer consulting business with a six-figure income.

The seventh player is Anne Howe. She's tall and slender with long brown hair and blue eyes. We met as graduate students and had a thing going for two years. Though the relationship cooled, we remained good friends. She completed her doctorate in 1970 and is now the head of the Department of Mathematics at Mills College in Oakland.

We've been playing poker on Monday nights for seven years. The game started after a housewarming party when I moved into my apartment, and we've been playing there ever since. The apartment is on the top floor of an old building in Berkeley, with a view of San Francisco, the bay, and the Golden Gate. The game is on the terrace when it's warm and in the living room with a fire going when it's cool. Of course, the primary function of the fireplace has to do with wine, music, poetry, and women.

Some players usually arrive early and have dinner. On this particular Monday, Jim, Anne, and Greg were due. It was 5:30 by the time the meal was prepared; I decided my students could wait until Thursday to get their exams back.

I put on Beethoven's Violin Concerto and took Hypatia (my pet guinea pig) from her cage. Guinea pigs are basically pretty stupid, having brains that weigh less than five grams. Hypatia's is probably closer to three, but she's soft and cuddly, and she likes music, especially Beethoven. She was named after the Greek mathematician and philosopher Hypatia, who may have been the last scholar to study in the library in Alexandria. The then young and growing Christian church considered the library to be a center of paganism and destroyed it, obliterating untold volumes of literature and scientific accomplishments. Hypatia was brutally murdered by a band of monks led by Cyril, the archbishop of Alexandria. Her writings have been lost; Cyril was made a saint. Hypatia's death in A.D. 415 may be taken as defining the beginning of the Dark Ages.

I put Hypatia in her cage and realized that I hadn't cleaned it in more than a week, although it ought to be done every three or four days. I let her run wild in the bathtub, carefully removed the newspaper from the cage (the *Chronicle* has many uses other than lining garbage pails and starting fires), and put in fresh paper. There was a short article about Brooklyn accompanied by a picture of the Brooklyn Bridge. I put the picture on top thinking she would enjoy the scenery and returned her to the cage.

I checked the food and prepared for the game. It's a fairly small-stakes affair—dime ante, three raises, fifty-cent maximum. I'm the most regular winner, but it should be noted that poker players are notorious liars—none has ever admitted to being behind for more than a single evening.

Anne and Jim came together at seven. Anne, as usual, went to pick up Hypatia, and Jim noticed that she was eating the newspaper. He said, "Hey, Danny, your guinea pig is eating the Brooklyn Bridge."

"What? Oh. Don't worry; newspaper is a mainstay of her diet. I understand the *Chronicle* is very nutritious. It's the only paper I ever feed her. Let's eat. Greg's coming, but you never know when he'll show up."

Greg finally put in an appearance at 7:30. We were almost finished. He sat down and said, "Hi Anne, Jim. How's the food? Where's the hot sauce?" He dumped some curry on his plate, gulped down a couple of mouthfuls, and said, "I hope I'm not interrupting anything interesting, but I have to talk to Danny. By the way, all of this is private and not to be repeated. We're dealing with a murder case."

Jim said, "A murder? You're kidding." And Anne said, "Not the Melton murder?"

"That's right." Greg turned to me and said, "Well?"

"I don't know. She could be guilty, but I'm assuming she's innocent. I'll have to interview all the guests at the dinner, not to mention the maître d', the waiter and waitress, the bartender, and probably some of the patrons. I'll also try to talk to the cop in charge. But it will surely be several months before it comes to trial, so there's time."

"Of course, Danny, should you find the real killer, there'd be no need for a trial."

I smiled and said, "I'll do my best. Have I ever let you down?"

"Ha!"

I ignored him. "Did you notice that everyone at the dinner was connected with Fabricon? I'd love to get a

19

peek at their books. Try to set it up, Greg. Maybe we can get Marilyn to come along—she'd know what to look for."

Greg nodded and went on eating. Jim and Anne assured us they would not discuss the case with anyone and then asked for details. I told them a little. I had a few more ideas to discuss with Greg, but the other players showed up, and we didn't get another chance to talk.

The game was a good one (that means I came out ahead). There was one hand that stood out, the last of the night. It was seven-card stud. Anne and I were each up by more than fifteen dollars. I was dealt a three and a five in the hole and a second three face up. Anne had an ace showing and bet it. My next two cards were queens, and Anne pulled another ace and a ten. Jim had three spades showing, Greg had a possible straight, and Anne kept betting her aces. Paul and Marilyn dropped, and Joel stayed in with nothing. I then got another three, Anne a second ten, and Jim his fourth spade. Anne kept betting as did Jim. I was sure he had the flush, which was fine with me since I already had a full house. But Anne made me nervous—she had bet her ace from the beginning and was likely to have the third one in the hole. Greg and Joel were nervous about everybody and dropped.

We pay royalties in our game, which means that if anyone gets four-of-a-kind or a straight flush, the other players each pay him or her fifty cents. It's a kind of icing on the cake. Such hands come up once every three or four weeks, which is to say not very often. I mention this because my last hole card was the fourth trey. Anne bet fifty cents, I raised, and for reasons I'll never understand, Jim bumped on his flush. When Anne bet the last fifty cents (only three raises are allowed), and I called, Jim began to worry, but he called.

Anne, as the last better, showed her hand first. She smiled and said, "Gentlemen, I'm afraid I have the third ace." She had every reason to be confident—only royalties could beat her aces full. Jim threw down his hand in disgust, and Anne began raking in the pot. I tabled my cards without comment.

Anne stopped, looked at my cards, looked at me, and without changing the expression on her face said, "May you wake up in the morning as an aardvark and find no ants in the sugar." Jim had taken a big swig of beer and started choking, spewing beer all over the table. That ended the game (it was after one o'clock), though I did manage to gather in my winnings.

$\int^4$ ELAINE HARRIS

I awoke early the next morning to prepare for my calculus class, which ran from nine to eleven. We were studying techniques of integration, and I needed examples to illustrate the use of trigonometric substitutions. For most topics it suffices to choose several examples from the homework problems in the text and to do them for the first time in front of the class. Some trig substitutions, however, can take an hour to complete, and the method may be lost among the details. As a result, the examples require careful consideration before presenting them in class.

I did manage to plan the lecture and to arrive in class on time. One student was waiting for me outside the classroom. He did have a question about calculus, but the real reason he was there was to see his exam. Some students become so hyper about tests they can't sleep until they know their grades; this one couldn't wait for me to enter the classroom. I promised to return the exams Thursday. (I did, in fact, make time Wednesday evening to grade them. Several of the students who had been suffering anxiety spasms then felt that if I had waited until the following Tuesday they could at least have had one last good weekend.)

I went up to my office after class to begin the Melton investigation. The easiest place to start would be with the police officer in charge. I dialed and a female voice answered, "San Francisco Police Department."

"I'd like to speak with Inspector Ashe."

"Please hold."

A male voice. "Sergeant Waymar."

"I'd like to speak with Inspector Ashe."

"Who's calling?"

"My name's Dan Brodsky. I'm calling in reference to the Melton murder."

"Hold on. I'll see if he's in."

Another male voice. "This is Ashe. What can I do for you?"

"My name's Dan Brodsky. I'm a private investigator working for Susan Melton. I . . ."

"Braden, if you think I'm gonna help you get that killer off, you're nuts!"

"It's *Brodsky*. Look Inspector, we both want the same thing: to discover the truth. I thought we could talk about it and help each other . . ."

"Sounds to me like I'd be doin' all the helpin'."

"Not necessarily," I said. "One hand can wash the other."

"Still seems like I'd be doin' all the washin', Borsky."

"*Brodsky*. I thought we could talk about it. Maybe we could meet somewhere."

"All right. Meet me across the street in an hour. How will I know you?"

"I drive a '52 Studebaker. You can't miss it."

"Okay. I'll be in a squad car. Be on time. I won't wait." He hung up.

When I reached the police station, there were several squad cars parked across the street. Only one was occupied, and I pulled up next to it. The man in the car got out and opened the door to my car. He was about six feet and two hundred pounds—it was not all muscle.

"Binsky?" he said. "I'm Ashe." He got in and said, "Drive."

"It's Brodsky, Inspector. *Dan Brodsky.*" I drove.

"Okay. Okay. Brodsky. Let's get down to business."

"How's a hundred sound?" I said.

"For that I'll tell you the charges."

"All right. Make it two hundred and I'll pay for lunch."

"For that I'll go to lunch with you," he said.

"How much, then?"

"Five hundred."

"You've gotta be kidding. I can't get that kind of money."

"The Meltons have it. This is a capital case, you know."

"There's no way I'm going to get five hundred. They don't even want me on the job. It's their lawyer who hired me."

"Okay, Brodsky. Make it three hundred."

"For that I want a copy of the file."

"You got it. When do you wanna meet?"

"How about tomorrow?"

"Fine," he said. "Get here before noon and we'll go to lunch."

After dropping him off, I called Greg and described the arrangement with Ashe.

"That's fine," Greg said. "I'd've expected to have to pay at least five hundred."

"Yeah, me too. Can I stop by your office for the money tomorrow morning? I suspect he won't take a personal check."

"Sure. Come by about eleven."

My next stop was an address on Balboa. I had made a real error in underestimating Delkin's secretary—I should have realized that anyone as powerful as Delkin would be difficult to reach. Unfortunately, he would now be aware that someone was trying to subpoena him, and it would be necessary to be a bit more devious. That first attempt was not a total loss. I had waited in the lobby and had followed a secretary who worked on the same floor as Delkin's office. She lived on Balboa in the Richmond District, and I went to her building and parked across the street.

I was sitting in my car when she arrived home from work and disappeared into her apartment. I was still working on my approach when she reappeared and walked to a supermarket. She was five-feet-six, slender, with auburn hair and green eyes—following her was not unpleasant. I took a cart and tracked her down an aisle containing bread and dairy products. She squeezed the sourdough French breads, and I eased my cart by to examine the cheeses. She moved toward me. I took a couple steps backward, banged into her cart, took a dramatic spill landing on my back, grabbed my ankle, and let out a terrific cry.

"Oh my god!" she screamed, bending over me. "Are you all right?"

She was genuinely concerned, which made me feel slightly guilty, but I ignored my feelings and said in obvious pain, "I think so. My ankle hurts." I stood slowly and "tested" it. By then the store manager was coming over to investigate, and I said, "Can you help me to my car?" I put my arm around her shoulders, and she led me to the parking lot. The manager watched us carefully, perhaps afraid I would sue.

She helped me into the car and said, "Will you be okay? Can you drive?"

"Probably. If I sit here a while. Fifteen, twenty minutes rest should do it."

"Oh no," she said in a soft and sympathetic voice. "You can't sit here like that. I live nearby—you can rest at my place."

When she parked my car in front of her apartment, I couldn't remember which ankle had been injured. Either I guessed right or she was amused by my ploy. In any case, she said nothing and helped me out and up the steps into her apartment. She lived on the first floor of an old renovated house. It was a small but pleasantly furnished one-bedroom flat.

"Should I make some coffee?" she said.

"Sounds great."

She helped me to the kitchen and into a chair. She got a second one to put my foot on. "I hope instant is okay?"

"Sure," I lied.

The difference between an insult and a casual comment is often a matter of timing. Suppose, for example, you're at a friend's house for dinner, and some delicious-looking bread is served. You spread the butter on thick, take a bite, and discover . . . margarine. If you remark on its unpalatability, your host will be offended. But suppose instead you wait until after dinner, turn the conversation to nutrition and cholesterol, and say, "Do you know that when they make margarine, they take unsaturated oil and change it to a saturated fat so it will harden? It's probably worse for you than butter." No offense. And if you're lucky, the next time you're there, they'll serve butter.

When the teakettle whistled but before she made the

instant junk, I said, "Maybe a cold drink would be better."

"How about some juice?"

"Perfect." And no insult. "By the way, I'm Dan Brodsky."

"My name's Elaine Harris." She handed me a glass of orange juice and made herself that stuff she called coffee.

"What do you do when you're not knocking people down?" I asked.

She smiled and said, "I'm a secretary. I work for Delkin Industries. It's a lousy job, but I can support myself. I'm also taking an evening course at San Francisco State. Computers."

"What evenings does the class meet?"

"Monday and Wednesday."

"Good. Then how about dinner tonight? Perhaps Le Petit Chateau."

"That's a pretty expensive place, isn't it?"

"It'll be worth it if you promise never to knock me down again." She laughed. "Actually, I'm working on a case involving Le Petit Chateau. With any luck, I won't have to pay for it."

"A *case*? What do *you* do when you're not *being* knocked down?"

"I'm an unemployed teacher and pay the rent as a private investigator."

"Are you working on the Melton murder?" she asked, her voice rising.

"That's right."

"I read about it. Isn't his daughter supposed to have done it?"

"Yeah, well, my job is to prove she didn't."

"And the Meltons hired you?"

"Their lawyer did."

"How exciting!"

"Shall we go?" I walked to the sink to deposit my empty

glass when I remembered my injuries. "Gee. My ankle's much better."

∫5
∫ JEAN MARTINOT

We drove to Le Petit Chateau, which is an expensive, highly regarded restaurant on Geary Boulevard in the western part of San Francisco. The maître d' was a short, dark-haired man with a small mustache and a French accent. He seated us in the front by a window.

As he held out menus I said, "Were you here last Saturday evening?" He was not very enthusiastic about the question and did not respond.

"I was hired by the Meltons to find out what really happened." He just looked at me.

"There's a good chance Susan Melton is innocent. Don't you want her to get a fair shake?"

Still nothing. I considered trying to pressure him by implying the Meltons, an important family in San Francisco, might not be pleased if he failed to cooperate. But I knew it would be an idle threat and said, "I'm sure you've been hassled by the cops and reporters. Perhaps in a couple of weeks you'll be able to help. Tonight we'll enjoy the food for which Le Petit Chateau is so well known."

He said curtly, "Enjoy your dinner," and left us to study the menu.

I surveyed the restaurant after ordering. It was one large room except for several private booths along one wall. The bar was toward the back with a wide passageway to its right leading to the restrooms. From our vantage point it was impossible to detect the room behind the bar. I walked to the bathrooms to survey the scene of the murder.

The room was about thirty feet square, the right-hand ten feet or so being the continuation of the passageway from the larger room. It was empty save for a single long table. The door to each john was set off by a partition that formed a kind of entranceway. The effect was that getting to the ladies' room required going into the back room, but the men's room could be entered from the front. As a result, a man who was not part of the Melton party would be more likely to be noticed than would a woman. There was an old-fashioned cubbyhole telephone booth outside the entrance to the men's room. I returned to our table.

I'm more of a gourmand than a gourmet—I recognize good food when it's put in front of me, and I can put away large amounts of it. Paul Hobart's wife likes to invite me for dinner because she knows I will appreciate and thoroughly enjoy what she serves. (Paul would as soon eat a bologna on white as the Chinese specialties his wife prepares.) I don't know how the kitchen at Le Petit Chateau compares with true French cuisine, but to me it was as good as any I've ever eaten. The meal was truly fabulous.

Coffee is something I do know about. We were served a rich blend of a Viennese roast with mocha and Java coffees, and it compared favorably with my own. Even Elaine noticed the difference from the garbage she makes. After her third sip she said, "This coffee is delicious! I wish it was possible to make it this way at home."

"It is," I said, "but it requires some effort. Someday I'll show you how."

She smiled and said, "What do you teach?"

"Mathematics."

"Mathematics? Yecchh. My worst subject in school." She

had a classic reaction. For reasons that are not at all clear, many otherwise intelligent people have a deep-seated fear of mathematics. On most college campuses, the department that gives the lowest grades is mathematics (chemistry is usually second). In the public schools, math courses are the ones most often avoided by students. It's such a common problem that it has been dubbed, "math anxiety," and special programs exist to help students overcome this difficulty. I explained this to Elaine, insisting that mathematics was not that bad. She didn't buy it.

I said, "Then why did you take a computer science class?"

"The company's paying for it. They pay an employee's expenses for taking certain courses. They mostly want the men to take them, but they don't want to appear as if they discriminate against women. They do discriminate, of course, especially when it comes to salaries and promotions. But as long as it was free, I figured I'd try it."

"How's it coming?"

"It was tough at first. But the teacher's great, and I'm beginning to get the hang of it. It's turning out to be a lot of fun."

"Elaine, that just proves my point. The kind of thinking that goes into writing a good computer program is similar to doing mathematics. I bet if you tried a math course now and went into it with an open mind, you'd find it fun, too."

"Perhaps. Maybe next semester," she said. She smiled and added, "If you'd help me."

During dinner I found myself enjoying her company. She was twenty-four and a native Californian, born and bred in Redwood City. She had worked for two years after high school and then gone to San Francisco City College (a community college) and earned a two-year degree. For the last two years she had been working for Delkin Industries. Her father was a bus driver and her mother a bookkeeper. She had a brother and sister, both older and married. I liked her and did not like my reasons for meeting her. I decided Delkin could wait.

The bill came to eighty-six dollars, and the tip made it an even hundred. Greg would love it.

We were working on our second cup of coffee when the maître d' came over and asked, "Was your dinner satisfactory?"

"Excellent," I said. "Truly exquisite."

He stood there a while, apparently expecting me to speak. He said, "Are you not intending to pressure me into answering your questions?"

I smiled and said, "No. I don't think so. Perhaps if I come back in a couple of weeks you'll no longer feel the strain."

"Your attitude is different from the reporters," he said.

"I'll bet they didn't eat here either."

"That is true," he said, smiling genuinely. He paused and then said, "I will answer your questions, Monsieur."

"Are you sure?" I said. "It doesn't have to be tonight."

"As you can see," he said, gesturing with his hand, "it is late and most of our customers have left. This is an excellent time."

"Thank you," I said. "I appreciate it. Are the waiter and waitress who served the Meltons here tonight?"

"They are. We can talk in the back room. That is where the, uh, incident occurred."

I said to Elaine, "Why don't you stay here and enjoy the coffee," and then followed the maître d'. He signaled to a waiter and a waitress, and they joined us. The waitress was taller than the maître d', very slender, with short brown hair. She spoke with a French accent. The waiter was blond, about six feet tall, and might have been a college student.

I said, "Let's start with your names."

The maître d' answered. "I am Jean Martinot, this is

Françoise Journet, and this is Elliot Fielder. Elliot is not French, but he is a fine waiter."

"Thank you. I'm Dan Brodsky." We shook hands. "Is the room arranged the way it was that evening?"

"Pretty much," Elliot said.

"Good. Let's sit down, relax, and try to picture things exactly as they were. Close your eyes and concentrate on Saturday. I know you've gone over everything with the police several times. Forget what you said to them and concentrate on visual images of the Melton dinner party." We sat at the end of the table near the bar, and they seemed willing to follow my instructions. I refrained from speaking for several minutes.

The maître d' began without prompting. "They had reservations for seven o'clock. Monsieur et Madame Melton arrived early with their daughter, a young man, and a tall, muscular man. The others came, mostly in couples, during the next half hour."

"Try to describe exactly what happened," I said.

Françoise said, "When they were all seated, we took orders for cocktails. Elliot took the orders of Monsieur Melton and that side of the table." She pointed to the side near the wall. "I took the orders from Madame Melton and this side. We went to the bar and gave the orders to the bartender. He made the drinks, and we brought them to the table."

"Did anyone have a second cocktail?"

She said, "Madame Melton and the big man sitting next to Monsieur Melton. No others on my side." (From the seating arrangement given to me by Susan and her mother, I assumed the "big man" meant Jason Bealer.)

Elliot said, "Melton himself had three more, and his son and the fellow sitting next to him each had a second."

"Do you remember what Melton was drinking?"

"Yes," he said. "He had whiskey sours."

31

Françoise seemed to blanch. "What is it, Françoise?" I said.

"Rien," she said, looking down at her hands.

"Françoise, that look on your face means something. Please tell me."

"But I cannot. You will get the wrong idea."

"I already have the wrong idea," I said. "What do you remember?"

She looked at Martinot, and he nodded. She said, "When all the commotion started, I was in the kitchen. When I returned to the table, many people were around Monsieur Melton, but I saw an empty piña colada glass in front of him. I noticed because the glass had fallen over."

Elliot said, "I didn't serve anyone a piña colada."

"But I did not either," Françoise said.

"Something like that is easy to forget," I said.

"I did not serve anyone a piña colada," Elliot insisted.

The maître d' said, "You should understand that for us the quality of service is as important as the preparation of the food. Eating at Le Petit Chateau is a total experience. Everyone who works here is carefully trained, and Françoise and Elliot are both very competent. They do not make mistakes. They did not make a mistake on Saturday."

"I'm sure you're right," I said. "The service tonight did match the food. So who could have served the piña colada? Perhaps the bartender?"

"No," the maître d' answered. "He would never leave the bar."

"Could a customer get himself a drink?"

"That's possible," Elliot said. "They often sit at the bar while waiting for a table."

"Of course," Martinot said, "it is very unusual for a customer to go to the bar after he has been seated."

"It's a minor point anyway," I said. "After all, the poison was in the wine. What happened after you served the cocktails?"

"We took dinner orders and brought them to the kitchen," Françoise said. "We returned with the wine, which they had asked us to bring right away."

"Do you remember who chose the wine?"

"Yes," Elliot said. "Melton. He selected a Pinot Blanc and a Chateauneuf-du-Pape."

"Two excellent French wines, Monsieur," Martinot said, obviously proud of their wine list.

"The Pinot is of course white," Françoise said, "and the Chateauneuf est rouge."

Elliot said, "I opened the white wine for Melton to taste. He said it was quite acceptable. The man on his left tasted the other and said it, too, was satisfactory. I poured the Pinot for those who wanted it, and Françoise poured the Chateauneuf. Then we brought second bottles of each and opened them. I put the white wine in an ice bucket on a stand next to Melton."

"You poured the first glass of wine for each person in the group, but not the second?" I asked.

"That is correct," Françoise said.

"What did you do after the wine was served?"

"We waited to see if anything else was needed," Françoise said. "Then we went into the kitchen for the hors d'oeuvres. I returned with my tray, and Monsieur Melton had fallen over. Everyone was shouting and crowding around him."

"Do you remember exactly who was near him?"

"The big man was bending over Monsieur Melton," she said, "and Madame Melton was there, too."

She paused, and Elliot said, "The tall guy was also bending over him. And there was someone from the restaurant."

"You mean someone not in the Melton party?"

"Yeah. She must have been using the restrooms and have come over to help when she . . ."

"*She?*"

He looked at me. "Yes. A woman. Probably forty or so."

"Tall? Short? Fat? Skinny?"

"I don't know."

"I remember her," Françoise said. "I think she was a doctor."

"Do you remember what she looked like?"

"Oui. She had brown hair and seemed, well, ordinary. Nothing special."

"But you would recognize her if you saw her again?"

"But of course."

"Good. What happened next?"

Elliot answered. "Jean came over, and he and I tried to keep everyone away from the table. Someone, I think the son, called for an ambulance, and it wasn't too long before one showed up."

"The police arrived shortly after the ambulance and started asking everyone questions," the maître d' said.

"The police?" I said. "Why were they asking questions? Why were they even here? It must have looked like a heart attack."

"I do not know, Monsieur. But they asked questions and more questions."

"There was a policeman eating here," Elliot said, "and he called for help. He also refused to let any of the patrons leave."

Still seems odd. I would have to ask Ashe about that. I said, "Did they remove anything from the table?"

"Mais oui," Martinot said. "They took everything—plates, glasses, napkins. Everything. It took them an hour to pack. 'Do not disturb the fingerprints,' they kept saying."

I took some notes and sat there trying to picture the situation. "What about the wine," I said. "The one Melton was drinking. What happened to the first bottle after you brought the second?"

"I removed it," Elliot said. "It was a large group, and the first bottle was finished quickly. It was empty when I brought the second."

"And what happened to the second bottle?"

"It was still in the ice bucket when the police took it."

The maître d' looked puzzled. "Monsieur," he said, "now that you mention it, there was a wineglass in the ice bucket as well."

"C'est vrai," Françoise said. "It was Monsieur Melton's glass; the police, they took it too. They asked me whose glass it was."

"How did you know it was Melton's glass?"

"I looked on the table and saw there was no wineglass at his place."

"Are you sure it was Melton's? Could someone else have taken Melton's glass after he collapsed?"

"Je ne sais pas."

"One last question. Do you remember anyone getting up before Melton collapsed?"

Elliot answered. "One of them did. The one next to Mrs. Melton."

"There were two people sitting next to Mrs. Melton."

He smiled. "Yeah. Right. The one to her left." That would be Roger Mayfield.

"Do you know why he got up?"

Elliot shook his head, but Martinot said, "He made a telephone call. I saw him."

"Could he also have stopped at the bar?"

"It is possible, Monsieur, but I did not see him."

"I'm under the impression," I said, "that at one point they all stood to toast and congratulate Melton. Do any of you remember that?"

"We might have been in the kitchen," Françoise said. "I did not see a toast."

"Me neither," Elliot said.

"Well, you've all been a big help. I do appreciate it—almost as much as I enjoyed tonight's dinner."

$\int 6$

DANIEL BRODSKY

I went straight to Greg's office the next morning. He gave me an envelope containing fifteen twenty-dollar bills and hitched a ride with me into San Francisco. I dropped him off and went to meet Ashe.

I'm not very comfortable in a police station, even when I'm there on legitimate business. The reason is simple: My experience with officers of the law has not been pleasant. I was arrested three times when I was a student at the University of California. All were political busts. The first occurred during an anti-R.O.T.C. demonstration at Harmon Gymnasium. This was one of many that turned into confrontations with police. The cops were dressed in riot gear, made free use of billy clubs, and filled the air with tear gas. I was arrested when half a dozen police charged, clubs flying. We ran; I didn't run fast enough. I was charged with disturbing the peace, resisting arrest, and assault with a deadly weapon (a felony). My bail was set at sixty-five hundred dollars!

That was a Thursday, which turned out to be very unfortunate because I was not arraigned until Monday, when my bail was reduced to five hundred dollars.

I remained in the Berkeley city jail for the entire weekend, and because of the large number of arrests on

Thursday, it was crowded. The cells were six feet by eight feet. Each cell had two bunk beds and accommodated four prisoners. There was a toilet without a seat and a small sink with no hot water. There was a single naked light bulb that burned continuously. We were fed twice a day at six o'clock—every six o'clock. Breakfast consisted of inedible powdered eggs, barely edible sausage, a slice of bread, and weak, black, instant coffee; dinner consisted of beans, something that was supposed to be meatloaf, a slice of bread, and the same weak, black coffee. Friends could send cigarettes, books, and small change. The coins were useful because the guards were willing to buy candy bars for the prisoners. By Saturday afternoon the vending machines were empty, and by Monday I had lost six pounds.

My case came to trial several months later. Two policemen testified for the prosecution and told two totally unrelated stories. I was acquitted.

My second bust occurred during a rally on campus when a student from SDS was having a disciplinary hearing. It was a peaceful demonstration, but twenty-seven of us were arrested anyway. This time bail was initially set at five hundred dollars, and I was out within a couple hours.

We were tried in three groups and defended by Halloran and Mackey, Greg's law firm. Mitchell Halloran and Timothy Mackey were young, left-wing attorneys at the time, and Greg was still in law school. He was already friendly with them, and he did some work on the case, but it was Mitch Halloran who handled the actual defense. The first group, mine, was acquitted, and then the other cases were dismissed.

The third and last time I was arrested was during the so-called People's Park Riots in May of 1969. The mass media would have us believe that the confrontations that took place on campuses in the sixties were student riots. This is not accurate. In 1964 and 1965 there were a number of student marches and protests. While there were always police present, they generally did not interfere or interact with the demonstrators, and there were few arrests and virtually no violence (except for certain special situations, notably in the South). In later demonstrations, the police began to disperse crowds with billy clubs and tear gas. Students were angered and fought back, and the police stepped up their attack. A more accurate description of those confrontations would be "police riots."

The People's Park incident is a good example. Of all the encounters between police and students at Berkeley, People's Park was easily the biggest and most violent. The issue involved was actually minor and ultimately unimportant. On Thursday, May 15, there was a student rally that the police attended in force. The Alameda County Sheriff's Department sent its deputies, known in Berkeley as the "Blue Meanies" because of their garb and because of their disposition. They came with shotguns. The rooftops along Telegraph Avenue were lined with Blue Meanies, shotguns poised. Scores of people were shot, including two reporters. The Sheriff's Department maintained that they were using birdshot, but doctors at Herrick Hospital who treated many of the victims said buckshot was used as well. On page 26 of the May 19, 1969, issue of the *San Francisco Chronicle* there is a picture of a youth fleeing an Alameda County deputy sheriff aiming his shotgun. The accompanying article said the young man was shot in the back. Fortunately he was not seriously injured. One student was mortally wounded that day and died on May 19.

The police violence led to larger demonstrations, including a march in memorial to the dead student. Then Governor Reagan called out the National Guard. Two thousand guardsmen were sent to Berkeley; a 10 P.M. curfew was enforced; Berkeley became a city under siege. The fighting continued. On May 20, seven hundred students were trapped on campus in Sproul Plaza and gassed from a helicopter.

I was among 482 people arrested on Thursday, May 22. It happened at a demonstration on Shattuck Avenue in downtown Berkeley. On that particular occasion I was more of an onlooker than a demonstrator, but that made no difference. Everyone in the area was arrested—demonstrators, shoppers, shopkeepers, reporters. More were arrested than the Berkeley city jail could handle, and we were sent in busloads to the county jail at Santa Rita. The atmosphere on the bus was jovial and spirited, filled with camaraderie.

The mood changed suddenly when we arrived at the gates of Santa Rita and the guard on the bus said, "Okay everybody. Move! And I mean move! The first bastard that moves too slowly for me is gonna get a stick up his ass." Believe me, we all moved quickly. We were herded into a compound where we saw several hundred men lying on their stomachs, their faces on the gravel-covered asphalt, more than one of them being jabbed with billy clubs and shouted at by guards. We were then forced to lie prone, face down, and told not to move a muscle. Anyone attempting to relieve the stiffness that quickly enveloped his body received the wrath of the guards in the form of a kick in the side or a billy club in the back. We were held that way for three hours.

Lest you doubt the accuracy of this report, let me refer you to the front page of the May 24 *San Francisco Chronicle*. There's an article entitled, "I Was a Prisoner at Santa Rita," written by a staff reporter who had the misfortune to be assigned to the demonstration that afternoon. The article includes the following excerpts:

At the far end of the four rows formed by the prostrate demonstrators, one young man was erect on his knees, a uniformed guard standing over him screaming and jabbing with his stick.

The pebbles of gravel dug sharply into your cheek, a chilly breeze blew past, and the flat angle at which you could see made it seem that much more frightening as the shiny black boots of the guards marched by, riot sticks tapping at their pant legs.

Throughout the more than two hours we lay on our stomachs . . . a fat gray-uniformed guard . . . shouted threats.

"Don't none of you move—we shoot to kill here."

. . . We were ordered inside an empty barracks, and told to sit on the bunks or the floor. All the windows were open to provide a chilly ventilation.

But first there was a search—the third of the day.

"Face the wall! Get everything out of your pockets and take your belt off, creep."

The rest of the night resembled a boot's first experience with the Marine Crops. First a friendly guard, then a savage one. First an assurance that you could "take it easy," then a snarling burst through the door and orders to "get on your feet—get by your racks."

In the next barracks we could hear people being warned to stay awake or they would be struck.

Occasionally someone was struck or shoved for looking the wrong way or smiling. "You think it's funny, you long-haired creep?"

After that incident, there was a court order restraining the Alameda County Sheriff's Department from beating or otherwise mistreating prisoners. Many suits were filed against the Sheriff's Department, and, if I remember correctly, charges against the demonstrators were dropped in all cases. The charges against me certainly were.

My record is clean: three arrests, no convictions. Still, you can understand why I am less than comfortable in the presence of police.

I arrived at the precinct at 11:45 and was asked to wait. I was seated in a very large room filled with desks and cubbyhole offices separated by glass partitions. Several doors appeared to lead to larger, private offices. The place was crowded and noisy with reports being typed, file drawers being opened and closed, cops coming and going. And everywhere I looked there were cops. Cops, cops, cops. The room seemed to be shrinking. I began to sweat. I kept saying to myself, "You're supposed to be here. You have an appointment. You will go home after the interview. Do not get up and walk out." A more daring soul than I would not have been perturbed by the situation; after twenty minutes I decided that Ashe's file wasn't that important anyway and got up to leave.

A voice behind me said, "Brodsky! Leaving already?" It was Ashe.

"No. I was, uh, looking for a water fountain."

"You just passed it. Ready?"

I tapped the pocket containing the envelope Greg had given me and said, "Shall we go?"

∫7
INSPECTOR JOHN ASHE

We took my car, and I handed him the envelope as we drove. He opened it, counted the money, counted it a second time, and put it in a hidden compartment in his billfold.

"Satisfied?" I said.

"Fine." He reached into his coat and removed a manila envelope that had been tucked into his pants under his shirt. "This is everything."

"Tell me, Inspector. What makes you so sure . . ."

"Hold it. We're almost there." He directed me to a small Italian restaurant in North Beach. "Pull up here."

"It's a fire hydrant," I said.

He smiled. "Don't worry. I'll fix it." He placed a plastic card on the dashboard and said, "That'll do it."

We went in and sat down. I said, "Why are you so sure Susan Melton is guilty?"

"It's open and shut. She's guilty as sin. There's no doubt about it. She killed her father in cold blood. She probably planned it for weeks. And I'll tell you something else. That guy Raskin's involved, too. We have him as an accessory."

"Yes, Inspector. I understand. But on what evidence do you base these conclusions?"

He held up his hand and said, "Okay. Okay. It's very simple. She had motive, method, and opportunity. It's a classic case . . ."

The waitress came over and we placed our orders. Ashe went on with his explanation. "She'll inherit a lot of dough, you know. And if you've seen the place she lives, she can use it. And she hated her father, you know. Lots of witnesses for that. And she hated his business and wanted to change it." He pulled the file from the manila envelope, leafed through it, and handed me a sheet of paper. "Here. Look at this. It's a sworn statement from the guy that sold her the poison."

The statement read:

 I remember them walking in. I was serving another customer, and they drew our attention because

they were speaking very loudly. I heard him say, "But he's your father. You don't want to break ties with your own family."

She said, "Why not? I hate him and everything he represents. All you're interested in is the Melton fortune."

He said, "We could put that money to good use. We could support all the causes we believe in."

They were almost shouting. I may not have the words exactly right, but this is pretty close.

She said, "Billy, that money comes from exploiting workers. Superexploiting them. You walked the picket line last spring during the strike. You remember all the stories we heard. Father's factory is the worst one in Chinatown. And there, they're all sweatshops."

The customer I was serving was embarrassed, but we could not help overhearing. I remembered the strike myself. It had been in the news. I remembered the things she talked about.

The boy said, "But we could change all that if we ran things. How much longer can your father live after the heart attack he had last year?"

She said, "Let's stop fighting about this. I will go to Father's birthday party at Le Petit Chateau tonight. Let's get what we came for and go home."

They came over and asked for some rat poison. The other customer was glad to have me serve them first. I sold them Rat Ravager.

After they left, the customer and I talked about it. The customer wondered if the rat they wanted to get was Bradford Melton. That's why I remember it so well.

After reading the statement I said, "It sounds a little pat," thinking she must be guilty. Raskin too.

Ashe said, "There's a lot more testimony like that, you know. From her friends. No, Brodsky. She's guilty."

"Perhaps," I said. "But don't you think it likely the shopkeeper embellished his story a bit after reading about the murder?"

"Maybe," he said. "But we have lots of corroborating evidence."

"Did the customer come forward, too?"

"No. But the shopkeeper gave us the receipt for the poison, and we found the girl's copy in her apartment along with an opened box of the poison. She's guilty all right. This was an easy one."

For the first time it seemed to me that Susan might be innocent. I never had much respect for her or for Billy Raskin, but nobody could be *that* stupid. I said, "Do you mean to tell me, Inspector, that Susan Melton went into a store and said, 'I hate my father. Can I have some rat poison?' Then she went home and carefully saved the receipt and the unused poison? Nobody in his right mind would behave that way."

"She could plead insanity."

"Yeah, right. It makes a lot more sense if we assume the killer wanted to frame her."

"You're grasping at straws, Brodsky. Sometimes people do incredibly stupid things, you know."

"But not that stupid." There was no point in arguing further, so I said, "You know that Rat Ravager was the source of the poison?"

"Oh yeah. The medical examiner said there was no doubt that arsenic trioxide was the cause of death. It was in his wine, you know. The lab boys had no trouble identifying Rat Ravager as the source. It's a common rat poison. Available all over the place."

"If Rat Ravager is that common," I said, "how can you be so sure the poison in Melton's wine came from the box Susan Melton had?"

"It's common enough, as a rat poison. But how many people use rat poison at all? And there's some direct evidence that she put the poison in his wine."

"Such as?"

"It was in his wine, but there was no arsenic in the bottle, so it was only in *his*. And Susan Melton poured for him."

That bothered me, and I was beginning to wonder again if she might be guilty. He was smiling, as if to say, "No answer for that one I see." I ate some spaghetti.

"There's one thing I've been curious about. There was a cop at Le Petit Chateau that night. That could be a coincidence. But he took charge as soon as Melton collapsed. Why would he have suspected anything? It must have looked like a heart attack or someone choking."

"He was there on assignment. To watch Melton . . ."

"To watch Melton? Don't tell me Susan Melton called you and said she was planning to kill him that evening?"

"No. But there'd been some threats."

The waitress brought coffee. It was acceptable but not good.

"What kind of threats?"

"We're not exactly sure. But ever since the big strike last spring, there've been a number of threats on Melton's life. Probably from disgruntled employees."

"And you've been keeping an eye on Melton ever since?"

"That's right," he said. "He was an important man in this town, you know."

"If those threats were taken so seriously, why do you ignore them now?"

"Because of the evidence, Brodsky. It all points to Susan Melton and Billy Raskin."

"You mentioned Raskin before. Will he be charged?"

"He was arrested this morning."

"For murder?"

"Only as an accessory for now. But we may charge him with homicide. You'll find out soon enough."

The waitress poured more coffee. I drank some and said, "Did it ever occur to you that Raskin's guilty and Susan is innocent?"

"It did. For about thirty seconds. She's the one that poured the wine."

I let it go at that and said, "Let's get back to the officer at Le Petit Chateau. He took charge as soon as Melton collapsed. I presume that nobody was allowed to leave without giving you his name."

"That's right. But there's nothing there."

"You checked out everybody?"

"As best we could. There were almost a hundred people, you know."

"What does 'as best we could' mean?"

"We made sure someone questioned each of them, and the result was that none had much to do with Melton."

"That doesn't sound quite the same as nothing at all to do with Melton," I said.

"There were a couple of former employees. But lots of people have worked for him."

"Maybe somebody was fired and . . ."

"You're reaching, Brodsky. Susan Melton killed the bastard."

"There was somebody who ostensibly went over to help Melton. Anything there?"

"Nothing. Just a doctor who had dinner there. She had been using the restrooms and tried to help. We've checked out everything."

"Then my job should be pretty easy," I said. "Did you know Ralph Cordova? He was apparently a cop before working for Melton."

"I'd never met him. It's a big department, you know."

"But you did check up on him."

"Yeah. He used to work for the narcotics squad. Supposed to have been a good cop."

"One last question. Susan Melton was arrested on Sunday. How were you able to act so quickly?"

"We had an autopsy performed right away because of the threats, so we knew he'd been murdered with arsenic. Then the shopkeeper called us Sunday morning, and that led us straight to Susan Melton."

I nodded and said, "Thank you, Inspector. I appreciate your help."

I drove Ashe back to the police station and picked up Greg.

"How did you do, Dan?"

"Not bad." I handed him the file and said, "Make a copy for me."

"Sure. Tell me about the interview."

"They have a good case . . ."

"Dan, we have to assume she's innocent. It's my duty as her attorney, and if you think she's guilty, you won't be very useful."

"Actually, Greg, I do think she's innocent. She *couldn't* be that dumb. It's all too pat. You might even be able to make a good case in front of a jury arguing that she couldn't have been as stupid as their case implies."

"I'd rather not depend on that sort of argument."

I laughed and said, "Hopefully, you won't have to. By the way, Raskin's been arrested."

"I'm not surprised. Are they charging him with murder?"

"Not yet, but I think they will."

"What next?"

"Interview lots of witnesses."

"Speaking of which," Greg said, "I made appointments

for you with Susan's brother tomorrow afternoon and with the Bealers tomorrow evening."

"Greg, tomorrow's Thursday."

"You gotta be kidding! This is an important case."

"Greg, you know I never do any detecting on Thursdays; that's my research day."

I still wanted an academic job, and having a long list of publications is the best way to be hired by a college or university. A "publication" consists of a written report of accomplished research appearing in a scholarly journal. Research in mathematics means developing new ideas, usually in a very specialized field. Few publications contain important work of general interest, and mine would never be one of those few. The only mathematicians interested in my work are the handful of analysts who care about bounded operators on Hilbert space. I had seven publications at that time, one of which I considered to be quite good.

I said, "If I stop doing research on Thursdays, I'll be a detective the rest of my life. This case won't come to trial for several months—one day won't make any difference."

"But you also never work on weekends, nor on Tuesday mornings. You usually play tennis with Jim on Monday morning and go to that stupid seminar in the afternoon. And then there's the poker game on Monday nights. That's a lot more than one day."

"Change the appointments, Greg. And don't make any for Friday morning because I'm playing tennis."

"Shit!" He laughed. "Who're you playing with?"

"Mitchell Halloran. You remember him—he's your boss."

"Oh god." It was more of a sigh than an epithet. He shook his head in disbelief and said, "What's doing with Delkin?"

"Coming along. I've made contact with a secretary in his office. I'll get him."

"How much is it going to cost me?"

"It already has. We went to Le Petit Chateau on Tuesday. You'll get the bill."

We reached his office in Oakland, and I said, "See you Greg. And keep cool. You don't want to get ulcers."

He got out, and I went home to grade papers.

∫8
∫ HERMAN

I have taught part time at the University of California for several years. The Department of Mathematics usually has a number of sections that cannot be covered by regular faculty or teaching assistants, and, although the pay is not very good, I have always made myself available. I enjoy teaching, and the experience looks good on a vita.

The vast majority of students are good kids. They come to class because they want to learn; some because they really like the material, others because the course is required. One of the more satisfying teaching experiences is to have a student begin a class caring only about grades, and by the end, decide to be a mathematics major. But whatever their reason for being in class, most students respect their instructors and regard them as individuals from whom they can learn.

Unfortunately, there is an occasional exception. There

is the pompous ass who comes to class prepared to prove that he is smarter than you. If, for example, you write "sin x" instead of "cos x," the typical student will raise his hand and say, "Excuse me, but shouldn't that be cos x?" You may be cute and say, "They don't make chalk the way they used to," or simply, "Thank you." The pompous ass, on the other hand, never raises his hand. He just says, in a tone of voice developed especially to show his superiority, "That *must* be a cos x. If it were sin x, it would violate . . ." He then goes into a long explanation, trying to demonstrate how much he knows. He's always ready to jump down your throat. In practice, he is often incorrect and succeeds only in disrupting the class; he is rarely one of the good students.

I returned exams Thursday morning and had a run-in with another type of annoying student—the one who always thinks you are grading him unfairly. He cheats on exams, and I suppose he assumes you must be cheating, too. The one in my calculus class came up to me after class, thrust his exam at me, and said, "You marked number four wrong. It's right." I looked at it and saw that his answer was different from what it had been when I had graded it—he had changed his paper after I returned it! It's not that hard to spot such changes because when a problem is wrong you have to examine it carefully to determine whether the answer deserves partial credit. The funny thing was that he had changed his answer from one wrong answer to another wrong answer—he couldn't even copy the right answer from the blackboard. I said to him, "This is no better than what you had when I graded it." I looked at him and said calmly, "Don't *ever* try to pull a stunt like that again." He started to argue, and I said, "If you think I'm being unfair, go to the dean. End of discussion." He turned red and walked out without saying anything; he caused no trouble after that.

I went to my office after class to do my own work. There was one particular result I'd been trying to obtain for several months. I was convinced that it was a valid theorem but had been unable to prove it. The week before I'd had an idea that I thought might do the trick, and I'd spent a lot of time thinking about it. My goal was to write it out that afternoon. Unfortunately, the best laid plans . . .

In other words, the afternoon passed quickly with no success.

There are certain modern technological devices that are especially disagreeable. One is the self-answering telephone, which talks to the caller but does not listen. Large businesses use them to put you on hold. They assume you need them more than they need you, which is probably true, and they don't care if you have to wait for ten minutes. The worst offenders in my experience are the airlines, with certain insurance companies a close second. Self-answering telephones are also used by individuals who can't stand the thought of missing a telephone call when they're not home. The only justification I can see for these machines is a one-man business in which potential clients might otherwise be lost. If you call me when I'm not in, the recording you hear is, "This is Dan Brodsky. I'm out at the moment, but I'll get back to you as soon as possible. Please leave a message when you hear the tone."

There had been four callers while I was in school, three of whom did not leave messages. Greg's was the last. He said, "I hate this thing, you dumb bastard. Call me as soon as you get in."

Greg's notion of "as soon as you get in" and mine probably differ. I took a long hot shower, had dinner, and looked at the *Chronicle* over coffee. Then I called. He answered on the first ring.

"Gregory Langley speaking."

"You're a very nervous man, Greg. You'll have bleeding ulcers some day."

"Where the hell have you been? Alice Melton is getting pissed."

"Greg, you have to learn to calm down. If not your stomach, then your heart. Be good to yourself."

"Dan, this is serious," he said, speaking more softly. "They want to know what's happening. She's upset because you didn't make the interviews today. She's wondering what she's paying you for."

"Tell her," I said, "that this is not my only case; that the preliminary hearing will not take place for several weeks; that the trial won't start for several months. Tell her I'm on the job and not to worry. Tell her . . . whatever you want."

"Dan, you're a real pain sometimes."

"I know. But what were you so anxious to tell me?"

"Several things. First, I couldn't set up anything for tomorrow. You can see Joe Melton and his wife Tuesday afternoon. He said he'd take off early, and you can meet them at their place at 3:30. Doris will be home by then. The Bealers will see you Tuesday evening at their home, but you should call first. I still haven't . . ."

"Slow down. I'm writing. Okay. You still haven't what?"

"Gotten in touch with Mayfield or Melton's brother, but Ralph Cordova will meet you at your apartment Wednesday morning at eleven. Raskin is being charged with murder. He's asked us to defend him—they want to be tried together."

"What did you tell him?"

"I recommended separate attorneys and separate trials, but they think they should stand together. I've been talking with Mackey and Arnold Miller. I think you've met Miller. He's the kid who just joined the firm. We haven't decided what to do yet."

"From my point of view," I said, "it could make a big difference. My job is to prove Susan innocent. That could mean proving Raskin guilty."

"You'd enjoy that, wouldn't you? Yeah. We have the same problem. Even if they insist on being tried together, and I'm sure the D.A. would love it, we may refuse to defend them both. Ignore the problem for now—we're not his attorneys of record yet."

"Fine. Anything else?"

"No," he said. "Are you going to Anne's barbecue Sunday?"

"Wouldn't miss it. She said I could watch the football game. I think she expects me to insist on putting it on, and then, as long as the TV is blaring, she'll watch the game herself. We used to go to the Cal games together."

"I remember. See you Sunday."

"Good night." He had already hung up. I went to sleep thinking about my lost theorem.

The next morning I awoke well rested and ready for tennis. Mitch Halloran is a fine tennis player, and though I usually play well against him I rarely win. I did not lose that morning. I did not win either—Herman wouldn't start. Herman is my '52 Studebaker, and I spent most of the day tinkering with him. He finally got going late in the afternoon.

You're probably wondering why I continue to live with an old wreck when a car can be an important part of my business. In the first place, the thirty dollars an hour I charge is not nearly as good as it sounds. I average fewer than twenty chargeable hours a week, and I have to pay my own fringe benefits. It's a good month when I'm able to pay the bills on time, and a very good month when I have cash to invest in Herman's future. Even were my financial condition to improve substantially, I would never trade Herman in. We've been together for fifteen years, and he has served me loyally. Most of the time.

I got my first driver's license in 1964 (you must be eighteen in New York). I can still remember my excitement when the license first arrived in the mail. *Name: DANIEL BRODSKY. Id:* (a bunch of numbers). *Height: 6 Ft 0 In. Weight: 165.* (That figure may be a bit higher now.) *Hair: BROWN. Eyes: BROWN.* My eyes are really hazel, but they could handle only brown or blue. A few months later, a neighbor had an old Studebaker he wanted to sell, and I grabbed it for sixty-five bucks. The body was in good shape, it started most of the time if it wasn't too cold, and it got me from place to place. The odometer read 32,654, which probably had very little to do with the actual mileage. When it reached 00000 in 1971, I named it Herman. Over the years, most of his mechanical parts have been replaced or rebuilt. He even has overdrive, and, when well tuned, gets twenty-four miles to the gallon on the highway.

Herman's problems occupied most of Friday, and I spent the rest of the weekend relaxing. Elaine Harris came over for dinner on Saturday, and I found myself liking her more and more.

The meal included matzoh ball soup, which is a Jewish dish, and when I served the coffee she asked me about my background. (Everyone seems to be concerned with his roots these days.)

"My grandfather was a Russian Jew," I said. "He got into trouble during the 1905 Revolution and came to the United States. He spoke no English then, and the customs officer who handled his case wrote down Brodsky, although his name was Broderevski. He ended up in St. Paul, Minnesota, and married an American Indian. They moved to New York in nineteen twenty-three when my father was seven."

"What about your mother's side?"

"She was born in Brooklyn and will probably die there. Her father was an Italian immigrant, and her mother a German Jew. That makes me an Italian-German-Russian-American Jewish-Catholic Indian."

"And I'm only an ordinary Anglo-Saxon," she said. "My ancestors go back three hundred years in this country."

"That's okay. I'm not prejudiced."

She drank some coffee and said, "You do make good coffee."

"Of course."

It was a cold, wet evening, and we spent most of it in front of the fireplace sipping cream sherry, listening to Beethoven chamber music, and reading poetry.

The weather cleared on Sunday, and Elaine went with me to Anne's barbecue. Anne can do terrific things with spare-ribs, and everyone present, which included most of the poker game and half the Mills College faculty, contributed something. We did not watch football because the Raiders were playing Seattle in the Monday night game.

My one fear was that Greg would ask me about Delkin in Elaine's presence. He didn't; the one business discussion we had was held in private. He had duplicated the file from Ashe and gave me a copy.

"Any ideas after reading this?" I said.

"Nothing special. Lots of witnesses."

"That there are. For now I'll stick to those at the birthday party. My assumption is that one of them is guilty."

"That's fine," he said. "Though you might check out the doctor who tried to help Melton."

"Maybe I will. I doubt if anything will come of it. It may eventually be necessary to check out that whole list, but I hope not."

"Did Ashe say the police spoke to every one of those witnesses?"

"He did, but I don't know how thoroughly, even with the manpower they have available."

"Keep pluggin'," he said. He never asked about Delkin, which was just as well.

It was a pleasant afternoon, and driving Elaine home that evening I found myself becoming more and more fond of her. I wanted to avoid getting to Delkin through her, and an article in Monday's *Chronicle* gave me a chance. The Delkin Foundation was establishing a home for runaway teenagers in San Francisco, and he was expected to attend the dedication ceremonies. I, too, would be there.

∫9

RACHEL JANEWAY

There was a message from Jim on the Record-A-Phone when I arrived home Monday morning. He said he could not play tennis but would make the poker game in the evening. That left several hours free, and I decided to follow Greg's suggestion and call the doctor who had tried to help Melton. Her name was Rachel Janeway, and she worked in a hospital in San Francisco. After a half hour of *please hold's* and *I'll connect you's*, I managed to get through, and she agreed to meet with me the following afternoon at one.

I was about to leave for San Francisco the next morning when a student came to my office for help. I don't know if he learned anything, but he did teach me the meaning of the word frustration.

"Professor Brodsky," he began, "I'm a little confused about this trig substitution stuff you've been doing recently."

"It's not very difficult. If you see a Pythagorean relationship under the integral sign, you draw a triangle the way I've been doing it and do the substitution."

"Well, yeah, but, I don't really follow it. I mean, how can you just substitute like that?"

"It's no different from any other substitution," I said.

"Have we done other substitutions?"

I looked at him in disbelief. "You know the chain rule?"

"Yeah, I guess. But isn't that for differentiation?"

I was beginning to wonder if he knew anything. "Of course. But there is a relationship between differentiation and integration. You do know that, don't you?"

"Yeah, sure. I mean, there's a theorem that says something about it, isn't there?"

"Yes. It's called the *Fundamental Theorem of Calculus*. You have heard of it?"

"Yeah, but I mean, maybe I didn't fully understand it."

I didn't have to wonder anymore: He knew nothing. "This entire course is based on that one theorem. If you don't understand it, you're in real trouble." He looked a little worried, and I said, "Do you come to class?"

"As often as I can. You see, I need this course to graduate. But there's also an economics course I need, and it meets at the same time. So I go to one sometimes, and the other sometimes."

I was bewildered but managed to remain calm. "Why didn't you take one of the other sections? This isn't the only Calc II."

"But the other teacher's supposed to be lousy."

"There's also an evening section," I said.

"It meets two nights a week. I can't give up two nights."

"You'd prefer to flunk?"

"No. But I think I can pass."

"What was your grade on the last exam?"

"Thirty-seven. But I'll do better next time."

"Not likely," I said. "In fact, given the questions you've asked me today, I'm amazed you did as well as a thirty-seven. Let me give you some advice. You have virtually no chance of passing this course. Why don't you drop now and try again next semester?"

"But I also need Calc III, and I have to graduate in May."

"Look. Even if you miraculously pass this course, there's no way you can learn enough to be able to handle Calc III."

"You mean I need this course for Calc III?"

"Yes," I said. "Calculus II comes before Calculus III. That may be why they number it that way."

"Oh. What do you think I should do?"

I gave it some thought and concluded that it would likely be deemed unprofessional to advise a student to commit suicide. "Drop this course and take it again in the spring. Then take Calculus III over the summer. It won't kill you to graduate in August."

He looked at me a while and said, "I'll think about it." He left my office, and I never saw him again. I drove to San Francisco for the meeting with Rachel Janeway, unable to understand why it is that education is the one product from which the consumer does *not* want to get his money's worth.

Janeway was a cardiologist working in a large hospital. She seemed to be quite harried when I was ushered into her office. She was a short woman in her forties with a friendly smile. My impression was that she was likely to be a competent physician. She offered me coffee, which I declined, not daring to try a hospital brew.

"You said on the phone yesterday that you're investigating the Melton murder?"

"That's correct," I said. "Melton's daughter has been charged, and I was hired by the family."

"To get her off."

"To find out what really happened."

"Is there a difference?"

"Hopefully not."

"I'm not sure how I can help," she said.

"You were there when Melton collapsed. As a doctor not involved with the Meltons, you can give me a relatively objective account."

"Maybe. What do you want to know?"

"What you saw. What your involvement was."

"My husband and I were having dinner, and I went to use the ladies' room. I saw Melton on the floor. My first reaction was that he was probably having a heart attack, so I went over to see what I could do."

"And when you got there?"

"Several people were crowding around him. I said I was a doctor, and they left room for me to attend him."

"Did you notice who was near him?"

"Three or four people. But I was concerned with the patient and not with the people around him."

"What was his condition?"

"The primary symptom was extreme stomach cramps. He was also sweating profusely, and his heart was beating rapidly."

"Did you still think it was a heart attack?"

"The symptoms of a heart attack can vary a lot," she said, "but I didn't think so. My guess was food poisoning. The severe cramping indicated a reaction to a toxin."

"What did you do?"

"There wasn't much I could do. I didn't have anything with me."

"You didn't try to induce vomiting?"

"No. That could be dangerous, and paramedics could pump his stomach. I told someone to call an ambulance, and one arrived within a few minutes."

"Did you go to the hospital with him?"

"No. I asked the paramedics where they were taking him and then called ahead to the emergency room."

"Is there anything else you can remember?"

"That's about it."

"You've been very helpful, Dr. Janeway. By the way. Did you know any of the Meltons before?"

She smiled, evidently amused by the question. "Mr. Brodsky. Physicians have sometimes had difficulty with malpractice suits in situations like that, but I've never heard of a doctor being accused of murder under those circumstances."

I held up my hand and shook my head. "You misunderstand me. I'm certainly not accusing you of anything. But I need as much background information as possible."

She obviously didn't believe me but said, "Okay. I didn't know any of them."

I thanked her and left to meet with Susan's brother, Joseph.

∫10
JOSEPH AND
DORIS MELTON

Joseph Melton and his wife, Doris, lived in the Sunset in San Francisco. This area is appropriately named because the fog makes it seem as if the sun is always setting, although the appellation probably stems from its location in the western part of San Francisco. Their home is one of the narrow four-story houses common to that part of the city. Because the West Coast does not have hard winters and is supposed to be warm year-round, these homes are not heated properly; and because of the fog, they tend always to be cold.

I arrived at 3:30 and was greeted by Joseph. He led me into a large living room with a twelve-foot ceiling and a big fireplace. It had modern furnishings, and I sat on a comfortable sofa. Joseph was very thin and three or four inches shorter than I. He had brown hair, at least what was left of it, and a small scar in the middle of his forehead. His wife was a short, blue-eyed, buxom blond with a warm smile.

They offered me a drink, which I refused, and a coffee, which I accepted. It was percolated and not very good. They were cooperative, and we talked for several hours. Their description of the birthday party confirmed what I already knew, but there was some useful information.

"After you all stood to congratulate your father, did anyone leave the table?" I asked.

"Roger Mayfield," Joseph answered. "He said he had to make a phone call."

"Anyone else?"

"I don't think so." He looked at his wife. "Doris?"

"Only Roger."

"How long was he gone?"

"It couldn't have been more than five minutes," she said.

There was one question that I felt had to be asked, although I was afraid of what their reaction might be. "Please don't be offended, but there is something that requires discussion." I paused and then said, "Mrs. Melton. You're a high school chemistry teacher?"

"Yes." She spoke slowly and carefully. "So?"

"You have a lab in school?"

"Yes."

"You have arsenic in the lab?"

Her face reddened, but she spoke calmly. "I did not

poison Bradford Melton. Neither did my husband. We have arsenic in the lab, but it is not rat poison. No special knowledge of chemistry is required to purchase rat poison or to put it in somebody's drink."

I wondered what made her say "drink" instead of "wine." Interesting. I said, "Of course. And the police have identified the source of the poison as a commercial product, not a laboratory chemical. But you understand, the question had to be asked?"

She stared at me and then relaxed. "I guess so. Is there anything else?"

"Yes," I said. "Who would have gained enough or despised your father-in-law enough to want to kill him?"

Joseph answered. "Frankly, Mr. Brodsky, my father was not a very nice man. There are only two people I would rule out. Jason Bealer is one, and my mother is the other."

"Why do you rule them out?"

"Bealer and my father went to school together and have been lifelong friends. He's the only man I know who's as ruthless as my father was, and he's the only man who could stand up to my father. They seemed to understand each other, and there was a kind of mutual admiration based on the knowledge that neither could dominate the other. I'm sure they were genuinely close friends. Bealer may well be capable of murder, but not of killing my father."

"And why do you rule out your mother?"

"For exactly the opposite reason. She hated my father, and I'm sure she's happy to see him dead. But you have to understand the nature of their relationship. They haven't gotten along for at least twenty years. Except for social functions requiring joint participation, they've led separate lives. He controlled the purse strings but was very generous with her. She could have anything she wanted. It was typical of the way he controlled people."

"Please don't misunderstand me," I said. "But you make it sound as if your mother had a very good motive."

"She did. But she could never have killed him. For one thing, she loses financially. She got the house but was otherwise left out of his will. The main thing is that she was too afraid of him, too dominated by him. She could never stand up to him, let alone kill him. Believe me, she could not have done it."

"Okay," I said. "Let's talk about the others at the party. From what you've said, you think any one of them might have killed him?"

"No. I said they all had motives. I know I didn't kill him, though I can't say I'm sorry he's dead. I'm also sure Doris didn't do it. Nor Susan. I'd pick Raskin if I had to pick somebody."

"Oh, Joe. You make it sound like a lottery," Doris said. She turned to me. "I can tell you the way I felt about him. 'Hate' is too strong a word. But I certainly disliked him."

"Why?" I said.

"Joe and I first met at Berkeley. We were in a chemistry study group. After we'd been dating a few weeks, Joe brought me home to meet his family. His father was arrogant and domineering, and . . ."

"What was his attitude toward you?"

"He never liked me very much because my family wasn't 'high society.'"

"Did he interfere with your relationship with Joseph?"

"Did he ever!" she said. "The night Joe first told his parents that we were getting married, Joe and his father had a long talk. Joe told me his father had said I was fine for having fun with—that's the way he put it, 'having fun with'—but Joe should marry someone worthy of his background and social status."

"That's true," Joseph said. "He made it sound as if she were a whore. He never forgave me for marrying her."

"Is that why you didn't get along with him?" I asked Joseph.

"No. It's much deeper than that. He always wanted me to go to Stanford, be a football player, attend law school, and take over Fabricon. His first disappointment with me came when I didn't grow big enough and wasn't aggressive enough. When I was around fifteen, he made a remark to me that I'll never forget. 'You'll never be big enough to play football. You'll always be too much like your mother.' That was a real blow to me because I knew how he felt about her, and we never got along after that."

"You mean one remark changed your whole relationship?"

He sat back and said, "No. That was the beginning. I had worshiped him before then, and I had tried to emulate him. He seemed to me to be strong, dynamic, and powerful. He was a man who knew what he wanted and usually got it. Thinking about it now, I realize that remark had very little to do with it."

"What did happen then?"

"No one thing. I began to grow up. I began to understand my mother and what my father had done to her. I had always assumed the problems in their marriage were due to my mother's inadequacy. I started seeing things differently, and I found myself despising him. Because of what he did to my mother. Because of what he was."

"I suppose your father's attitude toward Doris didn't help matters any."

"No. I went to Berkeley because he wanted me to go to Stanford; I majored in physics because he wanted me to go to law school. I made those decisions to spite my father, and the result was meeting Doris." He looked at his wife with a childish grin. "She's the best thing that ever happened to me."

"And yet you work in your father's business," I said.

"I don't want him involved with Fabricon," Doris said.

"But Joe has this idea that he can take over the company and change the way it's run."

"A noble idea," I said. "But if you want my opinion, which you probably don't, it's an impossible dream, regardless of your intentions."

"I want your opinion," Doris said, "because I agree with you." Joseph laughed, and she said, "He could have been a good physicist. We don't need his parents' money, and I'd just as soon say good-bye to the Meltons and to Fabricon."

"Does that include Susan?" I said.

"No. I like her," she said.

I must have grimaced because Joseph said, "I see by the expression on your face that you don't like my sister very much."

"Don't worry. I'll do my best to prove she's innocent."

"I'm sure you will," he said. "Susan's okay. I know she seems like a spoiled brat at times, but she's a good kid. She had it pretty rough. My parents led their own lives and gave her presents instead of affection. She . . ."

"You don't seem to have the same problems," I said.

"It was worse for her."

"Why?"

He said softly, "It was worse." He looked at his feet. Then he smiled and said, "You didn't know me before I met Doris. Susan is involved with that asshole Raskin."

I laughed and said, "I knew Raskin at Berkeley. He and I never liked each other very much, and he's on my suspect list. What can you tell me about their relationship?"

"I'm convinced the reason she got involved with Raskin," Joseph said, "was that he was the one man who would most offend my parents."

"Do you think she'll marry him now that your father is dead?"

"I don't know," Joseph said. "I doubt it."

"That's an important question," I said, "because Raskin doesn't have much of a motive if they don't get married."

"She doesn't know what she wants or how to get it," he said. "I don't know what she'll do."

"I can't be sure either," Doris said, "but I think it unlikely she'll marry him."

"You asked about motive before," Joseph said. "Susan and I had the same motive. I despised my father, and she hated him. We both stand to inherit, and together we could control Fabricon. Perhaps I should have killed him, but I didn't. Perhaps Susan wanted to kill him, but I'm sure she didn't. She's my sister, and I know her very well. She would never have done it."

I liked both Joseph and Doris. They were warm and friendly, and they were speaking candidly with me. I tend to trust people who trust me. Of course they did have access to arsenic and certainly had motive. Nonetheless, I didn't want them to be guilty and crossed them off my list.

Joseph's comments did strengthen the case against Susan, but I still could not believe anyone could be that stupid. Billy Raskin was another story. He was moving toward the top of my list. I made a mental note to talk to Greg to be sure he didn't defend Raskin. I also decided I wouldn't like Jason Bealer and put him on the prime suspect list. Alice Melton seemed like a good suspect, too. Joseph's remarks aside, she could have reached the breaking point.

"Tell me a little more about your parents' relationship," I said to Joseph. "I hope it doesn't sound like prying, but background information can be important. For what it's worth, I'm assuming you and your sister are innocent."

"My mother was a beautiful woman when she was younger. She came from a family that had been in San Francisco for several generations. They weren't really wealthy, but they were well established. My mother even came with a small dowry, which my father used to expand Melton Fashions, the precursor of Fabricon. He married her because he wanted an in with San Francisco society, and because he wanted her as a showpiece. He certainly never loved her, and I'm sure he despised her by the time I was born."

"Why did she marry him?"

"He could be very charming when he wanted to be. She must have regarded him as handsome and debonair, strong and masculine. She certainly saw herself as a society woman who would run charities and throw large affairs while my father took care of business. He would have seemed a perfect match for her."

"Things didn't work out very well for her."

"No. They didn't," he said. "She learned to hate him soon enough. If anything, 'hate' is too weak a word. They had very little to do with each other when I was born. That's probably why it was six years between me and Susan—they almost never slept together."

"Why didn't she divorce him?"

"She couldn't. Divorce didn't fit in with her self image. Over the years, she became very withdrawn. In public, she was the society woman she wanted to be. In private, she was a beaten woman, destroyed by my father."

"Well," I said, "you've certainly been very helpful. I stood and extended my hand to Joseph. "I'd better get going."

He shook my hand warmly, and Doris said, "Why don't you stay for dinner? It's getting to be about that time, and I want you to prove to Joseph that he can't change Fabricon."

I looked at my watch. It was almost seven o'clock. I said, "Thanks, but I have an appointment with the Bealers for eight-thirty."

"There's plenty of time," Joseph said. "The Bealers live

only ten minutes from here. And *I* want to know why you think I can't change Fabricon if I run the company."

I smiled and said, "You're on."

We all worked on preparing dinner. Doris made a salad, Joe whipped up a delicious stew from leftovers, and I brewed the coffee. I found a Melitta cone and used a paper towel as a filter. They only had a supermarket blend, but it was palatable. Doris noticed the difference from their usual percolated stuff; Joe said he thought it was too strong. No accounting for taste.

"So tell me," Joe said, "why can't I change Fabricon?"

"Because you can't operate in a vacuum. Your father may have been especially ruthless, but most businesses are run in pretty much the same manner. To compete, you have to keep expenses down, and that means low wages and lousy working conditions. That also means harassing workers so they'll be afraid to organize. That's what happens in Chinatown. Most of the workers are immigrants who speak little English; many are so-called illegal aliens afraid of being deported. They . . ."

"But why can't I change all that?" Joe said.

"I'm sure you'll try," I said. "But you won't be able to let your prices get too high. So you'll compromise. And you will change. Over the years, your ideals will be lost in the name of practicality. Have you read *The Godfather*? In the beginning, Michael is the good guy, untouched by the corruption around him. By the end, he's worse than his father."

"That's a great analogy," Doris said.

"Maybe," Joe said. "I'll think about it."

For the next hour we talked about politics, Berkeley, living in the Bay Area, and football. "The important question is," I said, "will the Raiders go all the way this year?"

"They could," Joe said, "the way the defense is playing."

"And Plunkett looks like he's back at Stanford," Doris said.

I decided they were definitely innocent.

11
JASON AND SARAH BEALER

The Bealer estate is near San Francisco City College and occupies three or four acres. It is surrounded by dense trees and a ten-foot brick wall. There is an electronically controlled gate at the foot of a long driveway, which leads to the house. I pressed a button outside the gate, and a voice said, "Who's calling, please?" I answered and the gate magically opened.

I would classify the Bealer home as a large house rather than as a mansion, but it was one classy joint. The entranceway was as large as my dining room, and the living room into which I was ushered had expensive paintings on the walls, beautiful rugs on oak floors, and objects d'art on teak tables. I knew many lawyers had good incomes, but I was surprised at this luxury. Something else bothered me. The butler who admitted me was well-mannered, but he looked as if he would be more comfortable in a boxing ring. He offered me a chair and said, "Can I get you something to drink, sir?"

"Perhaps some coffee. Black."

"Yes, sir." He left and I sat there for several minutes sensing that I was being watched, perhaps sized up. The place gave me a spooky feeling.

Jason Bealer came in and walked over to me with his

arm extended. He gave me a firm handshake and said, "Daniel Brodsky, I presume. I'm Jason Bealer. My wife will be down shortly." He was a large, portly man with graying hair. He would be tough in the clinches. He would be tough anywhere.

The butler brought coffee, and Mrs. Bealer soon followed. Bealer stood and said, "Brodsky, this is my wife Sarah. Let's get down to brass tacks. You're supposed to get Susan Melton off, and you want my help. I'm sure she's innocent, but the D.A. intends to push it. I spoke to him myself. He said he can't release her—too much publicity and all that. So Sarah and I are ready to give you all the help we can. What do you want to know?"

We discussed the birthday party at Le Petit Chateau, going over it in detail, but there was nothing really new. I was still assuming that Susan was innocent, and hence that there was something the police had missed. Their case depended on sleight of hand—Susan had to add the poison to Melton's wine in front of everybody. It is true that everyone was drinking and in a gay mood, so they might not have noticed. But it seems like a dangerous gamble to me. If the killer were desperate enough, such a chance might have to be taken, and certainly having a room full of suspects would be desirable. Nonetheless, if I had planned to kill Melton, I'd be considerably more comfortable if I could administer the poison with no possibility of being seen. The question then is, how was the arsenic put into the wine? Nothing any of the witnesses told me had provided an answer unless we accept the police explanation. If we reject it, then we must consider the possibility that other aspects of their case are in error. Was Rat Ravager really the source of the arsenic? Indeed, was Melton actually killed by arsenic? If he was poisoned, was the poison in his wine?

There was also the question of motive. The answer was beginning to look too easy: Everyone seemed to hate

Melton. But someone decided to kill him that evening. Why? Because of convenient circumstances? Some weird notion that he should die on his birthday? Perhaps a festering hatred finally reaching the breaking point? One other possibility that came to mind was some recent event that made it necessary for the murderer to take immediate action.

"As Fabricon's attorney and as Melton's personal attorney," I asked, "can you think of anything out of the ordinary in the last few weeks? Maybe an unusual argument involving Melton? Perhaps something new at Fabricon? Was Fabricon being sued, or were there problems with a new line? Financial difficulties; anything at all?"

"Not offhand," Bealer said. "Brad was a bit hot-headed and frequently had arguments. But nothing unusual. Fabricon has been sued by competitors a couple of times, but not recently. I don't normally look at the books, but I am a stockholder, and dividends keep coming in. The company is sound."

"What about the strike last spring? It lasted several weeks and must have had some effect on profits."

"Well, sure," he said. "It hurt the summer line. But not that much, and that was eight or nine months ago."

"Let's go back to the dinner," I said. "Had Melton eaten anything before he collapsed?"

"I'm not really sure," Bealer said. "There was bread on the table, and the appetizers had been served, but I can't remember if Brad had eaten anything. I doubt if he had any bread—middle-age bulge, you know." He laughed and looked at his own pot belly.

Mrs. Bealer said, "He ordered escargots, but I'm certain he hadn't touched them." She leaned forward. "I notice things like that."

"Then you're the right person to talk to. How much wine did he drink?"

"Three or four glasses," she said. "And at least three

cocktails. Brad was a drinker. Always whiskey sours. He had a sweet tooth."

"Did he ever drink piña coladas?"

"Occasionally," she said. "He liked sweet drinks. But usually whiskey sours."

"What about that night?"

She paused and then said slowly, "He may well have had a piña colada."

Bealer said, "She's right. I saw him drinking it."

"Do you remember who served it to him?"

He shook his head. "It was a week and a half ago."

Mrs. Bealer said, "I think it was the boy. He was the one who served Bradford the wine and the whiskey sours. It must have been him."

I sat back and said, "I'd like to get as much background as possible. You've known the Meltons a long time?"

"Yes," he said. "We went to school together. Stanford. We were both on the football team. Defensive linemen."

"So you knew him when he started with Melton Fashions?"

"Yes. His brother, Henry, was the artistic one and had been working for their father, Elias, for several years as a designer. Elias wasn't much of a businessman. It was after Brad started running the company that it really took off."

"That was after Elias died?"

"Even before. Brad took over the business end shortly after he started working. After Elias's death, Henry was the chief designer and Brad ran the company. They were an unbeatable team."

"Successful enough to incorporate."

"They made a lot of money and took over a couple of smaller firms," he said. "Then they incorporated. The company now grosses over a hundred million. He was a good man."

"You liked him," I said.

"He was the best friend I ever had. I know a lot of

people didn't like him. But it's a cruel world out there. Kill or be killed . . ." He stopped himself. Was it simply because of Melton's death, or was there something more sinister? He said, "Don't read anything into that, young man. It's just an expression. An unfortunate choice under the circumstances. But just an expression."

That could have ended the interview—my face must have given my thoughts away. Remind me never to play poker with Jason Bealer.

I needed to say something if I wanted their cooperation. "Mr. Bealer, from what I've heard, and not just tonight, you're one of the few people who had no motive. As you said, Bradford Melton was not well liked, and you and he were close friends. I knew that before I got here. While everyone at the dinner has to be considered a suspect, you're way down on the list."

He relaxed and I continued my questions. "You knew his family well. Tell me about his relationship with them."

Sarah Bealer spoke. "Mr. Brodsky. We've been good friends with the Meltons for a long time, and we know them very well. We've seen their children grow up; we've been involved with their business; we've helped them through difficult times. Bradford is dead. I don't think gossiping about the family would be at all appropriate."

"I understand," I said. "But Susan Melton is in serious trouble. *We* know she's innocent—the police and the district attorney think otherwise. Their case is not a bad one. I must find a hole in it."

"I have every confidence in you and her lawyer," Bealer said.

"That's nice to hear. But frankly, it may not be that easy to convince a jury. Greg Langley is a fine attorney and will defend her well. Even if he does get her off, if the real culprit is not found, there will always be doubt in the minds of her friends and family. Greg is not in any position to find the real killer. The police are, but they're not looking. That means that if the guilty party is to be uncovered, I'll have to be the one to do it."

"But why must you look into personal family matters?" Mrs. Bealer asked.

"Disliking a man is not usually enough motive for killing him. My feeling is that something happened recently that made Melton a danger to someone, and Melton probably knew what that something was. I want to get inside his head, to know him, to see what led to his murder. I need to have a sense of his family life and of his business life. The two of you knew him better than anyone outside his immediate family."

"All right, Mr. Brodsky," she said. "You asked about Bradford's wife. Alice was born into San Francisco society. She had a pampered childhood and led a sheltered life. She attended private schools and was brought up to be a society woman. When they met, Bradford was a handsome young businessman on his way up. He was ambitious and a little reckless in those days, and she found him exciting."

"I gather it didn't work out well for her after they were married."

"No. It didn't," she said. "He was too strong for her. She was a perfect Mrs. Bradford Melton in public, but she was unhappy at home. Their relationship deteriorated rapidly, and Bradford became more and more engrossed in the business. Divorce was unthinkable for Alice, and she led her own life, not part of Bradford's."

"I've heard that she hated him."

"They didn't get along well," she said, "but she didn't hate him. No, 'hate' is much too strong a word."

"Do you have anything to add, Mr. Bealer?"

"I don't think so. Sarah summed it up very well."

"How did Melton get along with his son?"

"Joe's a good boy, but I don't think Bradford was fully

satisfied with him," Bealer said. "They certainly argued enough."

"What did they argue about?"

"All sorts of things. Brad wanted him to go to Stanford; he went to Berkeley. Brad wanted him to go to law school; he studied physics. Brad wanted him to marry someone of his social class; he married a professor's daughter. Joe never did the things his father wanted him to do, and never was the kind of man his father wanted him to be."

"How do you mean that?"

"Brad wanted a strong, ambitious son to follow in his footsteps. Joe is easygoing and, well, kind of a softy. He couldn't hurt a fly."

His comments were consistent with my impressions of Joseph, and he remained at the bottom of the suspect list. Proving Susan innocent was the primary objective. I did not feel any closer to that goal.

"What about Susan?" I said.

Mrs. Bealer answered. "She's a troubled young lady. She could never deal with the fact that her parents didn't love each other. She blamed her father but was never close to her mother. I'm sure she felt unloved."

"Do you think she got involved with Raskin because of feeling rejected at home?"

"Certainly," she said. "She went to Berkeley only because it was a hotbed of radicalism. Everything she did there was to spite her father. She and Bradford were always arguing."

"I want to prove Susan is not guilty. That's what I'm being paid for. But everything I hear indicates she had motive, and the police have some real evidence. Can you tell me anything that would point to her innocence?"

"Only that I'm sure Brad loved her, and that in her own way she loved him, too. She could not have killed him."

I didn't believe Susan had loved her father, and I was sure Melton never loved anyone, but I refrained from commenting.

"What can you tell me about Melton's brother?" I said.

"Henry's a lot like Joseph," Bealer said. "He's meek and soft-spoken. But what he lacks in ambition he makes up for in talent. He's a fine artist, in addition to being an outstanding designer of women's fashions." He pointed to a painting above the fireplace and said, "He did that landscape." It was an ocean scene done from cliffs above the beach. I knew little about art but was impressed.

"How did they get along?" I said.

"They weren't what I'd call really close, but they got along fine. Their interests were very different."

"What was their business relationship like?"

"Brad was president of Fabricon, and Henry was in charge of design. They functioned well together, and Fabricon was very successful."

"Do you think it bothered Henry having his younger brother for a boss?"

"I don't think so," Bealer said. "Henry has done well financially and been able to pursue his artistic talents without being concerned with the day-to-day running of the company."

"His wife may have felt differently," Mrs. Bealer said. "She's the dominant force in that marriage. I know she always thought Henry was responsible for the success of Fabricon, and I think she believed Henry ought to have been president. Before you asked for information to help prove Susan's innocence. Check out Margaret Melton— she's a good suspect if you want my opinion."

"Aren't you being a little hard on her, Sarah?" Bealer said. "I know you never liked Margaret very much, but she's hardly a murderer."

Mrs. Bealer said nothing.

I said, "Fabricon has had a lot of bad press. Anything there that could be useful?"

"Everybody hates big business these days," Bealer said. "But Fabricon is no different from other corporations. It employs several thousand people. They complain about the way Fabricon treats its employees in Chinatown, but let me tell you something. If it weren't for Fabricon, those people would be on a slow boat for China in a week." He was getting angry and speaking louder. "Those commie chinks are always stirring up trouble. But those people are used to working hard. That's the way they are. And they're a lot better off here than they ever were in China. You better believe it. They accused Brad of being a racist. Ha! He gave those people a chance."

"They" were right, and you're worse, I thought. But I dared not reply. I didn't have it in me to agree with him, so I said nothing, hoping he would continue and change directions. He did.

"If you want somebody to check out," he said, "try Nancy Chou. She's the bitch that tried to unionize the workers. She got thrown out on her ass after the strike. Now there's someone with a motive."

"I will check her out," I said. "That could be the kind of lead I'm looking for. I don't suppose you saw her at Le Petit Chateau?"

"I'm afraid not," he said. "But she's tricky. She could have done it."

"Who else might have murdered Melton? After all, if Nancy Chou wasn't there, she doesn't make a very good a suspect."

"To tell you the truth, there's only one person that could have done it. Billy Raskin. He's capable of it. And he had motive. He wanted to take over Fabricon. He planned to marry Susan, you know. And of course, she and Joseph inherit."

77

"You may well be right, though proving him guilty and Susan innocent could be tricky. But that's my problem." I stood and said, "You've been very helpful. Thank you."

Bealer extended his hand and said, "Susan is innocent. If I can be of any assistance, please feel free to call on me."

∫12

∫ RALPH CORDOVA

It was after midnight when I arrived home. There were two hang-ups and one string of profanities on my Record-A-Phone but no messages. I called Greg and he answered on the second ring.

"Gregory Langley speaking."

"You sound like a recording, Greg."

"Oh shit. Who else would call in the middle of the night?"

"You were awake, weren't you?"

"Of course. But calling this late—it's low class. You're not a student anymore, you know. You've gotta learn to . . ."

"I know, Greg. I'll try."

"I assume you have a reason for calling."

"Yeah. I'd like you to do some checking for me. First, can you get an independent chemist to analyze that wine? I'd like to know for sure if Rat Ravager was the source of the arsenic, and I'd like to know for sure if it was in the wine."

"We should be able to arrange it. What else?"

"What do you know about Jason Bealer?"

"Bealer?" Greg said. "Nothing special. He's a big-time corporation lawyer. You think he could have killed Melton?"

"Probably not. But I had a funny feeling when I was there."

"Funny feeling? About what?"

"Greg, could he be connected?"

"Connected?"

"Yes. Connected. You know. The Syndicate. The Mafia. The guys with the violin cases."

"You've gotta be kidding."

"I hope so," I said. "Talk to Mitch or Tim. See if they know anything. And get back to me fast. I want to know what I'm up against."

"Will do. Anything else?"

"Have you decided to defend Raskin?"

"Not yet. Tim and I talked about it a little. I went to see Raskin this afternoon and suggested he find another attorney. I told him there might be a conflict of interest. But he insisted that he wanted us, and that he and Susan wanted to stick together."

"He's my best suspect," I said. "It would be wise if you didn't defend him."

"I'll talk about it with Tim in the morning. We'll take your suspicions into account. I don't want to defend him, but Susan insists we do. It's tricky. Do you really think it was Raskin?"

"I don't know. I don't have any hard evidence yet."

"Why would he do it before marrying Susan? If I were in that position, I'd worry that inheriting all that money would change my relationship with her."

"That bothers me, too," I said. "But you remember what an arrogant sonofabitch he is. He'd be confident that Susan would still marry him. He certainly had an 'end justifies the means' approach to politics. He easily could have thought Melton was a capitalist pig who deserved to die. And I'll tell you, Melton was rotten. I could have killed him myself."

"If you prove yourself guilty, I'll defend you."

"I can always depend on you," I said. "The biggest problem with proving Raskin guilty is proving Susan innocent. If he's guilty, she looks guilty."

"There's another problem. If, as you put it, 'no one in his right mind would leave such a trail of clues behind,' Raskin could not have done it."

"Maybe. Somehow it feels different with Raskin."

"Only because you think so little of him."

"I do have a couple of other ideas, but I want that chemist's report before pursuing them. Get back to me as soon as possible."

He called back in the morning. "I've been talking with Tim. We won't defend Raskin, so you're free to prove him guilty. I've spoken with a laboratory in Oakland, and they'll do the analysis."

"What about Bealer?" I said.

"You were right, Dan. Tim said he's a top lawyer for organized crime. Tread carefully. But remember, it is better to have tread carefully than never to have tread at all."

"Thanks." I didn't know if Bealer was guilty, but I had no intention of implicating him. I crossed him off my list.

"You're meeting Cordova today?"

"Yeah. He's due in a few minutes."

"Anything new with Delkin?"

"The Delkin Foundation Home for Wayward Girls is being dedicated today. Delkin himself is supposed to be there. I'll be waiting for him."

Ralph Cordova arrived on time. He was a tall, well-built man, a rather imposing figure. At the same time he was quiet and soft-spoken. I made coffee and we reviewed the events at Le Petit Chateau. His description was very precise, probably because of his background as a policeman, and was generally consistent with what other witnesses had told me.

"When Melton collapsed," I said, "there was a lot of confusion. Perhaps you can clarify some of the details."

"I had been talking to Henry and Margaret Melton and heard a noise. I turned and saw Melton had fallen over."

"Do you remember what your first reaction was? After all, it was your responsibility to protect him."

"I immediately went to see what the problem was, to see if I could help. My reaction was that he'd had a heart attack. I mean, he was overweight and a smoker."

"So you didn't feel that you had failed?"

"Certainly not. Not at first, anyway."

"And now?"

He shrugged and said, "He was murdered."

"Do you think there was anything you could have done to prevent it?"

"No. I wasn't really expected to protect him from his own family."

"So you think Susan Melton is guilty?"

"Not necessarily. But someone in the family must be."

"Why? There were a lot of people in the restaurant. Any one of them might have done it."

"Sure. But it's not very likely. Look. I used to be a cop. I don't believe in coincidences. So I find it hard to accept that someone happened to be having dinner and suddenly decided to commit murder."

"Couldn't someone have known that he would be there?"

"Maybe. Do you have any evidence to that effect?"

"No. Not yet," I said. "And I'm willing to reject coincidences. But not having the evidence doesn't mean it didn't happen."

"I'll believe it when I see the evidence."

"Let's say you're right and assume some family member

is guilty. That creates another problem. If Susan is innocent, then the murderer wanted to frame her as well as to kill Melton."

"Susan could be guilty. We don't have a bad police force in this city, and they don't make that many mistakes. On the other hand, there were a couple of people at the dinner who weren't Meltons and might not have cared about framing her. Roger Mayfield for example, or Billy Raskin."

"But Raskin's supposed to marry Susan. Would he have framed her?"

"He might not have intended to."

"Then he certainly didn't plan things very well."

"It wouldn't be the first time. And there's always the possibility someone wanted to get rid of both of them."

"I've considered that. But then what's the motive?"

He shrugged. "Susan was easy to dislike. Once the decision was made to kill Melton, it may have been easy to choose her as a patsy. But let me ask you a question. Do you really think Susan is innocent?"

"Yes. The case against her is too pat. She would have had to have been incredibly stupid not to have covered her tracks better."

"Then who do you think is guilty?"

"It's a little early to answer that question," I said. "I've just begun my investigation. But I would be interested in your guess."

"Do you care what I think?"

"Sure. You're not a Melton, and you are a trained policeman."

"What do you want me to do? Give you my analysis of everyone at the birthday party?"

"That'd be great," I said.

"Where should I start?"

"Why don't we go around the table; begin with Jason Bealer."

82

"A strong man, maybe capable of murder. But not a good suspect."

"Why not?"

"He was Melton's best friend. They genuinely respected each other. And I'm inclined to believe it was someone in the family."

"Why?"

"There's a lot of money to be inherited. In my experience, when there's money around, it's usually the motive."

I nodded. "Sounds reasonable. I think we're up to Sarah Bealer."

"Right. A very sharp woman. Hard to read. But not a Melton and not a good suspect."

"You're next," I said.

"I guess it would be easier if I confessed, but I didn't kill him."

I smiled. "I'm glad. But you can tell me a little about yourself. For example, how did you like working for Melton?"

"It wasn't bad. I can't say I was very fond of the man, but I was well paid, especially since I've been living on the estate."

"You live with the Meltons?"

"Yes."

"How long have you been there?"

"Maybe a year or so. It works out pretty well."

"Are you married? I was wondering if your wife liked living there."

"Divorced."

"Sorry. I didn't mean to pry. What will you do now?"

"I guess I'm out of a job, and I'll have to find a place to live. Maybe I'll go back to being a cop. That wasn't so bad."

"Sounds like a good choice. Shall we continue around the table?"

"Sure. Margaret and Henry Melton were sitting next to me. Henry is an artist with his head in the clouds, not a killer. Margaret's another story. She hated her brother-in-law and thought her husband should be president of Fabricon. She'd be a good suspect."

"I'll keep that in mind. Alice Melton is next."

"She and Melton didn't get along very well, but I doubt she killed him. She certainly wouldn't have wanted to frame Susan."

"Agreed. What about Roger Mayfield?"

"He's not a Melton, so I don't think of him as a good suspect. At the same time, I don't trust him. He was the company accountant. If he was doing something funny with the books and Melton found out . . ."

"Worth checking out," I said. "That leaves Joe and Doris, and of course Susan and Billy Raskin."

"Joe's a good man, and Doris is really nice. They surely make the worst suspects. Susan and Raskin we've already talked about. I still think he makes a good suspect. A good approach you might take would be to assume he's guilty but did not intend to frame Susan. If you can make the facts fit that assumption, I think you'll have a solution."

"I've thought about that," I said, "but I can't make the facts fit."

"Brodsky, let me ask you something."

"Shoot."

"I'd like to know who did it. As you said, it was my job to protect him. Suppose I worked with you? I mean, I was a cop for eight years and should be able to help out."

I considered the idea. I certainly had not eliminated Cordova as a suspect, but I didn't think it likely he was the killer, to some extent because of his manner and to some extent because there was no obvious motive attributable to him. Were he the killer, he might well want to stay close to my investigation. But his explanation was reasonable, and I decided to at least partly trust him. I said, "I'm sure your expertise would be very useful. I do have to do the legwork myself. Alice Melton may not . . ."

"Yeah, sure. I understand. But if we talk about the evidence as you gather it, I think I can help out a lot."

"You probably can. I'll keep in touch."

∫13

∫ JOAN CHAKELEY

The Delkin Foundation Home for Wayward Girls was on Divisadero Street, south of Geary, in an area of San Francisco known as the Western Addition. It was cordoned off when I drove up at 1:30, and I left Herman in a garage several blocks away.

There are two toolboxes in his trunk. One has the implements necessary to keep him running. The other has a pair of binoculars, a beat-up camera that doesn't work, a Nikon with several lenses that does work, a stack of business cards indicating anything from airlines to zipper repair, four not entirely valid driver's licenses issued to four different individuals, an entirely valid press pass, a .38 caliber revolver that I never touch, a set of lock picks whose technique I have yet to master, and a micro-cassette recorder. The beat-up camera was once worth six hundred dollars; it was smashed at a time when I needed it solely as a prop. I have since learned to carry my good camera only if I intend to take pictures.

I acquired the press pass a couple of years ago while teaching an evening calculus class at Hayward State College. One of my students was a housewife from Orinda who frequently came to my office for extra help. By the middle of the course, we were stopping for coffee after class, and by the end, we were going back to my place. The affair lasted six months, after which she decided to try to make her marriage work. She had a part-time job with a small newspaper, the *Orinda Weekly News*. She was able to get me a legitimate press pass in return for an occasional (twice a year) column about Berkeley. As a result I am a member in good standing of the Fourth Estate.

I took the beat-up camera and my press pass from my toolbox (I refer to the other one as Herman's toolbox). I walked the three blocks to the ceremony and had no trouble getting past the police cordon. I prefer the press pass to any of the business cards because I'm uncomfortable doing impersonations of questionable legality.

Herbert Delkin is one of the wealthiest and most powerful men in California, and he draws a crowd. There were hundreds of newsmen, cameramen, TV personalities, politicians, and onlookers. The building being dedicated was set back thirty yards from the street, and six men and women sat in front. I did not know what Delkin looked like, but I did recognize three others: the mayor of San Francisco, a Channel 4 newswoman, and Joan Chakeley, Delkin's personal secretary. I remembered her austere angular face from two weeks earlier when I first tried to serve the subpoena.

At two o'clock sharp, the Channel 4 newswoman stood, said a few words, and introduced the mayor, who, in turn, stood, said a few words, and introduced Delkin. Delkin walked to the microphone, cleared his throat, and began. "Many young women come to our fair city in search of . . ." He was a short, fragile-looking man in his late forties. He spoke for ten minutes and then took a gigantic pair of scissors and cut a red ribbon tied across the front door. The newspeople crowded in, and I knew I had him. I moved in slowly, thinking this would make the six o'clock news, which was perfect under the circumstances. I might even be interviewed and have a chance to explain PURE's position.

I was twelve feet from Delkin when Joan Chakeley caught sight of me and whispered something in his ear. He said, "Excuse me a moment," to the newspeople and whispered something to a man who had been sitting next to him. That man whispered something to a cop with all sorts of brass on his uniform. He whispered something to a sergeant, who whispered something to a patrolman. I was within eight feet of Delkin in the second row of newspeople, trying to push my way forward, when I felt a hand on my shoulder. "What d'ya think you're doin', Bub?"

I turned and saw a big, fat, ugly cop. "What's the matter?" I said. "I'm a member of the press; I've got credentials."

"You better come wid me, Bub."

"But I have questions to ask. I'm on a story."

"C'mon, Bub. Don't cause no trouble. It'll go easier on you." He led me back to the police cordon and said, "Now what'cha doin' here?"

I showed him my press card. "Like I said. I'm on a story." My pulse must have been over a hundred.

"What the hell is the *Orinda Weekly News*? I never heard of it."

"Just what it says. They're in the Yellow Pages."

"Maybe it is. Maybe it ain't. Why don't you just wait over there." He pointed to the other side of the cordon.

"But my story," I protested.

"Look, Bub," he said, "if you prefer, we can talk about this downtown. Now why don'cha go quietly." He turned to one of the cops and said, "Don't let this one through again. You guys gotta learn to be more careful." He gave me a final shove to prove how tough he was.

I watched Delkin from the distance, wondering what the hell I thought I was doing. At least I didn't get busted this time, but who cares about Delkin or Melton or any of it. I should be teaching calculus and complex analysis, not gallivanting around chasing bad guys. Were I Nero Wolfe, I would have Archie Goodwin round up all the suspects in the Melton case and bring them to my office. I would question them for two hours, announce who the murderer is, and send said individual to the police conveniently waiting outside. Then I would go up to my plant room and water my orchids while Archie collected my fifty-thousand-dollar fee.

Were I Perry Mason, I would be in my luxurious suite of offices at one o'clock in the morning working hard on a brief that *had* to be done that night for a wealthy client. Alice and Susan Melton would enter in tears. After explaining that I was impossibly busy and could not take on another case, I would call Paul Drake, who never sleeps, and send him to find clues that no ordinary human could uncover. The next morning I would go to court to defend Susan. I would be threatened with disbarment by Ham Burger, unveil the real killer, and, of course, charge no fee.

Were I Perry Mason and confronted with the Delkin situation, I would give the officer a bunch of habeas corpuses, writ subjicendums, and some other Latin stuff, walk past all the reporters saying, "I'm Perry Mason, the famous trial lawyer," and hand Delkin the subpoena. Then I would handle the trial and save the redwoods by citing as precedent Robin Hood's exploits in Sherwood Forest.

But I am Daniel Brodsky. I should be a professor of mathematics in a small university with an office in an ivy-covered tower. I should spend my days teaching and doing research, and at night go home to my wife, preferably a doctor, and three little Brodskys. I am a private eye by circumstance—not by design.

∫ 14

SHARON LANGLEY

I parked Herman in my driveway at four o'clock, angry and frustrated, suffering from a good case of millicopitis. My one rational thought was, "I need more publications." Without checking my Record-A-Phone, I had coffee, made a sandwich, and went to my office on the seventh floor of Evans Hall. Except for a pause to eat the sandwich at seven and a coffee break at nine, I worked straight through until midnight, concentrating on a question I had been thinking about for the last six months. The problem was to classify the invariant subspace lattice of a certain family of operators. There was a technique I had been trying to develop for two weeks that I was confident would yield the desired result. At ten it was beginning to look as if it would work, and by midnight I had it! It appeared that the technique would generalize to other classes of operators. I kept going. By 5:00 A.M. I had three more theorems, including the solution to a problem that a friend of mine at the Santa Barbara campus of the University of California had been working on for two years. This would easily be my best publication to date!

I slept for three hours in my office, taught my class, and started writing. I had a first draft of the article by the end of the afternoon. I Xeroxed the handwritten copy and sent it to Howard Williams, my friend at Santa Barbara. He and I had collaborated in the past and were generally interested in the same field of mathematics. On two occasions he had tried to bring me to Santa Barbara, but budget restrictions and my inclination to remain in the Bay Area prevented anything from working out. I was ready to move to Santa Barbara, and Howard had become chairman of the department. With this new work, a position there might be possible.

In case you are unfamiliar with hiring practices in higher education, publications and research potential is primary in the large universities. In most colleges, teaching and "university service" are also important, and in community colleges, research is at best tolerated. In the major universities, quality teaching counts for little: Hiring and renewal depend only on research. Hence the phrase, "publish or perish." New Ph.D.s are hired as assistant professors. If their research is satisfactory and they don't rape the president's daughter, they are promoted to associate professor and awarded tenure after three to six years. Promotion to the rank of professor results after three to six more successful years. For someone with my publication record, there would be a chance of being hired at the associate level with tenure.

With that and the Delkin debacle in mind, I came to an easy decision: I would quit the private eye business. Susan Melton was probably guilty anyway. After all, the only good reason for believing she was innocent was that she was my client. And it would take a better man than I to reach Delkin. On the other hand, even if Santa Barbara did not come through, I was bound to find an academic job with my new results.

I went home and checked my Record-A-Phone. There were two hang-ups, a call from someone who needed a private investigator but could not wait for me to phone him, a call from Elaine "just to say hi," and two calls from

Greg, the second of which included a lecture on returning calls and keeping in touch with him. I took Hypatia out of her cage and called Elaine first.

"I've got big news," I said. "I've spent the last twenty-four hours doing research and have come up with some good stuff. It should lead to the kind of job I've been trying to find for the last five years."

"Sound's great," she said.

"There's more," I said. "I have investigated privately for the last time. No more Meltons. No more . . . any of that crap." I almost said Delkin, which probably would have meant no more Elaine. "I was never intended to run around asking people stupid questions. I've had it. I quit!"

"That was sudden," she said. "What does Greg say?"

"I haven't told him yet. He may not be too happy. But he'll get over it."

"Are we still going to his house for dinner?"

"Oh sure. One has nothing to do with the other. I better call him. See you tomorrow." I hung up and said to Hypatia, "What do you think? Should I call Greg now or talk to him tomorrow? Maybe I should call now. Then you have to go home." I put her in her cage and dialed.

"Gregory Langley speaking."

"Daniel Brodsky speaking."

"Where the hell have you been?"

"Greg, you must learn to calm down. You're surely killing yourself. By the way, I quit."

"You what?"

"Quit. Q—U—I—T. Quit. You'll have to get yourself another pigeon. Dan Brodsky, private eye and persona extraordinaire, is turning into a pumpkin. I'm fed up, Greg. I never want to see a cop again."

"Did you get busted?"

"No. But it was close. That's not the point. I'm not cut out to be a gumshoe. It's not me."

"How do you plan to feed Herman?"

"Teaching and doing research. I've spent most of the last twenty-four hours doing mathematics, and I have some good results. Good enough to get me a job."

"So that's it. No sleep."

"Greg, I'm quitting."

"Fine. Get here by five tomorrow, and we'll talk more."

"Sure. But don't expect me to change my mind."

"Of course not. Have I ever asked you to do anything against your will?"

"Ha! Good night."

I was asleep two minutes after I hung up and slept for twelve hours. I had a dream in which I was driving down a long, narrow road on the way to my new job. I could see the university in the distance, high on a hill, among the clouds. As I approached, the highway was lined with men dressed in blue. They were cops in riot gear, all with shotguns poised. I reached the gates, and Delkin's secretary opened them with a hideous grin on her face. I parked in front of a twenty-story building and saw Greg in a monk's robe carrying a sign that read, "Enter Here and Ye Shall Be Betrayed." I went in and was met by Susan Melton, dressed in a nurse's uniform. She led me down a long hall, at the end of which was a small, windowless room containing a single, naked light bulb. She shoved me in, slammed and locked the door, and walked off. I could hear her high heels clicking on the floor as I woke up.

Greg has a beautiful two-bedroom apartment in an old building in Oakland. Elaine was to meet me there at 6:30, and I arrived an hour earlier. Greg's wife, Sharon, answered my knock. She is his exact opposite: Greg is short, overweight, and awkward; Sharon is tall, slender, beautiful, and graceful. Greg is a nervous worrier, always under pressure; Sharon is relaxed and easygoing. She and

Greg first met when they were both young attorneys with Halloran and Mackey. She was currently on a leave of absence because of the birth of their daughter.

"Hi, Dan," she said. "Greg's in the kitchen cooking up a storm. You're not really quitting, are you?"

"Yes. For real. You know I never liked this business." I followed her into the kitchen.

Greg looked at me with disgust and said, "So. You can't take it anymore."

"That's about the size of it."

"And Susan Melton? You never liked her very much anyway. So what if she spends twenty years in prison."

"She's probably guilty. Even if she's innocent, she's committed sins against humanity. Besides, Greg, I have great faith in your courtroom ability. You don't need me."

"You're wrong about that. The police have stopped investigating, and they have a pretty good case. I'm not at all sure I can win without uncovering new evidence."

"You can hire someone else. I'll tell him what I've learned so far, and I won't even bill you for my time. The same with Delkin."

"Okay," he said. "To tell you the truth, a couple of people thought hiring you was a mistake. You are inexperienced, after all. I argued that you're better than anyone I know at tracking people down, but you haven't come up with much after two weeks of investigating. Maybe they were right."

"They probably were," I said. "I'm not really qualified. My quitting may save Susan Melton."

"Goddamnit!"

I laughed. "You want me to fall for your dime-store psychology? If I were you, I would argue that I have a responsibility to PURE and the Redwoods, to Susan and to justice and the American Way, not to mention to apple pie."

"Would you change your mind?"

"No. But at least you'd sound sincere. Look, Greg. I'm serious about this. Delkin doesn't want to see any subpoenas. Even if he is served, it's not likely you'll find a judge who insists Delkin himself show up. His attorneys will argue that you're just harassing him, which is essentially true, and you'll never get him on the stand."

"That's PURE's tactic, and it's our obligation to serve the client."

"Your use of the word 'our' is questionable. Greg, it's no fun anymore. Delkin is a very powerful man—I don't want him mad at me."

"What about Susan?"

"Innocent people get convicted all the time. She may or may not become one of them. I'm not a knight in shining armor; I'm not the hero type. What it comes down to is, well . . . I quit."

"You left out one important point. You agreed to work on these cases. You committed yourself. If you want to quit when you've finished these jobs, that's fine with me. But you have some responsibility to your clients, not to mention to me." He was shouting, and his face was turning red. He looked at Sharon and said, "Will you talk to him? He's out of his mind. He gets like that sometimes. Ask him how he plans to pay the rent before this mythical job comes through."

To Greg she said, "If he needs it, he'll borrow money from us, and we'll give it to him." To me she said, "Dan, you really do have a responsibility. Greg came to you in good faith. You could have turned him down when he first asked you to take the cases. God only knows how many times you've done that before. But you did agree to help, and it seems to me that you should finish what you've started." Greg began to add something, but Sharon said, "Don't push him, Greg. He knows what he has to do."

I desperately wanted to come up with a counter argument, but I knew she was right. I stood there like a stubborn child. I said, "Okay. But these are my last cases. Remember that."

"You can always say no," Greg said. He looked at me, still angry. "Dan, why do you always do these things to me?" Then he burst out laughing, and I started laughing, too.

The baby began to cry, and Greg said, "Can you get her, honey? She's probably hungry, and I want to talk with Dan." To me he said, "What happened Wednesday?"

"I was a few feet from Delkin when his secretary spotted me. It would have been great. There were TV cameras all over the place. Had I served him, the TV people would have interviewed me, and PURE would have made the six o'clock news. Unfortunately, the police threw me out before I had a chance."

"Any more bright ideas?"

"There is Elaine," I said. "But I've gotten really fond of her—I hate to use her that way."

"Why not tell her the truth? If your relationship is worth anything, she'll understand."

"I suppose. I'll have to choose the right moment."

"What about the Melton case? Any progress?"

"Some. Not a lot. There's a question about whether the appetizers had been served and whether Melton had eaten his. Different witnesses say different things."

"Anything else?"

"Melton was drinking a piña colada, but nobody seems to have given it to him. That's not a whole lot to go on. We'll see. Did you set up a meeting with Melton's brother?"

"Tuesday evening. His house."

"And Mayfield?"

"He insists he's too busy, and he's going on vacation soon."

"Vacation? Now? Seems odd, what with Melton dead."

"Maybe, Dan. He did promise to meet with you when he gets back."

"That could run into January," I said. "I'm going to New York on December twenty-first and returning the third. When's the preliminary hearing?"

"A week from Monday, right after Thanksgiving. It looks like Susan will be bound over for trial unless you come up with something soon."

"I'll do my best. If Raskin's guilty, it may be tough to prove Susan wasn't involved. I'll try to talk to him before the preliminary. Does he have a lawyer?"

"Yeah. Guess who."

"Clarence Darrow."

"Alex Knight," he said. "The bastard who used to defend the University."

"Sounds like Raskin. Perhaps I should let you interview him. He hates my guts."

"Maybe, Dan. But he's mad at me for not defending him, and you've been doing all the interviewing. I prefer to keep it that way and then examine the witnesses on the stand. He'll talk to you. Any other suspects?"

"Everyone who was there. Mayfield is a possible because he was the only one to leave the table during the dinner. The waiter could conceivably be guilty. He served Melton but denies bringing him a piña colada. Maybe Jason Bealer did it—he's the only one without a motive. In other words, I have no idea."

Greg's other guests began arriving, ending the discussion. We forgot about the Meltons and enjoyed an excellent meal. Greg let me make the coffee.

Elaine watched the Raiders' game with me on Sunday afternoon. Their opponent was Philadelphia, who had been eating up the league. The Raiders led 7–3 in the

96

fourth quarter when a fluke turned a ten-yard play into a long gainer. The Eagles won 10–7.

We built a fire after dinner, and I knew it was time to talk to her. "Elaine," I said. "I have a confession to make."

"Yes," she said, smiling, not expecting anything special.

"Maybe we shouldn't talk about it now. You'll get mad."

"I won't get mad. What is it?"

"Some other time. Let's enjoy the fire."

"Daniel, I won't get mad."

"You will," I said.

"I'm getting angry now. I won't if you tell me what's on your mind."

"Okay," I said. "You remember I told you that serving subpoenas led to my private investigating?"

"Yes. So?"

"Well, that's also how we met. It was like this. I had this subpoena. For Herbert Delkin."

At first she didn't react. Then she realized the significance of what I'd said, and she exploded. "What! You mean you've just been using me all this time?"

"I knew you'd get mad."

"I'm not mad. I'm . . . I'm outraged!"

"I knew you'd get mad."

"How could you use me like that? Take me home. No. I'll get a cab."

"We could talk about it."

"How can I talk when I'm mad?"

"I knew you'd get mad." She laughed, though she was still angry. I said, "Can we talk now?"

"Talk."

"One of Delkin's companies is cutting down redwood trees in northern California, and one of the environmental groups wants to save the redwoods. They plan to put Delkin on the stand, and I'm supposed to serve the subpoena. When I went to the Delkin Tower, I couldn't reach him, and I saw you. You looked like someone I'd like to know a little better, and I thought you might be able to give me a line on him."

"You mean everything that happened in the supermarket was a charade?" She was obviously amused, though still angry.

"As a matter of fact, I thought it was pretty good. You're here, aren't you?"

"I don't know whether to laugh or cry. Haven't the last two weeks meant anything to you?"

"A great deal. That's why I'm talking to you now, and why I haven't asked you about Delkin."

"But?"

"But nothing. That's it."

"So you no longer want me to help you get him?"

"I didn't say that," I said. "If you feel uncomfortable about it, fine. If you're willing to help, better. The main point is I care a lot about you, and I want to be honest with you."

She looked at me for a long time. I kissed her and held her close to me. After a while, she smiled broadly and said, "What the hell. How can I help? Let's get the bastard!"

"Delkin is a difficult man to reach. I came close Wednesday, but . . ."

"What happened Wednesday?"

I gave her the gory details, and she said, "What do you want me to do?"

"Keep your eyes and ears open. Don't start asking questions—that will only get you in trouble. Listen for office gossip. What I need to know is when he'll be in a public place. Wednesday was almost a perfect setup. Unfortunately . . ."

"You blew it."

∫15
HENRY AND MARGARET MELTON

The next day was Monday, November 24. It was a sunny, warm day, and I felt great. I could do anything. My tennis game was sharp, and I handily won three sets from Jim. I knew I would solve the Melton case shortly, serve Delkin with the subpoena, and be offered a position at Santa Barbara. And there was Elaine. Something special was happening.

As usual, I went to the Operator Theory Seminar at Berkeley in the afternoon. There is normally a one-hour lecture on current research (an hour lasts fifty minutes in academic circles). Anyone who wants to may give a two-minute talk at the beginning. A two-minute talk consists of raising a question, describing a recent paper, or outlining the speaker's own work, and lasts about five minutes. (If it were a five-minute talk, it would run ten minutes.)

I gave a two-minute talk on my new results. Paul Hobart, to whom I had briefly described the work on Friday, asked a few questions. Several others followed suit; my two-minute talk lasted forty-five minutes; the scheduled lecture was postponed a week. I went home knowing that nothing could stop me.

There was a message on my Record-A-Phone from Howard Williams in Santa Barbara asking me to call him at home in the evening. I tried at six. A female voice answered.

"Anita?" I said.

"Yes."

"This is Dan Brodsky. We've met a couple of times."

"Oh yes. I remember. Howard isn't home yet. Should I have him call you?"

"Yes. Please do. I'll be home."

Jim Berkowitz and Paul Hobart came over for dinner before the poker game. We were discussing the oil crisis when the phone rang at 7:30. It was Howard Williams.

"Your paper arrived this morning," he said. "It's nice. That technique looks useful."

"It took a long time to push it through. I was lucky."

"Listen, Dan. I've been talking with a couple of people in the department. We may be ready to hire you. Are you prepared to come down?"

"Perhaps. I could give you more of an answer if you could be more definite."

"I can't make an offer without speaking to the dean. If we do, it should be at the associate level."

"With tenure?"

"I think so. Interested?"

"Very likely," I said. "Certainly if it's a tenured associate professorship."

"Good. I'll meet with the dean after Thanksgiving. Probably on Monday. I don't anticipate any problems, but you never know. We weren't planning to hire an analyst, and he's always worried about the budget. I'll call you next week."

"Talk to you then."

I went back to the dinner table, and Paul said, "Was that Howard?"

"Yes." I said to Jim, "He's a mathematician at Santa Barbara. He called about a recent paper of mine. And to offer me a job."

"It's about time," Paul said. He had been my dissertation advisor and had spent a lot of time trying to convince people to hire me. "What kind of offer?"

"Nothing definite," I said. "Probably associate with tenure. He said he'd have to clear it with the administration because it's an extra position."

I called Elaine and made arrangements to celebrate with her after meeting Henry Melton Tuesday evening.

I found it difficult to get interested in the game, and I did not play well. I lost twenty-three dollars but afterward felt better than if I had won a hundred.

Henry and Margaret Melton live in Walnut Creek, a wealthy suburb of San Francisco east of the Berkeley Hills. In the summer, when a cold wind blows through a foggy San Francisco, it is sunny and hot in Walnut Creek fifteen miles away. They have a large, expensive home situated at the end of a cul-de-sac. Henry Melton answered the door when I knocked at eight o'clock Tuesday evening.

"Come in, Mr. Brodsky. I'm Henry Melton." He was a short, slender, bespectacled man with thinning hair. I knew he was fifty-eight, but he looked older, moving slowly and speaking softly. I followed him into a large living room furnished in the colonial style. "Sit down," he said. "I'll get my wife." There were many paintings on the walls, mostly landscapes, and all were signed, "Henry." He returned shortly with his wife. She was a white-haired obese woman in her late fifties.

Their description of the Melton birthday party was similar to that of previous witnesses, though they did add a few interesting details.

"Did anyone leave the table before your brother collapsed?"

"Not that I recall," Henry Melton said, "but I'm not sure. Margaret?"

101

"I don't remember anyone getting up," she said.

"What about cocktails? Do you remember what Melton was drinking?"

Mrs. Melton said, "He always had whiskey sours. He had two or three that night. Bradford liked his liquor."

"Did he ever have piña coladas?"

"Maybe once in a while, but he's been drinking whiskey sours ever since I met him thirty-five years ago," she said.

"That's right," her husband said. "Always whiskey sours."

"Do you remember if the hors d'oeuvres had been served?"

"That I do remember," Mrs. Melton said. "I was quite hungry and wanted the food service to begin. The waiter served the other side of the table, but our side was not served."

"What about your brother-in-law? Had he gotten his appetizer?"

"Yes," she said. "He was also served by the waiter."

"That's right," her husband said. "After he served the hors d'oeuvres, he bumped into Roger Mayfield. Now I remember."

"So Mayfield left the table?"

"Yes. He had gone to make a phone call. He brought back a piña colada for Bradford. Roger said it was on the house. For Brad's birthday."

"Did Mayfield give the drink directly to your brother?"

"No," he said. "Roger's seat was at the other end of the table. He handed the drink to Margaret, and she passed it to Jason Bealer. Jason gave it to Bradford."

"Mrs. Melton," I said, "do you remember Mayfield handing you the drink?"

She paused before answering and then said, rather cautiously I thought, "I do believe that's right. And I did give it to Jason."

"Mr. Melton, you're sure the drink was a piña colada?"

"Yes. Brad said something. He didn't really want it."

"But he did drink it?"

"Yes. Is that important?"

"No. The poison was in his wine. But the details help fill in the picture."

He said, "Will that kind of detail help Susan?"

"It's hard to say what will help. We know she's innocent, but the police have a strong case that must be countered. So I'm trying to find out all I can about the dinner and about your brother. What can you tell me about him? Please be frank."

"Mr. Brodsky, my brother is dead. He had good and bad traits. You're asking me to comment on his bad traits—after all, you want to know why someone killed him. It's not easy for me to speak badly of him now."

"I understand. Let me say that what you tell me will be held in the strictest confidence, and nothing will go beyond this room unless it has a direct bearing on the case. Your niece is in trouble, and I need the information."

He looked at me, stared at the ceiling, and sighed. "You're correct; Brad was not well liked. He sometimes could be ruthless in his dealings with people. He was strong and arrogant, dedicated to building Fabricon, willing to do whatever he thought necessary to achieve that end."

"Would you say he was unethical? It's been said he was rather devious in business."

"That's not accurate. He was brilliant when it came to business, and very successful. We took over several competing firms, and the new division usually did very well. Because of Bradford. Some of the previous owners felt they'd been cheated, but they were on the brink of bankruptcy before we bought them out."

"So you would say that his reputation was not deserved?"

"On the whole, no. He could be ruthless at times. If he was double-crossed, he would attack without mercy. But if you were straight with him, he gave you a fair shake."

His wife spoke up, quite sharply. "Henry, you know that's not true. He was absolutely ruthless at all times. He spied on the competition and stole their designs. He forced smaller companies out of business and then bought them up for a fraction of their true value. Hiding the truth will not help Susan, and it's obvious that Mr. Brodsky already knows what kind of man Bradford was. We don't want Susan convicted, and we must be candid now." She turned to me. "Bradford was a devil. The company was started by Henry's father, Elias, and Henry worked for him as a designer. Henry was always very artistic." She looked at him and smiled. "Look around this room. All these paintings are his."

"What happened when Bradford Melton joined them?" I said.

"Bradford assumed control, leaving design to Henry and the management of the factory to Elias. Bradford took over more and more of the operations. He slowly forced Elias out. Elias made out well financially, but Bradford took his company away from him. Elias died when he was fifty-nine years old, a defeated man sent out to pasture. When I met him in 1941, he looked more like Henry's brother than his father. When he died in 1950, he was an old man."

"You make it sound as if Bradford killed Dad," her husband said. "I know you never liked Brad very much, but Dad had cancer. He had to retire. Brad didn't force him out. Let's not be unfair."

"You're too easy on him, Henry," she said. "You always have been. Your father retired two years before he got sick." She looked at me and spoke with increased vehemence. "I'll tell you something else. It was not Bradford's business sense that built Fabricon. It was Henry's design.

Henry was and still is the finest designer of women's fashions on the West Coast."

She did hate Bradford Melton. I said, "So you think Fabricon's success will continue without him?"

"Yes," she said. "If anything, it will be more successful. Bradford's son, Joseph, will share control with Henry, and they will do very well together."

"I hope you're right, Margaret," he said. "I'm not so sure. For all his faults, Brad knew how to run the company. Maybe he wasn't entirely ethical with everybody he dealt with, but I could always depend on him."

I was happy to have them argue and said nothing. He continued. "I'm not very strong, physically or emotionally. Brad always looked out for me, even when we were kids. I remember once when I was sixteen or seventeen—he would have been thirteen or fourteen. I was having trouble with a bully. A big fellow, much stronger than I, and bigger than Brad at the time. The boy was trying to pick a fight with me, calling me names and shoving me. Brad came along like a little tornado and tore into the boy. The boy ran away crying, and Brad asked me if *I* were all right. He was always tough. And he was always loyal to me."

"Is that why he cheated you out of twenty percent of the company?" she snapped. She looked at me. "That's right. Fabricon absorbed Prince Jeans, but somehow all the Prince profits went to Bradford. Henry got nothing out of it. And Prince is now almost a quarter of Fabricon's business. It was that Roger Mayfield. He connived with Bradford to set it up that way."

"Margaret, stop!" He raised his voice for the first time. "That was a private deal. After Brad took over Prince, we agreed to merge. But Brad bought out Prince on his own. It was perfectly legitimate."

"Henry, you never stop defending him. But he cheated you, and you know it." She was getting very angry. Then

105

she calmed down, as if suddenly aware of my presence. She said, "Mr. Brodsky. I don't want you to get the wrong idea. Bradford Melton was ruthless in business, even in regard to his own brother. But I think I may have overstated the situation a little. We have done very well financially. We certainly have nothing to complain about."

That effectively ended the interview, although there were other questions I wanted to ask. I moved Roger Mayfield and Margaret Melton up a notch on the suspect list. It bothered me that Jason Bealer had handled the piña colada, but I still had no intention of proving him guilty.

∫16

∫ HAVALAH SPINELLI

I felt that I was getting closer to a solution of the Melton murder when I left Walnut Creek, but I was certainly unable to name the killer. I called Greg and asked him to hurry with the chemist's report, and I called Elaine to say I would be there soon. She was waiting with a bottle of champagne and a cake on which she had written, *which way is santa barbara*. We celebrated in grand fashion. She wondered if the party were not premature. I assured her that it was, but next week there might be nothing to celebrate.

She had succeeded in learning some potentially useful information: Delkin frequently went to Oregon, where he had a ranch on the coast, and every year he took a group of "disadvantaged children" to the Super Bowl.

Elaine left for work in the morning, leaving me alone in her apartment with nothing better to do than work on the Melton case. I called Jason Bealer's office. He said he was leaving early since it was Thanksgiving Eve and would meet with me at his home at two o'clock.

I went to Le Petit Chateau at noon, hoping to talk to the waiter and waitress who had served the Meltons. The restaurant was closed, but the maître d', Jean Martinot, was there. He was not unfriendly and was willing to answer a few more questions. I indicated that I wanted to talk to Elliot Fielder and Françoise Journet. He said that Elliot did not work on Wednesday, and that Françoise did not come in on Monday, but both were there every other day except Sunday, when Le Petit Chateau was closed.

I said, "You told me the police cleared the table."

"Oui. They took everything, even the tablecloth. They still have it all."

"Did they give you a list of what they took?"

"Mais oui. Would you like to see it?"

"Yes, if I could." He led me into a small office behind the cash register and pulled a sheet of paper from a filing cabinet. I glanced at the list, handed it back to him, and said, "Can you tell whether hors d'oeuvres had been served?"

He studied the list. "Six were served, monsieur." That was consistent with Elliot's side having hors d'oeuvres.

"Did anyone have a piña colada?"

He looked at the list again. "Oui. There was one."

"Can you remember if Mr. Melton was given a complimentary cocktail?"

"It is not likely," he said. "We had prepared a special cake for the affair, compliments of the chef. We would not have given him a cocktail as well."

"How do you keep track of customer bar bills?"

"The waiter takes the orders and writes them down. It is the same as with the dinners."

"Then," I said, "if a waiter wanted to give a customer a complimentary cocktail, you would have no record of it?"

"That is correct, but our waiters would never do such a thing without asking me."

"I understand. Of course a customer could get himself a drink from the bar, and you would have no record."

"The customer would pay the bartender, and it would be rung up on the cash register tape."

"But you would have no way of knowing which customer ordered which drink."

"No."

"The same would be true if a customer was drinking at the bar while waiting for a table."

"Oui."

I said, "May I see your wine cellar?"

"But why, monsieur? It is impossible for customers to go downstairs."

"Nonetheless, I'd like to see it." He led me through the kitchen and down a narrow stairway. The cellar was large, containing an impressive selection of wines. I looked around but saw nothing of interest. There was a door near the stairs, and I asked him where it led.

"Nowhere. It is a utility closet." He opened the door and switched on a light. There were various cleaning products, a mop, and two mousetraps. I was closing the door when I caught sight of a red box with a skull and cross bones—it was Rat Ravager! He didn't seem to notice my surprise and was apparently unaware of my discovery.

"Do all employees have access to this closet?" I said.

"Oui. They do. But only the janitor goes in there."

I thanked him and said that I would return to talk to Elliot and Françoise.

My next stop was the Bealers, and I felt uncomfortable as soon as I pulled up in front of the electronically controlled gate. It opened without my ringing as a voice said, "Come in, Mr. Brodsky."

Bealer greeted me with a firm handshake and a broad smile when I got out of my car. "I see that old heap of yours is still running. Come in. Come in."

His wife was waiting inside. She extended her hand and said, "Hello, Mr. Brodsky. I hope you've been well."

"Yes, fine, thank you."

"Will you be able to prove Susan is innocent?" she asked.

"I hope so. That's why I'm here."

"How can we be of assistance?"

"Roger Mayfield left the table to make a phone call."

"Yes," she said. "His mother had been ill."

"Can you remember what happened when he returned?"

"Is that important?" Bealer asked. "I'll be darned if I can remember."

"It might be important," I said. "I don't know yet. Let me put it another way. The last time we spoke, you mentioned that Melton was drinking a piña colada. It's not entirely clear how he got it. He didn't order it himself. What I want to know is . . ."

"That's right!" he bellowed. "Mayfield brought it back with him. He said it was on the house. For Brad's birthday, you understand. He handed it to me—I was sitting next to Brad."

"Are you sure he handed it directly to you?"

"No. I didn't remember the incident until this minute."

Mrs. Bealer said, "He didn't give it to you, Jason. He handed it to Margaret, and she passed it on to you. You then put it down in front of Bradford."

"You may be right," he said. Then he looked at me. "You can trust her, Brodsky. She has a much better memory than me. But how can this help Susan? The poison was in the wine, wasn't it?"

"Yes. But I don't like loose ends."

He gave me a long stare and said, "Loose ends, my

foot. You think the poison was in the drink." He laughed heartily. "It wouldn't surprise me one bit if you were right, too. You may well be the right man for the job." His face lit up suddenly. "Say. If you're right, Susan would be off the hook. Can you prove it? Why would the police say the poison was in his wine if it was in his drink?"

"Mr. Bealer, I wish I were as optimistic as you are. I don't know if the poison was in his drink, and if it was, I don't know if it can be proved. An independent chemist will do an analysis. We'll see. Let me ask you one last question. When Melton collapsed, who went over to him?"

"I did," Bealer said. "As soon as he collapsed. I was sitting next to him. Ralph was there immediately after me. Susan jumped up and screamed but didn't come near him. I think Raskin came over, probably to be sure he was dead. There were a couple others. Do you remember, Sarah?"

"Margaret came over to him, though not right away. There was also someone from the restaurant, a doctor I think."

"I'd like to be sure," I said. "Was there anyone else?"

"I don't think so," she said. "Roger went to get help, and Joe followed him. Doris and Henry stayed in their seats. So did I. Maybe Alice. I'm not sure."

"Thank you," I said. "You've been very helpful."

"We want to be, Brodsky," Bealer said. "And don't be afraid to call on us again. I have a lot of connections and will use them if need be. We don't want to see Susan convicted."

We shook hands and I left. Driving down the driveway I noticed an old pickup truck with what looked like garden tools in the back parked by a shed at the side of the house. Herman stopped, and I walked over. A short, elderly gentleman looked up at me and said, "Howdy."

"Hello," I said, extending my hand. "You must be Jason's gardener." He nodded, shaking my hand. "Jason was telling me how pleased he is with your work. Are you too busy to take on another home? My place is much smaller, maybe half an acre, but we could sure use some help, what with the trees and the flowers."

"Might be possible," he said. "Give me a call sometime. That's the number." He pointed to the door of his truck, which said "Sam's Gardening" and listed the phone number.

"I'll do that," I said, turning to leave. Then, as an after-thought, I said, "Say, maybe you can give me some advice. We have a rat problem in the basement. My wife can't stand them. I'm not too fond of them myself, to tell you the truth. What do you recommend?"

"I use my own mixture. Been in the business for forty-five years. Your missus ain't unusual, and I've handled a few rat problems in my time. A cat's the best thing, though. Get yourself a cat."

"I'm allergic to cats," I said.

"That's a shame. Cats 'r' nice animals. Solve rat problems quick, let me tell you. You could try one of the commercial products."

"Which one do you like?"

"Like I said. Use my own mixture. Used something called Rat Ravager couple a times. Don't like it much. It kills rats all right. But it kills dogs, too. Too dangerous for me. Nah, I like my own. Much safer. Effective, too. You betcha."

"Jason ever had a problem with rats?"

"Not since I been here. No sir. Not since I been here."

"You wouldn't happen to carry some of that Rat Ravager stuff on your truck. Or maybe your own mixture? Be glad to buy it from you."

"Like I told ya. Don't like that Rat Ravager. Too dangerous. And I don't carry my own 'less I need it."

111

"Okay. Thanks for the information. I'll call you soon."

I wasn't sure if I was disappointed or relieved to discover that Jason Bealer didn't have Rat Ravager handy. Maybe I was too nervous, but he sounded too innocent. He and his wife were the only ones at the dinner besides Ralph Cordova on whom no suspicion had been cast. I didn't know what I would do if I turned up evidence pointing to Bealer's guilt. I guess I did know—I would suppress it. I later met with Ralph, and he thought it was ridiculous to write him off as a suspect.

I said, "If Bealer had killed Melton, and if I were close to proving it, do you honestly think he would refrain from acting again? With his connections? Ralph, you prove he did it. Just don't tell me anything about it."

He laughed, and we discussed the day's events; we didn't turn up anything interesting.

I went home and spent the evening cooking and cleaning. I was expecting twenty-three guests for Thanksgiving, and quite a bit of preparation remained. Thanksgiving has always been one of my favorite holidays, filled with good food, good friends, and good cheer. This one was no different.

The Thanksgiving of two years earlier was one I'll always remember. My maternal grandmother, Havalah Spinelli, had died the previous summer, and the weekend was a memorial to her. She was a German Jew who had emigrated to the United States in 1907 at the age of fifteen. She married my Italian grandfather in 1911. They had four children, eleven grandchildren, and, counting my eight-month old niece, seventeen great grandchildren. She was the last of my grandparents, and she had become the family matriarch. She was loved and admired by everyone who knew her. We all were deeply affected by her and mourned her loss.

But enough sentimentality. I spent Friday recovering from Thanksgiving, and Saturday and Sunday preparing the final exam for my calculus class. I had it reproduced in school Monday afternoon.

Mitchell Halloran called me in my office. He said in a cheerful voice, "How's tricks? Hope you had a good Thanksgiving."

"Mitch, you're trying to butter me up. What is it?"

"I've got a hot case for you. Should be a bonus in it."

"Have you spoken with Greg?"

"You mean the other cases you're on? Don't worry. Greg says a few days won't hurt."

"That's not what I meant, Mitch."

"He did say something about you planning to quit. But how many times have said that in the last five years?"

"I'm serious this time. Can't you find another detective?"

"Sure. We could. But we have a working relation with you. We know what we're getting."

"I'm sure you can find someone you can trust."

"I suppose. But this case is right up your alley, and you won't start teaching for six months."

"I want to get out of the business," I said.

He said nothing, and I said, "All right. Tell me about the case. I'll get back to you in a couple of days. I can't start work on it before Wednesday anyway. I'll call you tomorrow if I decide to do it."

"That's fine," he said. "You should know there's a five-thousand-dollar bonus in it. You'd be able to do something about that wreck you drive."

"I'll let you know tomorrow. What's the job?"

"Most of our work, as you know, is union and political cases like the ones we've handled for you. They don't provide much income, but we do have some legitimate clients. One of them is a man named Ezekial Jones. He's in his seventies and dying. He hasn't seen his son in five years and wants to find him before he dies. He's wealthy and will be glad to pay time and expenses—any reasonable expenses. And if you can bring his son to him, there's a five K bonus."

"I'll consider it. But no promises."

"One other thing. There could be a connection with the Melton murder. It's pretty remote, but you never know. I'll tell you about it tomorrow."

"If I do it."

"Okay. But Dan, Jones has been a good client for us. I'd appreciate it if you would do it. As a personal favor."

"That's playing dirty, Mitch. Talk to you tomorrow."

I didn't want to take on another case, but Mitch Halloran had put a lot of groceries on my table. I sat in my office trying to come up with an excuse for refusing when the phone rang. It was Howard Williams.

"I met with the dean this morning," he said, "and I didn't want to keep you waiting. I'm afraid he said 'no.' I spent two hours arguing with him, but he said that budget constraints would not permit hiring another mathematician at this time. We have to hire two computer scientists. There's some chance things will change in April or May, but there's nothing we can do now. I'm really sorry, Dan. We would have liked to have you here. Me especially."

We chatted a while, but that was that. It was not the first academic position not offered to me, but I was depressed, much more so than in the past. I spoke to Paul Hobart, whose office is one flight up from mine, and we went to the Doberman Club, a deli-pizza-beer parlor on Telegraph Avenue. We became very philosophical about the whole thing after a pitcher of beer. He's a good friend. I would survive.

I felt better that evening winning thirty-two dollars in the poker game while the Raiders beat Denver 9–3 on Monday Night Football. The defense took command, but Plunkett was not sharp for the third week in a row. The

114

offense would have to improve if Oakland were to go all the way.

$\int$ 17

MITCHELL HALLORAN

Howard Williams's phone call ended immediate hopes of the academic life. I called Mitch Halloran Tuesday morning, and we agreed to meet for lunch on Wednesday and to see Ezekial Jones afterward. Nothing could be done on Tuesday because I was proctoring the calculus final.

The best students will complete a well-conceived three-hour exam in two-and-a-half hours, and the average student requires close to three hours. There are frequently one or two who realize they have learned nothing, accept their F, and leave in less than an hour. There is usually at least one student who will sit and work on his exam until his paper is taken away from him. This test was typical, and after three-and-a-half hours the last two students reluctantly handed in their exams.

It was two in the morning before I finished grading the finals, making up the grades, and filling out the various required end-of-quarter reports. I try to be objective when determining grades. During the quarter, there were two one-hour exams, each of which was twenty percent of the final grade; eight short quizzes, which counted twenty percent together; and the final, which was forty percent. To receive an A, a student had to achieve a 90 average, a B was an 80, and so on. Those break points

115

were not absolute—one student with an 89 average was given an A.

I had promised to post the grades on my office door by ten on Wednesday morning and to be in my office until eleven. Half the class stopped by. A few looked at their grades and left, and several came in to thank me. Six or seven wanted to look at their exams, including the two best students in the class. Their scores were 94 and 97, but they still wanted to see the mistakes they had made. One of them, Marie Arnot, told me she was a biology major but enjoyed her math courses more than her bio courses. We discussed the possibility of her switching to math, and I emphasized the need for more women in mathematics.

There was only one student who complained about his grade—he wanted an A instead of a B. His name was Arnold Pratt, a short blond with scraggly hair. He came in while I was talking with Marie Arnot, glanced at the grade sheet on the door, and said in an aggressive tone, "I don't think my grade is fair."

"If you like," I said, "I'll discuss it with you in a few minutes. I'm busy at the moment."

"But I'm in a hurry. We have to talk now."

"When I'm done."

He looked angry, but waited outside my office. During the ten minutes I was talking with Marie, he paced back and forth in the hall, looking at his watch each time he passed the door. When Marie was finished, he came in and said, "I deserve an A." His tone did not leave room for discussion.

I picked up my grade book and examined his record. He did have a 96 average on quizzes, but his exam scores were 81 and 73, with a 74 on the final. His semester average was 79.6—barely a B. I explained my grading system to him, indicating that a B was already generous. I showed him the scores of the A students and made it clear that he was not close to them.

He was not satisfied. "But look at my quiz grades. We had a quiz every week, so they're the best measure of how much a student learns. Only one of the A students had better quizzes."

"The quizzes are not the best measure of a student's performance, and certainly not the only measure. Moreover . . ."

"Then what is the best measure? It's the only thing we did every week."

"As I began to say before you interrupted me," I said, no longer hiding my annoyance, "the final is the one time when you must put the whole course together. That's why it's forty percent of the grade."

"It's not fair to give one exam that covers the whole course."

"A three-hour final is required."

Suddenly he became contrite. "But you see," he said, putting his hands in his pockets, "this is my first quarter at Berkeley and I must maintain a three-point-six cume for my major. Electrical engineering. I don't want to start out behind the eight ball." The "cume" he spoke of is the cumulative index, which is an overall average of grades received. An A is a 4.0, a B 3.0, down to 0.0 for an F.

"You're not close to an A," I said.

"But there are a lot of math majors in the class. It's not fair to grade me on the same basis."

"Why not?"

"Well, because . . . because math is their major."

He went on for twenty minutes, arguing that he deserved more points on various exams, and that his quizzes should count more and his final less. I finally agreed to look at his exams again and meet with him Thursday morning. He still wanted to argue, but I said I had a

117

luncheon appointment and had to leave immediately. He reluctantly gave up. For the moment.

I met Mitch Halloran for a dim sum lunch in Oakland's Chinatown. "Dim sum" refers to the style of service as well as to the type of food. Waiters carry trays containing small plates with food that can best be described as Chinese hors d'oeuvres. Customers simply point to the dishes they want, and at the end of the meal the bill is tallied by counting the plates. The food is usually excellent.

Mitch is tall and lanky with curly black hair. He is relaxed and easygoing—I can't remember seeing him losing his temper. We're not close friends, but we have had a good professional relationship and have always gotten along well.

He greeted me in front of the restaurant with a broad smile and a warm handshake. He commented that he was happy I had decided to take the case, and we chatted a while about tennis and the Raiders. (He's an ardent Forty-Niners fan, but they weren't going anywhere.)

"It's time to get to it," he said, putting down his chopsticks and picking up his teacup. He sipped and said, "Ezekial Jones was a furrier for many years. He started his own business in the fifties. Prince Furs. The business did well, and after ten years or so they expanded and started selling jeans. By the late sixties, jeans sales far exceeded fur sales.

"We became his attorneys because he'd been a left-winger. Most of the work was routine. In 1975 Melton made a move to take over Prince, which by then was doing very well in the jeans market. While Zeke was very friendly with us, he didn't think we were the right attorneys to deal with Melton. The lawyers he did hire couldn't or wouldn't handle Melton, and Zeke came back to us when he saw his company being stolen from him. I won't go into the legal technicalities, but when we got into it, it was too late to save the company. We did manage to salvage something, and there was a cash settlement. Three million bucks. But Melton did get Prince."

"Is this an introduction to the case, or do you think there might be a tie-in to the murder?"

He sipped his tea. "The connection sounds remote. Zeke certainly was not at Le Petit Chateau when Melton was killed. On the other hand, more than one person lost money because of the Melton takeover of Prince—it's possible someone carried a grudge a long time."

"If everyone who disliked Melton were a suspect," I said, "we'd have a million of them. Jason Bealer seems to be the only living person who didn't hate Melton. But I'll keep it in mind." I sat back and said, "What do you want me to do?"

"Zeke didn't marry until he was forty-three. He and his wife had one child. A son, Peter. He left San Francisco State in 1976. He and Zeke got into a big fight about something—I don't know what—and Zeke hasn't seen him since."

"And I'm supposed to find Peter?"

"You got it. Zeke has a bad heart. He doesn't know how long he'll live and wants to patch things up with his son before he dies."

"What about the boy's mother?"

"She died twelve years ago."

"We should begin by talking to Jones," I said.

"Fine. Let's go see him."

I leaned forward, resting my elbows on the table, and said, "And the deal is time and expenses with a five-thousand-dollar bonus should I bring Peter to his father?"

"That's right, Dan. And you can be free with the expenses. But don't get ridiculous."

"I see you've been talking to Greg."

"He did mention something about a hundred-dollar dinner."

"All in the line of work."

∫18

EZEKIAL JONES

Ezekial Jones was in a small private hospital in Berkeley. His room was on the fourth floor, and he was asleep when we arrived. Mitch shook him gently, saying, "Zeke . . . Zeke."

"Maybe we should let him sleep," I whispered.

"No. He'll feel a lot better if he knows you're out there looking for his son." He prodded again. "Zeke . . . Zeke . . . Wake up." Jones began to stir, and Mitch said, "Wake up, Zeke."

He opened his eyes, looked around, and said in a groggy voice, "Hello, Mitch. It's good to see you." He looked at me. "Who's that?"

"This is Dan Brodsky, Zeke. He's going to find Peter."

I extended my hand and we shook. He looked me over and said, "You think you can find my boy?"

"I'll do my best, Mr. Jones."

"Mitch, is he any good?"

Mitch smiled and looked at me. "He's a bit ornery at times, but he's the best man for the job."

Jones looked at me again. "Mr. uh . . . Mitch, wha'dya say his name was?"

"Brodsky," I said. "Daniel Brodsky."

"Brodsky, huh? You'll have to do." He pressed a button at his side, and the head of the bed slowly rose, leaving him in an almost sitting position. "I'm an old man. I'm dyin'. Bad ticker." He tapped a finger on his chest. "I've

120

worked hard all my life and never cheated nobody. All that's left is some money and a missing son. Not much for an old fogy. I want my son. He's a good boy. We had a little fallin' out a few years back. One thing led to another. I ain't seen him in four years. Find him for me. Before I leave this world."

"Tell me about Peter," I said.

He reached into the drawer in a small table next to the bed and pulled out a billfold. He fished through it and handed me an old, wrinkled, black and white snapshot of a young man. "That's Peter," he said. "Course he was much younger then. That was taken when he was fifteen, and he's twenty-five now."

"Could you describe him for me? This picture only shows his face."

"He's a big boy," he began, smiling at the thought of his son. "'Bout six feet tall. Broad shoulders. Weighed around hundred eighty-five last time I saw him. He had long blond hair then—looked like a hippie to me." He grimaced and went on. "Let's see. What else can I tell you? He has blue eyes and a small mole on his neck. Just below his left ear."

"That should do," I said, "along with this picture." I looked at the picture again. It seemed familiar, but I couldn't place the face. "What else can you tell me?"

"Wha'dya wanna know?"

"Start with hobbies, special things he liked to do."

"Well," he said, rubbing his chin, "he liked sports. All kinds. Baseball, football, basketball. Used to swim a lot. And water ski. He loved to go to the mountains by himself."

"Do you know any of his friends or acquaintances?"

"No."

"He went to San Francisco State College?"

"Yes."

"Did he graduate?"

"In seventy-six."

"Do you know what his major was?"

"His major? Let me think . . . social something or other?"

"Sociology?" I said.

"Yeah. That's it."

"Do you know what he intended to do when he graduated?"

"He wanted to save the world," he said in a disparaging tone.

"Can you be a little more specific?" I said. "Did he plan to find a job or to continue school? Anything like that?"

"I think he used to talk about more schoolin', but I don't know what he did. He used to say he wanted to help people—give them counseling. He was a dreamer."

"That should be enough to get started," I said. "I'll talk to you again if I need more information."

Mitch and I said our good-byes and were leaving when Jones called out, "Mr. Brodsky. Please find my boy."

I turned and smiled. "I will."

In the elevator Mitch asked, "What do you think, Dan? Can you find him?"

"He hasn't been seen for four years. He could be in Nepal or Tibet, and he could be dead. But most likely he's findable. I'll do my best. He's a nice old man." We walked to our cars, and I said, "Give Greg a message for me. Ask him to get the chemist's analysis as fast as possible, and tell him to be sure the chemist is very thorough."

"Sure. Anything else?"

"Yeah. Ask him to get a CPA to look at Fabricon's books. Try Marilyn Greene."

"Who is she?"

"Greg knows her. She's very sharp, but people underestimate her because she's overweight. Have him tell her to pay particular attention to Prince Jeans."

"Prince Jeans?" he asked, rather surprised. "You don't really think there's a connection?"

"I doubt it. But this is the second time Prince has been mentioned. We might as well check it out."

The place to start looking for Peter Jones was San Francisco State, but it was after four when I reached home and too late to accomplish anything that afternoon.

The appointment with Arnold Pratt the next morning was at eleven, and I reached my office at nine and telephoned San Francisco State.

A nasal female voice answered, "San Francisco State College."

"Could you please give me the name of the chairman of the Sociology Department?"

"Please hold." A few seconds later she said, "Professor George DeWitt. Would you like me to connect you?"

"Please do."

Another phone rang and another female voice answered. "Department of Sociology."

"May I speak with Professor DeWitt?" I said.

"Who's calling, please?"

"My name is Harrison Emory. I'm calling from the State University of New York at Stony Brook." I have been known to fib on occasion. All in the line of duty of course.

"Please hold." I did not wait long. Generally speaking, one can get through quickly when calling long distance. A male voice said, "This is George DeWitt."

"My name is Harrison Emory. I'm calling from SUNY Stony Brook."

"What can I do for you?"

"We're in the process of hiring someone to counsel students. One of the candidates is a man named Peter Jones. He's among the top three applicants. We consider the position important and want to check carefully before making a final decision. Peter Jones graduated from San Francisco State in nineteen seventy-six, and we were hoping you might remember him."

"Don't you have references?" he asked.

"Of course. We have four, and all are praiseworthy. But we do want to check further because of the importance of the position. None of his referees are from San Francisco State. Not that we expected any. After all, he hasn't been there in four years."

"Quite frankly, Mr. Emory, I don't remember him. But we do have a lot of students. You might try Carl Collins. He knew many of our majors, and he was here four years ago."

"Thank you," I said. "I appreciate your help. Could you give me back the operator? I'm calling long distance. I'm sure you have the same budgetary restrictions we have."

"Don't we ever. Sorry I couldn't be of more assistance."

I went through the same story with Carl Collins but did no better. He suggested I try Raymond Boulanger, who was not in his office. His secretary told me he would be in after two.

I called Greg.

"Halloran and Mackey."

"Could I speak to Greg Langley, please? This is Dan Brodsky."

"Please hold." The world seemed to be on hold.

Greg picked up his extension and said, "Hi, Dan. Say something to make me happy."

"No news is good news."

"That doesn't make me happy," he said. "What's up?"

"Did you talk with Mitch this morning?"

"Yeah. We had to get a court order for the independent chemist. The analysis should be ready next week."

"That'll be fine."

"I spoke to Marilyn, and she'll be happy to do what you want. She sounded as if she thought it would be fun to play detective."

"She should be very good, Greg."

"No doubt. Anything on what's-his-name?"

"Peter Jones. Not yet. I've just started. I'm supposed to call somebody this afternoon who might have some information. Tell Mitch I'll keep in touch."

"Will do." Then, as if suddenly surprised, he said, "Are you working today? It's Thursday."

"But Greg. I'm working for Mitch." I hung up quickly.

Arnold Pratt showed up at eleven on the dot. He appeared to be less aggressive. "What have you decided?" he said.

"I've looked at your exams and your average very carefully," I lied, "and I see no basis for changing your grade."

He was not pleased, but he didn't show any anger. He said contritely, "Yesterday when I said I was new at Berkeley, that wasn't exactly right. I already have two Bs and a C in my major. I can't afford a B in this course." It is not at all uncommon for students to have sob stories to justify grades higher than they deserve, and under some circumstances I will give a student a somewhat higher grade than he has earned. But not when a student has two, contradictory stories.

"There's nothing I can do," I said.

He went back to his arguments about quiz scores and being compared to math majors. Besides, my exams were too hard—he could have had 90s if they'd been fair. His quiz scores proved that. The discussion lasted thirty minutes until I said, "I'm not changing your grade; I won't debate with you any longer."

He wasn't done yet. "Will it reflect badly on you if I appeal my grade? I wouldn't want to get you in trouble." As if he cared. Or did he think it was a threat?

"You may do whatever you want," I said. "But I am not changing your grade. That's final." He left and I spent the next hour calming myself.

Nothing more could be accomplished on the Jones case until two, so I went home and had lunch. I succeeded in reaching Raymond Boulanger at State and gave him the same story.

"Oh sure," he said. "I remember Peter very well." Paydirt! "He was a fine student; the type that makes it clear why we work so hard at this job."

Unlike Arnold Pratt. I said, "Could you tell me a little about him? There are two things I would particularly like to hear your comments on. One is, how well do you feel he will work with students in need of counseling; the other is, do you think his training is adequate?"

"He was well liked by both students and faculty. He majored in sociology because of a genuine concern for people. He went to Lawrence largely on my advice because of their counseling program. By the way, did he finish his degree?"

I thought quickly. Lawrence would be the University of Kansas. I decided that Jones did not finish a Ph.D. and said, "He has his Masters."

"He didn't complete the Ph.D.?"

"No," I said, "but that's not a requirement for this position. The most important requisite is the ability to relate to students. Some members of the selection committee actually feel that a Ph.D. would be overqualified. I don't happen to agree, but I don't see a Ph.D. as essential either."

We discussed Peter Jones and the position at Stony Brook for another few minutes, but he had no more useful information. It bothered me deceiving Boulanger that way because he obviously cared about Jones. If I found him, I would be sure to have him get in touch with Boulanger.

I put a call in to Mitch Halloran, but he was not in the

office. His secretary said he would check in later in the afternoon, and she would have him call me. He called an hour later.

"Any news on Peter Jones?" he said.

"He went to the University of Kansas after graduating," I said. "That's as far as I've gotten."

"Great. What's your next move?"

"That's what I wanted to ask you about. I'll probably have to fly out to Kansas, even if he's no longer there. There's only so much you can do over the telephone."

"Do what you think's best," he said. "If you're worried about expenses, there's no problem with traveling."

"First class?"

"Coach."

"Okay. I'll probably fly out Sunday."

"Why not go tomorrow?"

"With the time difference and a four-hour flight, not to mention picking up baggage and a car, I'd arrive too late to do anything tomorrow. I might as well wait until the weekend. It's even possible a few phone calls will make the trip unneccessary."

"It's your show, Dan. Your only restriction is time. Zeke is anxious to see his son, and Greg wants you back on the other cases."

"Be in touch, Mitch."

I had a friend named Nicholas Zorn in the Department of Mathematics at Kansas, and I called him at home.

"Nick? This is Dan Brodsky."

"Hey, Dan, how ya doin'? Still a gumshoe?"

"Yeah. That's what I'm calling about."

"Sorry. We don't need any analysts."

"That's not what I meant, Nick. I'm trying to find somebody."

"You serious? You want me to help you on a case?"

"More or less. I need some information."

"What's the case?"

127

"An old man has not seen his son in four years," I said. "I'm supposed to find him. The old man's dying. The kid apparently went to K. U. in nineteen seventy-six."

"How can I help?"

"You have some kind of counseling program. Maybe several. I'd like to know in which departments."

"The School of Education has one. Supposed to be a good one. A friend of mine's in it. I could give him a call."

"That'd be great, Nick. Ask him if he's ever heard of a Peter Jones."

"I'll call him and get back to you tonight. You home?"

"Yes. Talk to you later."

It didn't take long for Nick to contact his friend, and the phone rang a few minutes later.

"Hello," I answered.

"Is this Daniel Brodsky?"

"Yes." It was a long distance call, but not Nick.

"My name is Alex Hermes. Nick Zorn called me."

"Ah yes," I said. "I thought you might be he calling back."

"Nick said you were looking for one of our students. Something about his father looking for him?"

"That's right. His name is Peter Jones. I've been led to believe he went to K. U. to study counseling, and he might have been in your department. His father is anxious to see him. They had a fight four years ago and haven't had any contact with each other since. The kid's name is Peter Jones."

"I think I remember a Peter Jones a couple of years ago," he said, "but I doubt if he's still a student here."

"That's okay. I'm trying to trace him. Can you tell me anything about him?"

"I didn't know him that well. I could find out tomorrow."

"Terrific," I said. "I'm thinking of flying out on Sunday. Could I meet you at school?"

"I'll be in Monday," he said. "My office is 203 Baily Hall. How does ten sound?"

"Fine. If you're unable to find out anything, could you call me back? I'd rather not make the trip if I don't have to."

"Sure. But someone around here will remember him."

"Good. See you Monday morning."

I called Mitch to report, made plane reservations, and ordered a rent-a-car. This one might be easy.

∫ 19

ANGELA ELDIN

There was little to do on the Jones case before leaving for Kansas, and I called Susan Melton Friday afternoon.

"Susan, this is Dan Brodsky. How are you holding up?"

"I'm okay. I wish we could get this thing settled already."

"It takes time," I said. "We are making progress, and I don't think you need worry. I called to ask a couple of questions."

"Sure. What do you want to know?"

"On the afternoon of your father's death, did anyone visit you after you came home with the Rat Ravager?"

"My parents came by. Mother wanted to check last-minute details for the birthday party. Roger Mayfield drove them. They were waiting for us when we got home."

"Did they see the Rat Ravager?"

"Yes. Roger said something about 'rats in the belfry.' He thought it was funny."

"One other question. When your father collapsed, who went over to him?"

"Billy and Jason Bealer were sitting next to him, and they tried to help. I think Aunt Margaret and someone from the restaurant was there, too. I can't remember."

"That's fine," I said. "Don't worry. We are progressing. I think we'll have the whole thing cleared up before your trial."

I spent Saturday with Elaine, and she drove me to the airport Sunday morning. The flight was uneventful, and the rented car was waiting for me when the plane landed. It was sixty miles to Lawrence, and I wasn't settled in a motel until after nine. I finished the Agatha Christie novel I had started on the plane, hoping for inspiration from Poirot. I went to sleep, uninspired, realizing that Poirot would have solved the Melton murder with no difficulty.

I appeared at Alex Hermes's office at ten and was greeted by Nick Zorn. He made the introductions and said, "I hope you don't mind if we tag along. This looks like fun."

"It's not," I said, "but you're welcome."

Alex, who had stood to shake hands, sat behind his desk, and Nick and I took straight-back chairs in front of it. His office was cluttered with books, journals, and newspapers. Alex had curly red hair and was as unkempt as his office. Nick is short and dark with meticulously manicured hair and beard.

"I have some information for you," Alex said. "Peter Jones was a student here from nineteen seventy-six to nineteen seventy-eight, when he received an M.A. His adviser was Gale Windsor, but Gale doesn't know what Jones did when he left."

Nick interrupted with a smile. "Then we did some detective work. Gale knew a student who was still here and had known Jones. We spoke to the student, and she didn't know where Jones went."

"That's detecting?" I said.

"Aha!" Alex said. "We didn't stop there. We do have his last known address."

"You guys are real pros."

"Is that the place to start?" Nick said.

"As good as any."

Alex rose with his hands on the desk and said, "Let's go then."

"You're both nuts," I said. "Come on."

We went in the rental, and they directed me to an address on Tennessee Street. "You two will have to wait here," I said. I put on a coat and tie and walked up to a modern apartment building with twelve units and a security door. I pressed the button of number one, which was marked "manager" under the name Joanne Lesley. I did not see the name Jones among the tenants. The door buzzed, and I pushed it open and went to apartment number one. My knock was answered by a young woman.

"We're all filled up," she said.

"I'm not looking for an apartment. A man by the name of Peter Jones used to live here. I'm trying to find him."

She eyed me suspiciously and said, "What do you want him for?"

"My name is Hamilton Powell," I said, handing her a business card that indicated that the bearer was an attorney. "Mr. Jones's father died recently in San Francisco, and there's a rather large inheritance."

"Are you on the level?"

"I assure you, Miss Lesley, I am. If I can find Peter Jones, he will be quite a wealthy young man."

"You're not a cop?"

"Not a cop. If you can help, it would simplify matters a great deal. Jones's father had a brother and a sister who want to get their hands on his money. If we can't locate Peter, there will be a court battle."

"I'd like to help," she said, "but I didn't know him. I've only been here a year. If he left before that . . ." She snapped her fingers. "Maybe Bob Korman knew him. Bob's been here for three years. He lives in number nine. That's upstairs."

"Thank you, Miss Lesley."

I turned to look for a stairway when she called me back. "You won't find him now, Mr. Powell. He won't be in until this evening."

I returned to the car, and Nick said, "Well?"

"The manager's been here only a year and doesn't know Jones. He must have moved out right after he finished his degree."

"What do you do now?" Alex asked.

"Come back this evening. There's a tenant who's lived here for three years."

We drove back to the University and Alex said, "It's been fun, guys, but I've got work to do. You'll have to do your own investigating, Dan."

I thanked him, and Nick and I went to lunch. We spent the afternoon in his office discussing mathematics, and we returned to the apartment on Tennessee Street at 6:30. Nick remained in the car. I pressed the button for number nine, and a voice came out of the wall. "Who's there?"

"My name is Hamilton Powell. Joanne Lesley may have mentioned I'd stop by?"

"Yeah, she did. You're the lawyer." The door buzzed, and I went up to his apartment. He was waiting for me in the hall, and I handed him a Hamilton Powell card.

He glanced at it and said, "C'mon in." He was a student

type in his early twenties. I followed him into a small living room with beat-up old furniture. "Sit yourself down," he said, and I sat on a couch with stuffing oozing out. He reclined himself in a large chair in similar condition.

"So Pete Jones is coming into some money," he said.

"If I can find him. His aunt and uncle have hired attorneys and are contesting his father's will. His father, Ezekial Jones, did leave a will designating Peter as his sole heir. But if we can't locate Peter . . ."

"I'll tell you what I know," he said. "It's not much."

"Whatever you can tell me."

"Pete used to live here." He stood and began pacing the floor. "He moved out a couple years ago. He'd just finished his master's. He told me where he was going. Let's see. I remembered it when Joanne was here . . . Kansas City! He got a job with welfare." He stopped pacing and looked at me. "Will that help?"

"It could. Did he leave a forwarding address?"

"No. We weren't good friends. I mean, we were friendly all right, and maybe had a beer together or something. But not really close, if you know what I mean."

"Yes. I know what you mean."

I thanked him and went back to the car. I filled Nick in and said, "Want to take a trip to Kansas City?" He declined, and we went to dinner and spent the evening drinking beer.

Kansas City is really two cities, one in Kansas, one in Missouri. There are a number of welfare offices, and I called them one by one.

"Welfare."

"Could I speak to Peter Jones? He helped me out quite a bit a year ago."

"Please hold . . . I'm sorry we don't have a Peter Jones working here. Can anyone else help you?"

"I don't think so."

The next two calls were almost identical, but the response to the fourth was, "I'm sorry, Peter Jones is no longer with us." The conversation then duplicated the others. I decided to wait until the next day to visit that office—I didn't want anyone to remember the phone call when I started asking questions about Peter Jones.

The office was on the second floor of an old building in downtown Kansas City, Missouri. There was a long counter opposite the elevator, and behind it was a large room with perhaps twenty desks. There was a flurry of activity and three long lines when I arrived. I walked up to a harried woman behind the counter, thrust a business card at her, and said, "My name is Hamilton Powell, the attorney. I must get in touch with Peter Jones. It is a matter of some urgency."

She looked up and said, "Excuse me?"

I repeated myself. She pointed to a door marked "Private" at the end of the counter and returned to the form she had been filling out. I went to the door and knocked. A high-pitched female voice said, "Enter." The office was small, and a very thin woman in her forties peered up at me through horn-rimmed glasses. She sat behind a cluttered desk with a cigarette in her hand; the large ashtray in front of her was full. The name plate on the desk read Henrietta Gruen. I gave her a card and explained that I was looking for Peter Jones, who stood to inherit if he could be located.

She put the cigarette in her mouth, stood, went over to a filing cabinet near the window, and said, "I remember Peter. He was a caseworker, and a good one. He wasn't with us very long." She pulled out a file, saying, "Ah, here it is." She sat down again and stubbed the cigarette in the ashtray. It was still lit, and a thin trail of smoke rose between us. She shuffled through the file and said, "He started working for us in July of nineteen seventy-nine and left in May of nineteen eighty." She looked up and said, "That's last spring." She leafed through the folder again. "It doesn't say where he went. As I recall, he said he felt he wasn't helping anyone. He was too idealistic to work here. I don't know what happened to him." She lit another cigarette.

"Is there anyone in the office who might know him?"

"Try Burt Franklyn. He has the desk near the water cooler in the back."

I was happy to leave her office and made my way for the water cooler. "Mr. Franklyn?"

The man behind the desk was in his late thirties. His jacket hung on his chair, his tie was loose, and his shirt sleeves were rolled up to his elbows. He said, "Yes?"

"Mrs. Gruen said you might be able to help me," I said, handing him one of my cards.

"Yes?"

"I'm looking for Peter Jones. She said you might know him."

"I do. What do you want him for?" I explained one more time, and he said, "He told me he wanted to return to San Francisco. But I don't know if he actually went back. I'll tell you who might, though. There was a girl he got pretty friendly with. Let me see." He took an address book from the top drawer. "Here it is." He wrote the name "Angela Eldin" and an address on a sheet of paper. I thanked him and left.

I had passed through Kansas City a couple of times on cross-country trips, but I was unfamiliar with the city. I got lost trying to find Angela Eldin's address and stopped for lunch, more than somewhat annoyed that I had not bothered to obtain a street map. It was after two by the time I found the place, a lovely old building with six apartments. She did not answer my ring, but the building manager was in. He told me she was a school teacher and would likely be home by 3:30.

It turned out to be fortunate that she was out because I discovered I had given away all the Hamilton Powell cards. I sat in the rented car trying to determine what ploy to use. I looked through the business cards I did have. A plumber? No. I could be a computer consultant or a computer technician. Perhaps appropriate for the Welfare Department, but not for a teacher. A stockbroker. That might do it. How's this? Jones bought a stock that has gone way up—it should be sold now—I needed his approval. Yes! But who would believe a stockbroker would look up someone's old girlfriend. Maybe a real estate agent? No good.

I really liked the inheritance stratagem. Most people are reluctant to help you find someone because they don't want to cause anyone trouble. They react quite differently if they think you have money to give away. Being a lawyer seems to legitimate the story better than being a private investigator does.

I could be Dan Brodsky and still use the inheritance. That was almost the truth anyway. I could even be completely straightforward with her. Of course, being honest would make me uncomfortable.

I had decided that honesty was the best policy when I rang her apartment at four o'clock. An attractive brunette opened the door a crack and asked, "What can I do for you?"

"Are you Angela Eldin?"

"Yes?" She sounded suspicious. If only I had Hamilton Powell cards.

"My name is Dan Brodsky. I'm trying to locate Peter Jones."

"What do you want him for?"

"May I come in and explain?"

"No. What do you want him for?"

"His father wants him. They haven't seen each other for four years."

136

"What's his father's name?"

"Ezekial."

That seemed to mollify her. She said, "Come in," and opened the door. She led me into a nicely furnished studio apartment and said, "Sit down," indicating the sofa. "What did you say your name was?"

"Brodsky. Dan Brodsky. Peter's father is having heart problems and is anxious to see his son before he dies. Four years ago they had some kind of argument, and now Zeke wants to patch things up. He hired me to find Peter."

"How did you find me?"

"I started with San Francisco State College," I said, "and ended up at Welfare in Kansas City. Someone there knew you."

"Burt Franklyn."

"Yes. He wanted to help Peter. After all, Peter's father is wealthy. But money has nothing to do with Zeke wanting to find his son. He's a cantankerous old man, but I like him. It would be good if they could talk."

"Peter's back in San Francisco," she said. "He never gave me his address."

"You have no way of getting in touch with him?"

"He's called a couple times." She stood and said, "He told me he changed his name."

"What else did he tell you?"

"He was happy to be back home. He had a job as a waiter. Not much else."

"You don't have his address or phone number?" She hesitated and I said, "Miss Eldin, if I find Peter, I won't force him to see his father. But he should know his father is looking. Let me have the chance to talk to him."

She sat down and looked at her hands, clasped in her lap. She said quietly, without looking up, "I know his phone number."

"May I have it?"

She continued to stare at her hands. "All right." She wrote down the number and said, "He never did give me his address."

"Do you know what name he's using?"

"No."

"Thank you. I do believe Peter will be happy to see his father."

I drove to the airport and was able to book an 8:40 flight. That left two hours to kill, and I called San Francisco. Two years earlier I had helped a woman named Jane Abbott who worked for Ma Bell. A man had smashed into her parked automobile and driven off. A witness got the license plate, but the address listed with the Department of Motor Vehicles was not current, and the police checked no further. She hired an attorney, and he hired me. I found the driver, and she was able to sue successfully, the award being large enough to cover legal expenses and a new car. She was grateful, and on more than one occasion has assisted me. When I spoke to her from the Kansas City airport, I gave her Jones's phone number and asked for the name and address. At work she had available the most up-to-date cross listings of names and phone numbers, and she said she would call me at home in the morning.

∫20
∫ PETER JONES

It was two in the morning when I reached home and was tucked safely into bed. I slept soundly until I was cruelly awakened by the blast of a ringing telephone. It was Jane Abbott.

"I've got the information you wanted, Danny."

"What?" I said in a groggy voice.

"Did I wake you? Oh, I'm sorry. I have the information you wanted."

My brain began to function. "Let me find a pencil . . . Shoot."

"The name is Elliot Fielder and . . ."

"What!" Peter Jones was the waiter at Le Petit Chateau. Small world.

"The name is Elliot Fielder. Wake up, Danny, and don't shout."

"I'm awake. The name's a bit of a surprise. What's the address?"

He lived on 27th Avenue, north of California—the northwest part of San Francisco. I considered calling Mitch but decided against it since I had promised Angela Eldin that I would not force Peter to see his father. Herman gave me no trouble and brought me to Jones-Fielder's place, which was on the second floor of a duplex. He answered my knock and admitted me to a modern, sparsely furnished one-bedroom apartment.

"Hello, Peter."

He stiffened, almost imperceptibly. "What did you call me?"

"Your father is dying. He wants to see you."

He started to say something but just sighed. He walked to a window and closed it.

"Peter, this has nothing to do with the Melton murder. Your father hired me to find you. I didn't know you were Elliot Fielder until this morning."

He sat down, leaned back, and clasped his hands behind his head."

"How did you know I was Peter Jones?"

"I didn't. I traced Peter Jones to Kansas City, found out that he'd returned to San Francisco. All I had was a phone number. It was yours."

He laughed. "Can't you leave well enough alone?"

"Peter, I promised Angela Eldin that I wouldn't tell your father I'd found you unless you were willing to see him. If you don't want to see him, I won't force you."

"Then I don't want to see him."

"I know he's pretty hard-headed. But maybe you should give him a chance. I don't know what you fought about four years ago, but he is your father."

"Is he really dying?"

"I don't know," I said. "That's what he told me. He's in the hospital with a heart problem. But he may live another twenty years for all I know. He struck me as a tough old coot."

He smiled. "That he is." He stood and looked out the window. "He didn't tell you what we argued about?"

"No."

"It was over a woman. I was engaged. He didn't like my choice. I wanted to marry her anyway. In the end . . . well, I guess . . . I don't know. The marriage never happened."

"Was it your father's fault?"

"No. He was probably right about Betty. But he should have let me . . . You see, the fight was bigger than that. He would never let me lead my own life, make my own decisions. He . . . You don't understand." He opened the window and stared out. "Is he really that sick?"

"I think so. I could drive you now."

He turned and looked at me. "I don't know. I . . ." He paced the floor in front of the window. "How did you find me anyway?"

"I started with San Francisco State. I talked to a man named Raymond Boulanger."

"Boulanger? He was one of the best teachers I had over there. I went to K. U. because of him."

"I know. He told me. You should look him up. He'd like to see you."

"Maybe I will. I guess he told you I went to Kansas."

"Yes."

"And there you met Albert Ermine, who told you I'd gotten a job in Kansas City."

"No. I never met him, though I did go to the Welfare Department."

"Then how did you get there?"

"It doesn't matter. Let's go see your dad. You've grown up. And now you do make your own decisions."

He was staring out the window again. He sighed and said, "Okay."

"Good. Let me make a phone call first." I picked up the receiver and dialed.

"Halloran and Mackey."

"This is Dan Brodsky. I'd like to speak with Mitch Halloran."

"He's in conference."

"Tell him it's urgent."

"Please hold . . . He'll be with you shortly."

I put my hand over the mouthpiece and said to Peter, "I'm trying to get Mitch Halloran. He's your dad's attorney, and . . ."

Mitch came on the line. "What's up, Dan?"

"Can you meet me at the hospital in half an hour?"

"You found him! Fantastic!"

"Don't call Zeke. Let Peter handle it. By the way, he's a waiter at Le Petit Chateau."

"Christ! He wasn't involved with the murder, was he? Dan, don't do anything stupid."

"You're beginning to sound like Greg. Can you meet us, Mitch?"

"Not really. This meeting will last a couple more hours. You go ahead without me. I'll get there or talk to you later."

I hung up and said to Peter, "Ready?"

"As ready as I'll ever be."

We drove back to Berkeley, and I asked him, "What

went wrong in Kansas City? Angela Eldin seemed pretty nice."

"She was okay. We were never that close. I left because of my job."

"What happened?"

"I was a caseworker, which I thought would mean helping clients. It meant screwing people. Most of the caseworkers cared, especially the younger ones. The older ones had given up. I didn't want to become callous. I didn't want to fill out forms and forget there were real people in trouble."

"Was it really that bad?"

"Worse. There were so many people in trouble, and so much red tape. It was as if they were blamed because there were no decent jobs around. And then there was the bitch who ran the place. If you tried to cut through the red tape a little, maybe to feed some hungry kids, she'd jump down your throat."

"You mean Henrietta Gruen?"

"You met her. She's the one."

"I only spoke to her a few minutes," I said. "She seemed okay and said nothing bad about you."

"Believe me, if you'd worked for her, you'd understand."

Herman pulled up in front of the hospital, and I said, "Here we are. Your father's in room 411."

"Dan, I'd appreciate it if you'd come up with me. Sort of to make introductions or something."

We were a little early for visiting hours, and a guard so informed us, rather rudely I thought. I flashed my investigator's license, which has no significance whatsoever, said, "Official business," and walked by him.

Zeke was eating lunch when we entered his room. His bed was in the inclined position; there was a tray on his lap and a fork in his hand. He became motionless when he saw Peter, the fork frozen three inches from his mouth. Peter stood in the doorway, hands in his pockets, saying nothing. Zeke put the fork down and said in his gruff tone, "Well, are you comin' or goin'?"

Peter smiled and said, "You'll never change, Pop." He was wrong—there was a tear in the old man's eye. "You okay?"

"They ain't got me yet. Brodsky, take this tray away! Can't stand the food anyway." I didn't know whether to laugh or cry. I just moved the tray.

"I see you finally cut your hair, son."

"I had to. For my job. Maybe I'll let it grow again."

"Damn you will! What kind o' work ya doin'?"

"I'm a waiter. Le Petit Chateau in San Francisco."

"Never heard of it."

Peter laughed and said, "You wouldn't. You're still the same cheap old buzzard." They lapsed into silence.

Peter said, "I wanted to see you, Pop. But I couldn't."

"I know. You're pig-headed like your old man." Zeke smiled for the first time. "I'm glad you're here, son."

"Me too."

"C'mere, Peter. Let me get a good look at you." Peter walked over and gave his father a hug. I left quietly, closing the door behind me, and waited in the hall.

A nurse came by and said, "What's going on here? Visiting hours don't start until two. And that door should be open." She was a heavyset, middle-aged, officious looking woman. A pin on her pocket said Supervisor.

"It's all right," I explained. "Mr. Jones's son is with him. They haven't seen each other in four years."

"He'll have to wait until two. Those are the rules. And that door must be open." She moved to open the door, but I held it closed.

"Those aren't Zeke Jones's rules," I said. "Give them a chance to talk."

"This is a hospital."

"That's right," I said. "It's not a prison."

"We'll see about that," and she marched off in a huff.

"Brodsky! Get in here!" I went in as he was saying, "Peter, get my jacket outta the closet." Peter retrieved the garment while Zeke took a pen from a table near the bed. He reached into a pocket, removed a checkbook, and started writing. He handed me the check and said, "That ought to take care of you." It certainly would—it was made out for ten thousand dollars!

"That's very generous," I said.

"Generous, nothin'. You did good. I'm the first one to admit it. Might need you again someday. Good business, that's all. Good business."

The nurse burst in, followed by a doctor and a guard. I looked at Peter and said, "Trouble."

"Mr. Jones," the doctor began, "you have to take it easy."

"Easy? Hell! I ain't felt this good in months. Why don't you look after someone that's sick. Peter, get my clothes. We're goin' home."

"I don't think we're ready for that," the doctor said.

"Maybe you ain't, but I am."

The guard began to laugh, and the nurse gave him a forbidding stare. The doctor said, "We have to take good care of your heart. I'm sorry, Mr. Jones, but we can't let you leave yet."

"This ain't no prison, and we're gettin' outta here!" Where had I heard that before? The slightest grin appeared on the nurse's face.

"All right. But *I* will not take responsibility for *your* health. Nurse, will you prepare the papers?" With that he turned on his heels and left. The nurse followed. The guard winked at Zeke and walked off.

"Showed them a thing or two," Zeke said, and Peter and I burst out laughing. "Brodsky! Did I pay you enough to get a ride home." It was not a question.

"I'll get the car and meet you in front."

144

I walked out but Peter stopped me in the hall. "Dan, thank you. I'm only sorry you didn't come after me sooner."

"Maybe you wouldn't have been ready sooner."

"Maybe. Hey, why don't you come to Le Petit Chateau tonight? It's on me."

"That'd be great."

I sat in my car, staring at the check, very pleased with myself. I thought about Melton and realized that Peter Jones–Elliot Fielder had motive and opportunity, and there was a supply of Rat Ravager in the wine cellar. Nonetheless, I crossed him off my list.

Ralph and I met that weekend. He thought my technique for eliminating suspects left something to be desired. He felt that a pretty good case against Jones-Fielder could already be built. He reminded me of our first conversation in which he had indicated that he would consider someone not in the Melton party a good suspect if there was hard evidence, and here it was. I liked both Joneses and refused to consider the possibility that Peter might be Melton's killer. Ralph partly agreed, saying that Jones was probably not the murderer, but nonetheless insisting that he remain a suspect.

∫21

MARILYN GREENE

Marilyn Greene had finished her research, and we met with Greg at my place.

"I think I've got what you want," she said, "and it's juicy."

"Good beginning."

"Greg set things up so I'd have a free hand with the books. I don't know how he did it. I've never found a client that helpful."

"It was simple," Greg said. "I spoke to Alice Melton and to Henry Melton and told them both the same thing: If they wanted to see Susan acquitted, they would be sure you were given whatever assistance you required at Fabricon."

"Whatever, I was able to examine the company's records in detail. Danny, is there any more coffee?"

"Of course. Continue."

"As you know, public corporations are required to have independent audits by CPAs. That's why there are so many large accounting firms. The purpose of such audits is not to expose fraud, but rather to verify the accuracy and reliability of the financial report. Under some circumstances, the audit might turn up an embezzlement or other illegal activity. Generally not. The point is, I didn't find any clear fraud, but there still could be."

I leaned forward and said, "But you do have something interesting to report."

"Yes. I paid particular attention to Prince, as you suggested. I don't know what you had in mind. Nothing outright illegal is going on, but it's a little peculiar."

"What's peculiar?" I said.

"Prince is controlled by Fabricon—forty percent of the stock. It's not a wholly owned subsidiary."

"There's nothing unusual about that," Greg said.

"No. What's strange is the cash flow between the two companies."

"How so?"

"Prince accounts for about twenty percent of Fabricon's profits. Almost two million dollars. More than that—over three million—has been going back to Prince."

"That's not illegal?" I said.

"I don't think so. If there were a lot of R and D at Prince, it might be natural. There could be a legitimate reason. I didn't know much about the running of clothing corporations, but it made me wonder."

"From the look on your face," I said, "you know a lot more now."

"Right you are, Danny. In fact, someday I may go into partnership with you."

"Someday," I said. "Right now, I'm on the edge of my seat."

"If you're going to be sarcastic, you can get yourself another moll."

"I'll be nice. Go on."

"You'll never be nice," Greg said.

She continued anyway. "I have a friend—a stockbroker. I met him during an audit."

"Is this a purely professional relationship," I said, "or is this the unnamed mysterious stranger alluded to when you throw quarters on the table?"

"Dating a client is a no-no," she said. "They say it could be a conflict of interest. So we never talk about personal relationships with clients."

I said, "Okay. What did the mysterious stranger tell you?"

"He knows a lot of people in the fashion industry. They all agree the Fabricon-Prince arrangement is at best unusual. There could be fraud, though it appears that nothing strictly illegal is going on. The interesting thing is that not only was Bradford Melton president and chairman of the board of Fabricon, he held the same positions at Prince."

"So," Greg said, standing, making a small circle, and coming to rest with his hands on the back of his chair, "Melton could take the extra income from Fabricon and pay it to himself as salary for being president of Prince."

"I guess he could have," she said, "but he didn't. You have to realize that salary is the most public and most taxable form of income. No, what he did was much smarter. The income from Fabricon was used to buy up Prince stock from smaller stockholders. Then Prince awarded him stock options at a very low price."

"Is that legal, Greg?" I said.

"I don't know. I'm not up on corporate law. It sounds fishy enough."

"On the face of it," she said, "it's not that fishy. Corporate presidents are frequently given stock options, and it's natural enough for Fabricon to want to acquire outstanding Prince stock. What's fishy is the amount of money involved."

"Wouldn't that show up in the audit?" I said.

"Not necessarily. Fabricon and Prince are over-the-counter stocks and don't come under as close scrutiny as, say, a stock listed on the New York Stock Exchange. A routine audit would be unlikely to uncover the nature of these transactions."

"You mean the other stockholders would have no way of knowing what was going on?" I said.

"That's hard to say. In most corporations where there are only a few stockholders, the major stockholders are actively involved with the company, and they do know what's going on. On the other hand, Fabricon profits have been going up, and it's possible nobody saw any reason to look closely. Especially if Melton had help from the right person."

"Such as the comptroller." I said.

"Roger Mayfield!" Greg shouted.

"Yes," she said. "He's comptroller of Prince as well as Fabricon, and he's gotten his share of stock options—no pun intended. He now owns eight percent of Prince."

"Wouldn't the scheme eventually be discovered?" I said.

"Very likely," she said, "But Melton would have a lot of stock by then."

"Were you able to determine how long they've been at it?"

"It appears the stock options have existed ever since Fabricon acquired Prince. So have the stock purchases from small stockholders. Funneling Fabricon money into Prince is evident for the last two years."

"So," I said, "the big losers would be Fabricon stockholders. If the scheme were recently discovered, it could provide a motive for murder."

"Millions of dollars are involved," she said.

"I presume, knowing how thorough you are, that you have the names of the major Fabricon stockholders."

"I do. About ten percent is held by small and institutional investors. Bradford Melton owned forty-two percent, and each of his children has about five percent. His wife has no stock at all, by the way."

"Who else does?" I said.

"Margaret Melton holds fourteen percent, and Henry Melton nine percent."

"Henry Melton owns only nine percent?"

"That's right. There's one other large stockholder, but he's not a Melton. He has twelve percent."

"What's his name?"

"Jason Bealer."

I sat back and sighed. "I was afraid you'd say that."

"Two years sounds like plenty of time for Bealer or Margaret Melton to have discovered what Melton was doing," Greg said.

"Margaret Melton told me that Melton was cheating them with Prince. Bealer is tough and street-wise. Either one of them might have known." I shook my head. "So Bealer did have motive."

"We don't know that yet," Greg said.

"It doesn't matter," I said. "I have no intention of implicating him in the murder."

"What's the big deal with Bealer?" Marilyn asked.

"You don't want to know," I said. "One thing I do want to know is how Fabricon took over Prince. Did you find out anything about that?"

"Of course. I told you I was a good detective. Come to think of it, accounting is not that different from detective work. You have to follow clues, you have to . . ."

"Marilyn. What did you find out?"

"Prince used to be controlled by a man named Jones. He held a quarter of the stock. He had started the company, and it boomed in the sixties. It grew too fast for him, and he went public and sold a lot of stock to raise capital. Melton was one of the buyers. In nineteen seventy-five, Melton brought suit against Jones for mismanagement. There doesn't seem to have been any real basis for the suit, but Jones lost anyway."

"Mitch was involved," Greg said. "He thinks the judge and Jones's attorneys were bought off. After Jones came to us, Mitch was able to force them to buy Jones's stock. They were close to getting his stock for next to nothing. Mitch did a helluva job."

"The more I learn," I said, "the longer the suspect list becomes. Anything else?"

"Isn't that enough?"

"Too much."

"I'm sure you can handle it," Greg said.

"Well, gentlemen," Marilyn said, "I've got a date tonight. See you Monday."

"One last question," I said. "How did Mayfield react to your audit?"

"He didn't. I saw him only for a few seconds. He said he was busy and would leave me on my own." She bade us good-bye and left.

"When will we have the chemist's report, Greg?"

150

"He promised Monday."

"I'll call him. What about Mayfield? I still want to talk to him."

"He still says he's busy. Maybe next week. Have you talked to Raskin yet?"

"No."

"C'mon, Dan. He's available. I know you're not too fond of him, but you have to talk to him. Maybe you can prove him guilty. Think how much you'd enjoy that."

"Okay. Okay. Tomorrow."

"I better get going, too," Greg said.

"Talk to Mayfield and ask him to meet with me Tuesday. I'm leaving for New York on Thursday."

"You can't leave now, not when things are coming to a head. And you haven't served Delkin yet. That trial is set for February seventh."

"I've been planning this trip for three months. Christmas in New York is important to me. My sister will be in town, and it's the only time the whole family can get together."

"Couldn't you at least wait a week?"

"No."

∫22

∫ BILLY RASKIN

I approached the interview with Billy Raskin with some trepidation. We had known each other in the student movement at Berkeley in the sixties. I never liked him—not personally and not politically. Some background is required to understand our differences.

Virtually every political movement in history has been fraught with controversy and internal strife, and the movement against American involvement in Vietnam was no exception. SDS, the largest student group of that period, was itself an amalgam of groups and philosophies. Each faction naturally wanted its own point of view to prevail. There were essentially two approaches to handling these differences. Most factions put their positions forward in a healthy spirit of debate; others insisted that SDS be dominated by their philosophy.

The result of the latter approach was a split in SDS when a large but minority faction walked out of the 1969 national convention in Chicago and formed a group called the Revolutionary Youth Movement (RYM). RYM itself then split into several groups. One of the splinter organizations became known as the Weathermen, and they went crazy after the Chicago convention. The terrorist actions attributed to SDS were executed by the Weathermen. Their lifespan was fortunately short.

Lest this discourse become a political tract, let us return to Billy Raskin. A split similar to the one in Chicago occurred a year earlier at Berkeley when one faction deserted SDS and formed the Radical Student Union (RSU). Raskin was among its leaders. I felt that they had weakened the antiwar movement at Berkeley by dividing SDS, but my antipathy for Raskin went beyond political differences. He was an arrogant, egotistical individual who cared more for building his own image than for ending the war in Vietnam. He opportunistically used the student movement for self-aggrandizement and came into conflict with anyone who opposed him. I was one of the conflicts, and he was no more fond of me than I of him. We did not get along well before the split, and we did not get along at all after the split.

When I parked Herman in front of Billy and Susan's apartment late Sunday afternoon, I had not seen him in ten years and would have been happy not to see him for the next twenty. Even the sweet taste of the Raiders' victory over Denver earlier that afternoon could not assuage the uneasiness I felt as I rang the bell. Susan answered the door and said, "Hi, Dan. Come in. Billy's waiting for you."

Billy Raskin was short and stocky with a shock of unkempt black hair and a bushy handlebar mustache. He was sitting in an old overstuffed chair when I followed Susan into a drab, shabby living room. He neither stood nor offered his hand when he saw me; he merely said, "Well, look who's turned into a pig."

I smiled and said, "And guess who wants to become a big capitalist."

"If I ran the place, Brodsky, you can damn well bet there'd be some changes. For the better!"

"I imagine so," I said. "With you at the helm, Fabricon would do about as well as RSU—and last about as long."

He always had a temper, and he was probably still angry at me from our last meeting. He jumped up and moved toward me menacingly. Susan intervened, grabbing him and saying, "Billy! Stop! He's here to help us."

"Let him go, Susan," I said. "I wouldn't mind another chance to break his nose." I have been in exactly one fistfight since I was a kid, and that was with Billy Raskin. It was after a large, open political meeting at Berkeley. He took offense at some of my remarks, and he attacked me as I left the auditorium. I'm not much of a fighter, but I am a lot bigger than he. I threw one punch (in self-defense) and his nose is still rounder than it used to be.

He continued to make threatening gestures but allowed Susan to restrain him. I said, "Look, Raskin, we never liked each other very much, and as far as I'm concerned, you can spend the next twenty years in San Quentin. Susan's my client, and I need to talk to you to help her. Unfortunately, proving her innocent will probably get

153

you off the hook, too. If you'd prefer to fight, that would be fine with me, but it would be more useful for both of us if we talked."

I would like to think he was afraid of me, but he was probably satisfied to have made clear his opinion of me. Whatever the reason, he plopped himself into the chair and said, "Okay, Brodsky, what's on your mind?"

I sat on a lumpy sofa and watched a cockroach scurry across the wall. Susan perched herself on the arm of Raskin's chair, and we proceeded to discuss the events leading up to Melton's murder. As much as I dislike him, I must admit that he is not a stupid man. He remembered the details with much greater clarity than the other participants, and his responses to my queries were immediate and precise. We carefully reviewed what I considered to be the key issues.

"Had hors d'oeuvres been served?" I asked.

"Some," he said. "The waiter had brought some; the waitress hadn't. Susan's father had snails. He never ate any."

"Do you remember the wine?"

"Yeah. Some French stuff. Classy. He was drinking white wine. Had several glasses."

"And Susan poured?"

"She did, but she didn't put anything in it." He glared at me. "What are you askin' about that for? You're s'pposed to help."

"I still have to know exactly what happened. Do you remember what else Melton had to drink?"

"Whiskey sours. Three of them. And a piña colada."

"A piña colada?" Susan said. "Father always drank whiskey sours."

"Yeah, well, he had a piña colada that night. Mayfield brought it. Don't you remember? He got up to call his mommy and came back with the piña colada. He said it was on the house."

154

"Did he give it to Melton?"

"Nah. He gave it to Aunt Margaret. There's a winner for you. Ol' Aunt Margaret."

"Billy!" Susan protested.

"You love her alluva sudden? She's an old bitch. You've always said so."

Susan looked at her feet and said nothing. I said, "What did she do with it?"

"She gave it to Bealer. Tough old bird. He put it down in front of Daddy Melton."

"Did Melton drink it?"

"Sure," he said. "He drank anything. Man, he could put the stuff away. Could handle it, too."

Susan said, "Excuse me," and went into the kitchen.

Raskin watched her go and said, "Now that he's dead, she loves him. She always hated his guts. She hated her whole family. Except for her brother. Joe's all right. Idealistic, you know?"

"We've met," I said. "I liked him. I liked Doris, too."

"She's okay," he said. "A little pushy for my taste."

I felt like commenting about left-wingers and sexism but refrained. I said, "Did Melton finish the piña colada?"

"I don't know. It was a pretty big glass, and he collapsed maybe ten minutes after he started it. There might've been some left."

"When Melton collapsed, who went over to help?"

"Bealer was sitting next to him, and so was I. We both tried. Then the bodyguard pushed me out of the way."

"Anybody else?"

"Susan's mother and Aunt Margaret. But they just stood there. There was a doctor in the restaurant, and she sort of took over."

"Who do you think killed him?"

"I don't know. Everyone hated him."

"Everybody?"

"Just about," he said. "Look, Brodsky, you and I have our

155

differences, but we both understand the way he exploited people. He was a lot worse than just a boss. His father started the business, and Melton drove him out. Fabricon was successful because of Henry Melton, but he never got any credit. Melton destroyed his wife; he was always putting his son down. You wouldn't believe what he did to Susan."

"Try me. I've heard enough to believe anything."

"He raped her. She was fourteen. Can you believe that sonofabitch? Of course she hated him. If she had killed him, it would be justifiable homicide." He stopped and looked at me. "Don't worry. She didn't."

I shook my head. For the first time I felt sympathy for Susan. "Who else knew about this?"

"Susan doesn't talk about it much. Her mother certainly knew. Probably her brother. Maybe nobody else. I'm not sure."

"It may not matter," I said. "It may be a good reason for committing murder, but if that were the motive, he'd have been dead ten years ago."

"Don't tell Susan you know."

"I won't. Unless it becomes necessary."

"Any more questions?"

"A few. Can you describe exactly what happened to Melton. I know he collapsed, but that's pretty vague."

"He said something about his stomach bothering him. Then he grabbed his stomach, like he had bad pain. He was sweating a lot. He doubled over. When I bent over, he was breathing funny, and his heart was beating, well, sort of not right. Does that sound like arsenic?"

"I don't know," I said, "but I'll find out."

"Brodsky, can you get Susan off?"

"I think so. I have my theories, and they eliminate her. You, too."

"Do you know who did it?"

"I have my theories," I said. "But I'm not sure yet. I'm not even sure I know how he died."

"You don't think it was arsenic?"

"I don't know. I doubt every aspect of the police case."

He sat up and smiled. "Brodsky, how the hell did you become a private snoop?"

"By accident. It's a living. I wouldn't knock it if I were you. After all, I am your savior."

He sat back and said, "What else do you wanna know?"

"Who knew you bought the Rat Ravager?"

"Susan's parents and Roger Mayfield stopped by to see us about the party. They were waiting for us when we got home. They must've seen it. The bodyguard stayed in the car, but he might have noticed. I think Susan mentioned it to her brother on the phone. She might've told anybody. You'll have to ask her."

"I did," I said. "Her memory isn't that clear."

"She's been upset."

"One thing bothers me. If Rat Ravager was indeed the poison, it would seem the killer wanted to frame Susan. That doesn't make sense."

"That's easy," he said. "They probably wanted to frame me. It was Susan's dear ol' Mom who suggested I sit next to the old buzzard. She said I should try to smooth things over with him. So he'd accept me as his son-in-law. But anybody would probably figure Susan would not be accused, and I'd be a good patsy. They didn't like me too much. They might have seen my being convicted as fitting justice."

Simple enough. The fact that Susan was accused does not mean there was an attempt to frame her. Once she was arrested, it was not likely the killer would come forward and say, "You arrested the wrong person; I intended to frame Raskin."

There is another possibility. The killer may not have intended to frame anyone. I said to Raskin, "It's possible the use of Rat Ravager was a coincidence. The murderer

157

may simply have had some in the bathroom. Do you know if anyone had a supply handy?"

"No."

"Before I asked you who you thought might have killed him. Let's look at it the other way. Who was unlikely to have committed the crime?"

"In my opinion," he said, "anyone is capable of murder if the motive is strong enough. Henry's a weakling and Joe's an easygoing guy, so they're less likely than the others. Bealer's the toughest one, but he was the only one who really liked Melton. If he had reason, he'd have done it. I'd say Bealer's capable of anything he believes necessary."

Susan rejoined us and said, "Dan, would you like a beer or some coffee?"

"No thanks. I'm almost done. I do have a question for you. Who knew you bought the Rat Ravager? Besides your parents and Mayfield."

She sat on the arm of Raskin's chair and said, "I don't think there was anybody else."

"What about your brother?" Raskin said. "Didn't you talk to him on the phone?"

She colored slightly and said, "I guess so."

"No others?" I said.

"No. I'm sure."

"What about Ralph Cordova?"

"He was in the car. Maybe."

"Okay," I said, standing. "I'll keep you informed."

Ralph called me the next morning to say that he had found an apartment in Oakland and was moving in that day. We discussed the interview with Raskin, and he thought that Mayfield and Margaret Melton looked like our best suspects, but he still didn't trust Raskin. I was confused.

158

∫23

ARTHUR SACHLYND

"Kalnor Labs."

"Dr. Sachlynd, please."

Click. Ring. "Dr. Sachlynd's lab."

"May I speak with Dr. Sachlynd?"

"Who's calling?"

"Dan Brodsky."

"He's expecting your call, Mr. Brodsky. Hold on."

Pause. "Brodsky? Sachlynd here. Got your report. Come by after lunch. Two o'clock." He hung up. What if I were busy at two? I wasn't.

It was Monday, December 15. It was Herman's day. I had promised him a substantial portion of the Jones fee, and I brought him to the doctor. "Jake, be good to him. Whatever it takes. I'll pick him up next year." He gave me a loaner, and I sought out Kalnor Labs.

Kalnor Laboratories is an unobtrusive poured-concrete structure resembling a small fortress at the end of a long driveway in the Oakland Hills. It is not visible from the highway; the only evidence at the bottom of the driveway indicating that you have come to the right place is a small sign with the street address.

The receptionist who greeted me made a phone call, handed me a badge marked Visitor, and led me to The Galileo Conference Room. She told me to make myself comfortable, and Dr. Sachlynd would be with me shortly.

The room had no window and contained an oblong table surrounded by a dozen leather chairs. The table was bare save for a single ash-tray and the morning *Chronicle*. I opened to the sports pages and savored the Raider victory.

The door opened, and a tall, dark-haired man wearing a lab coat entered. He extended his hand and said, "Brodsky? Arthur Sachlynd." We shook hands, and he took a chair next to mine. He handed me a manila file and said, "It's all there. You may have some questions."

"Did you have any problem doing the analysis because of the time gap between the murder and your investigation?"

"No, not really. The police lab handled everything properly. They used refrigeration and airtight containers."

"Good," I said. "You found arsenic?"

"It's in the report. Yes. Arsenic trioxide. Enough to kill a human."

"Where did you find the arsenic?"

"In a liquid that I understand came from an ice bucket."

"I see. Anywhere else?"

"No. I tested the escargots, the bread, and the butter. There were traces in a wineglass."

"What about the wine bottle?" I said.

"There was no bottle."

"No. bottle?"

"No. I was sent a package to analyze. There was no wine bottle in the package."

"That's unfortunate," I said. "Were you able to determine the source of the arsenic?"

"Rat Ravager. It's a commercial product, commonly available. There's no doubt it was Rat Ravager. I could throw some technical terms at you, but to make it simple, Rat Ravager is not pure arsenic. There are enough other chemicals present to uniquely identify the product. It's in the report."

160

"The police say the poison was in the wine. Does your analysis support that theory?"

"That's not an easy question to answer," he said. "The simple answer is yes. There was arsenic in the wineglass, and apparently there was arsenic in the body."

"But there's another way of looking at it?"

"Yes. If you assume the arsenic in the ice bucket got there when the wineglass fell over, there's no problem with the police theory. But if there were arsenic in the ice bucket from another source, and if the wineglass were placed in the ice bucket, there would be traces of arsenic in the wineglass. It's the old chicken-or-the-egg problem."

"So one possibility," I suggested, "is that the killer put arsenic and the wineglass into the ice bucket to confuse the issue."

"That's a possibility," he said. "Frankly, though, I don't buy it."

"Why not?"

"That would leave the question of how the arsenic was administered."

"And you didn't find arsenic in any of the other food."

"Right."

"That's fine," I said, "because what you've told me so far is consistent with my theory. Let me ask you this. Was there anything present in the liquid from the ice bucket other than wine, water, and Rat Ravager?"

"Yes!" he said, leaning forward and pounding his fist on the table. "There was coconut, sugar, cream, rum, and . . ."

"A piña colada," I said.

"Right!" he said. "Do you know that he had a piña colada?"

"Yes."

"Of course you understand my findings show the arsenic could have come from the wine or the piña colada. There would be no way of determining which."

161

"Suppose there were traces of arsenic in the piña colada glass?"

"There were traces in the wineglass, too," he said.

"But the wineglass was in the ice bucket; the piña colada glass wasn't."

"That would do it."

"Did you analyze the piña colada glass?"

"I don't know. If I did, there was no arsenic in it."

I made a rough sketch of the glass and asked, "Did any of the ones you did analyze have this shape?"

He looked at it and said, "No. None of the glasses they gave me looked like that."

"One last question. Wouldn't the poison in a drink have alerted Melton?"

"It might, but not necessarily. You have to realize that a bad-tasting poison would also alert rats. That's why it's so easy to poison a dog with these products."

"And I suppose if he'd had a couple of drinks already, it would make it harder for him to taste it."

"Very likely."

"There's another point here," I said. "Melton was drinking an expensive white wine with a delicate flavor. It seems to me that anything in the wine would have affected its taste. On the other hand, a piña colada is very sweet with a strong rum flavor. Much more likely to conceal the taste of the poison."

"Sounds reasonable to me," he said. "Though that's really outside my field of expertise."

"But just between you and me," I said, "if you wanted to use rat poison to kill someone, a sweet cocktail would make the poison harder to detect than a white dinner wine would."

"I can't disagree with you," he said, smiling. "But you don't have to convince me; you have to convince the police."

"Or a jury. Will you testify?"

"If need be."

∫24

MARY CLARK

I called Greg's office from Kalnor Labs. He was out, but I left a message for him to be at my house by seven. I would have called Ralph but didn't know his new phone number. I did have the address, and though the loaner Jake had given me was certainly not Herman, it did manage to locate the place.

My knock was answered by an attractive thirty-five-year-old brunette. I said, "Isn't this Ralph Cordova's apartment?"

"Yes. He's not in at the moment."

"My name's Dan Brodsky. I . . ."

"Oh, of course," she said. "Ralph has mentioned you several times. He'll be back shortly if you'd like to wait."

"Sure." She escorted me into a modern apartment with boxlike rooms. I didn't like it very much, but it was certainly livable. Cartons covering most of the floor provided ample evidence of Ralph's recent move.

He had maintained adequate sitting space on the sofa in the living room into which she led me. "My name's Mary Clark. Do I dare offer you coffee?"

"Ralph *has* been telling you about me. Sure."

She disappeared into the kitchen. Her name sounded familiar, but I couldn't place it. When she reappeared I said, "Have we met before? I know your name from somewhere."

"You do. I was at Le Petit Chateau when Melton . . ."

"Of course! You were on the police list of patrons. Quite a coincidence."

"No. Not really. I was there looking for Ralph."

"So you knew him before the murder?"

"I'm his ex-wife. You see, I wanted us to be, well, at least friends. I'd called him several times, but he refused to talk to me. I was hoping to catch him there, knowing he wouldn't make a scene in public."

"Were you able to talk to him?"

"Not then. The place became a madhouse. But he saw me there and called the next day."

"I see you were able to make it a friendly divorce."

She smiled. "Yes. We may even get married again."

"I'm glad," I said. "Tell me, did you know any of the Meltons?"

"Only Bradford and Alice, and not very well." She stood up, saying, "The coffee must be ready. How do you take it?"

"Black."

I followed her into the kitchen where there were more boxes to be unpacked. There was some space on the table, and she filled two cups with her brew. It was distinctly mediocre.

Optimistically she said, "How is it?"

Saved by the bell. Ralph walked in at that moment, his arms filled with groceries. "Dan! Hi! I see you've met Mary."

"Yes. She's been telling me that you may get back together."

"I think so."

"Sounds good."

I described the meeting with Arthur Sachlynd, and he said, "That's great. Let's hope the police still have the piña colada glass. On second thought, maybe better not. What if there are no traces of the poison?"

"I'm pretty confident," I said. "And even if there are none, this should be enough to guarantee an acquittal."

"You're probably right." He turned to Mary. "You should ask Dan about that thing you were reading about."

"Oh yeah. It was in a magazine article. Something about Furmatts problem?"

"It's *fair mah*," I said. "Pierre de Fermat. A seventeenth-century French mathematician. The problem is known as *Fermat's Last Theorem*."

"The article said it was very simple to describe, but I couldn't understand what they were saying."

"Do you remember the *Pythagorean Theorem* from plane geometry?"

"Not really. Math wasn't one of my strong points."

I smiled. "That's all right. A collection of numbers such as three, four, and five is called a *Pythagorean triple* because three squared plus four squared equals five squared. Do you have paper and pencil?"

"Here's a pen, but I'm not so sure about paper."

They did have napkins handy (the napkin is a traditional tool of the mathematician), and I wrote:

$$3^2 + 4^2 = 5^2$$

"There's nothing deep there," I said. "It simply means that nine plus sixteen is twenty-five."

"So what's the problem?" she said.

"I'm getting there. There are many such triples. Five, twelve, thirteen. Six, eight, ten. In fact, there are infinitely many. Now, Fermat asked the question, 'Can you do the same thing with larger exponents?' For example, using three, can you solve the following equation using positive, whole numbers?" I wrote:

$$x^3 + y^3 = z^3$$

and said, "The question is only interesting if x, y, and z are positive, whole numbers. Otherwise, there are trivial solutions."

She said, "Can it be done?"

165

"Not for three. That is, there is no set of three positive whole numbers that satisfy that equation. Fermat made a comment in the margin of a notebook that he had a proof that the equation could not be solved for any exponent greater than two." I went back to the napkin, writing:

$$x^n + y^n = z^n$$

"Let me emphasize that for the theorem to be true, the equation must be *un*solvable."

"If there's a proof," she said, "why is it a famous question?"

"Fermat *claimed* that he had a proof but never wrote it down. If he did have one, nobody has ever seen it. Many mathematicians have spent a great deal of time trying to prove this theorem over the last three hundred years, but none has been successful."

"That's amazing. Have you ever tried?"

"No. I have no delusions of grandeur."

"And still nobody knows the answer?"

"That's right. It's known to be true for many specific exponents. For example, as I mentioned before, it's true for n equal to three. That is, the equation cannot be solved if the exponent is three. But it's unknown for arbitrary exponents. It is easily the most famous open question in all of mathematics."

"Do you think Fermat really had a proof?"

"That's hard to say. A lot of very smart people have worked on the problem, so it seems likely that he was wrong. But he was one of the greatest mathematicians. He might've had a proof."

"If he was so great, how come I never heard of him?"

"That's the lot of mathematicians," I said. "For a mathematician to be famous, he has to do something besides mathematics. Isaac Newton invented the calculus but is well known for the work he did in physics."

"The apple falling on his head and all that?" Ralph said.

"Yeah. Something like that. Do you know the name David Hilbert?"

"No."

"He was a contemporary of Einstein with an equally productive life. Everyone knows Einstein's name; very few non-mathematicians know Hilbert's."

"Why is that?" he said.

"I'm not entirely sure. Maybe because there's no Nobel Prize in mathematics."

"There isn't?"

"No. That's the way Nobel set it up."

"How come?"

"That's not entirely clear, but he apparently hated a Swedish mathematician by the name of Mittag-Leffler. Some say that Mittag-Leffler had an affair with Nobel's wife."

Mary laughed. "I didn't know mathematicians were such a racy lot."

∫25

∫ ALICE MELTON

It was poker night, and Greg arrived forty-five minutes early to talk before the game.

I made coffee, and he said, "Did you get what you wanted from Sachlynd?"

"Not entirely, but enough."

"What was missing?"

"Sachlynd didn't have the glass that contained the arsenic."

"They didn't send him the wineglass?" he said incredulously.

"They did, but I'm not talking about the wineglass."

"Danny, will you talk straight for once?"

"You won't have any difficulty getting Susan off."

"Are you serious? Fantastic! . . . Are you sure?"

"Oh yeah. No problem."

"So who did it?" He was getting insistent.

"I don't know." I sat back and drank some coffee.

"Well?"

"Well what?"

"What the hell did you find out?"

"You needn't shout, Greg. You mean you want me to hand you your case on a silver platter? Right now, when I'm planning to enjoy an evening of poker?"

"Yes, if you want to live long enough to play tonight."

"All right," I said, leaning forward and clearing my throat. "It's really quite elementary."

"Get to the point, Sherlock."

"The D.A.'s case depends on a few major points. First, motive. It's easy enough to show that everyone had motive. By 'everyone' I mean all the participants in the Melton birthday party, Peter Jones, and half of California. Melton was not one to win a popularity contest."

"I already knew that," he said.

"The next point in their case is the Rat Ravager. Susan and Raskin bought the stuff the afternoon of the murder. Both Roger Mayfield and Alice Melton knew about the Rat Ravager. So did Joe Melton, and Le Petit Chateau keeps it in the basement."

"I already knew that, too."

"The key point in their case is the fact that Susan poured his wine. Their argument is that she was the only one with the opportunity to spike the wine."

"I see we're getting somewhere. Where?"

"The arsenic was not in the wine."

168

"Can you prove that?" he said excitedly. "That would do it."

"It certainly would. And the answer is: probably. Roger Mayfield left the table to make a phone call. He returned with a piña colada, which he said was on the house. He handed the drink to Margaret Melton. She gave it to Jason Bealer, and he put it down in front of Bradford Melton. Susan never handled it. The Rat Ravager was in the piña colada."

"Are you sure?"

"Virtually. The problem is Sachlynd didn't have the piña colada glass to analyze. You should be able to force the police to analyze the glass. Even if the test comes up negative, the fact that they waited so long to perform the analysis will make it easy for a classy shyster to invalidate the results. Either way, you win."

"How sure are you that the poison was in the piña colada?"

"Almost certain," I said. "The piña colada was emptied into the ice bucket. Sachlynd was able to establish that much."

"Wait a second," he said. "If the poison was in the piña colada, why were there traces of arsenic in the wineglass?"

"The piña colada and the wineglass were both dumped into the ice bucket. The wineglass picked up traces of the arsenic after Melton was poisoned."

"Couldn't the piña colada have tipped over when Melton collapsed?"

"Possibly," I said, "but not likely. Moreover, he was drinking an expensive French wine. It would have a delicate, subtle flavor and wouldn't hide the taste of the poison. The piña colada, on the other hand . . ."

"That's good, Danny. Very good." He paced the floor, rubbing is chin. "Yeah, that should do it . . . That should do it . . . I'd still prefer to know the killer." He sat down.

"Will you be able to uncover the murderer before the trial?"

"Uncover the murderer? I wasn't planning to try. Do you want me to keep working on this? My job was to provide you with the evidence to guarantee acquittal. I've done that. I don't care who killed him. The murderer deserves a medal."

"There are problems with that, Danny. If you unmask the killer, we can be certain of acquittal. This will give us a strong defense, but you can never be certain of how a jury will act."

"Greg," I said, "why do I always have the feeling that you're pushing me into working for you? I'm flying to New York Thursday and want to forget the Meltons. As far as I'm concerned, this one is ready to be filed under success."

"Unless you keep working," Greg said, "this one goes in the partial success file."

"I don't distinguish." He glared at me, and I said, "I'll tell you what. If the Meltons will pay a bonus for completely solving the case, I'll do it."

"How much?"

"At least five thousand. Try for ten."

"You're nuts!"

"You're right," I said. "I didn't want to do it anyway."

He gave me one of his looks and said, "Should I call Alice Melton now?"

"The phone's still in the kitchen. I'll listen in the bedroom."

He dialed; the phone was ringing when I picked up the extension. A man answered and said, "Melton residence."

"May I speak with Alice Melton? This is Gregory Langley."

"Just a moment, sir."

The man put the phone down, and Greg said, "You there, Dan?"

"I'm here. I won't say anything."

Alice Melton picked up the receiver and said, "Mr. Langley?"

"Yes. I wanted to give you a progress report. Dan Brodsky has uncovered quite a bit of evidence, and I'm confident that Susan will be acquitted."

"That's wonderful. What is the nature of this evidence?"

"It's complicated. But don't worry."

"Does Mr. Brodsky know the identity of the real culprit?"

"No, but he's poked enough holes in the D.A.'s case. The only way we could have a stronger case would be if the murderer were caught."

"I see," she said.

"The question I have is, do you want Dan to continue with his investigation?"

"I don't understand."

"The point is, if Dan identified the real killer, we'd be absolutely certain of Susan's acquittal. On the other hand, if the murderer is not identified, even if we win the trial, there will always be a cloud of suspicion over Susan's head in some people's minds."

"Mr. Brodsky doesn't know who the killer is?"

"No. The problem is that Dan doesn't want to spend any more time on the case. I think he can succeed in finding the murderer if we keep him working. However, to get him to continue, a substantial bonus may be required."

"To be candid, Mr. Langley, if Susan can be acquitted, Mr. Brodsky's services will no longer be necessary. The police, with all their facilities at their disposal, should be able to solve the crime. I see no value in paying Mr. Brodsky more than he has already earned."

"That may be a mistake, Mrs. Melton."

"Mr. Langley," she said, her voice rising, "I see no need to pursue this matter any further. Please thank Mr. Brodsky for me. Tell him to send me a bill for his services to date. Thank you for calling." She hung up.

Greg said to me over the phone, "You heard?"

"I heard. Strange. I wonder why she was so adamant."

"Who knows? I'll try Susan."

The advances of modern technology. It was essential I pick up the extension before Susan answered, or she would hear a click and know someone was listening. Before the advent of touch-tone phones, Greg would not have been able to dial with an extension off the hook. Once again technology has come to the rescue of the snoop.

Raskin answered. He sounded reluctant to put Susan on. I wondered why he was suspicious. He finally called Susan, and a few seconds after she said "hello" I heard the telltale click—Raskin was listening on *their* extension.

Greg began as he had with Alice Melton. "I think we're okay, Susan. Dan has uncovered evidence that should insure your acquittal."

"Oh that's great! What about Billy? Will this clear him, too?"

"I should think so."

Another click, and then a shouting voice came through faintly, "All right!"

"Does Dan know who did kill Father?" Susan asked.

"Not yet," Greg said. "Unfortunately, he doesn't see any reason to continue investigating. He thinks . . ." Click. "We seem to have a bad connection." Click. *Good show, Greg.* "As I was saying, Dan thinks he's done his job and is not interested in working any more on the case."

"That's terrible," she said. "The police won't do it. Greg, you have to talk to him."

Click.

"I've tried, Susan, but he can be pretty stubborn."

Watch your mouth, Greg. "To be honest with you, while we now have a very strong defense, I'd be a lot more comfortable if the murderer were identified."

"I would, too," she said.

"The problem is, Dan's the right man for the job. There may be better private eyes, but it's kind of late to bring in a new man." *I'm warning you, Greg.*

"Isn't there anything we can do?" Susan pleaded. "Maybe if we paid him more money?"

"That might work. He is pretty mercenary." *I'll break your face, Greg.*

"Then tell him we'll pay more."

"It will probably require a five-thousand-dollar bonus." *You son-of-a-bitch, I told you to try for ten.*

"I'll have a lot of money soon."

Raskin suddenly broke in. "Are you crazy, Susan?"

Greg said calmly, "I didn't know you were listening, Raskin. And I didn't know you controlled Susan's funds."

"I don't. But she doesn't have to throw it away. What business is it of yours anyway?"

"Be quiet, Billy!" Susan said. "Greg, tell Dan we'll be happy to give him the bonus."

"I think that's wise. I'll talk to Dan right away."

∫26
THE BRODSKY CLAN

The next two days were occupied preparing for Christmas in New York. I stopped at my office in school to check my mail and found a notice from Reed College in

Portland announcing a position in the Department of Mathematics. They wanted someone with knowledge of computer science. I had no training in that area, but I had learned a fair amount while tracking people down. Enough to fake it. I sent them my vita and standard letter of application.

On Thursday morning, it was off to New York. My brother, Lawrence, met me at Kennedy Airport with his four sons, ranging in age from two to ten. Larry and his wife, Naomi, have worked at establishing good nutritional habits in their children, but I've always claimed the uncle's prerogative to corrupt the parents' influence. I promptly found four Hershey bars in my pocket, and the kids greedily consumed them as Larry gave me a dirty look. We piled into his Toyota, and he maneuvered his way through heavy traffic to Brooklyn.

Larry is largely responsible for giving our sister, Jessica, and me the opportunity to get college educations. He quit school at seventeen and went to work, contributing a substantial portion of his income to the family budget. It would otherwise have been infeasible for Jessie and me to attend Brooklyn College. Jessie went on to medical school, borrowing thousands of dollars to do so. She easily repaid the loans with the outrageous income typical of her profession.

My parents, Martin and Sophia Brodsky, live in southern Brooklyn near the Belt Parkway. They have lived in the same house since shortly before Larry was born. When I ran out of money at Berkeley, they took out a second mortgage to lend me five thousand dollars to continue my studies. I have been writing them checks whenever my bank account permitted it, and I presented them with a check for three thousand dollars when Larry and I arrived at the house.

The two weeks in New York passed quickly. The Raiders' final regular season game was against the Giants in

New York, and my father and I went with Larry's oldest. The Raiders won handily, bringing their record to eleven and five and guaranteeing a playoff berth. San Diego defeated Pittsburgh, which meant the Raiders would be a wildcard team. But they were in. Houston would be their first opponent, and the game would be in Oakland. I was confident.

Jessica, who lives in North Dakota with her husband, Michael, and two children, arrived on Tuesday evening. She, Larry, and I were up all night talking. Since Jessie is a doctor, she was able to give me some useful information.

"Jessie," I said, "do you know anything about arsenic?"

"As in the poison?"

"Yes."

"That's not my specialty."

"If you asked me about group theory, I wouldn't say I was an analyst, not an algebraist."

"I wouldn't ask."

"I would," I said. "Arsenic. What are the symptoms?"

"They're different with different victims. It depends on the dosage, what he'd eaten, his health. Under some circumstances, in small doses, it can have medicinal value."

"He probably hadn't eaten anything for several hours," I said, "and there was a large dose in a piña colada, which he drank after three cocktails. Assume no food and a fair amount of alcohol."

"It still depends on the particular arsenic compound," she said.

"Arsenic trioxide."

"Arsenic is not a fast-acting poison. Symptoms typically appear one to three hours after ingestion. The conditions you describe would probably mean the lower figure. The first symptoms would be stomach pains and difficulty swallowing. Violent stomach cramps would follow, and there might be convulsions. If the . . ."

"Wait a second. He apparently started feeling the effects within ten or fifteen minutes."

"That doesn't seem likely from what I know. Of course, I'm not an expert, but I'm pretty sure I'm right."

"Jessie, this is important. If you're right, it could change everything."

"One of my old professors is a pharmacologist. William MacHenry. I could call him."

"How about right now?"

She looked at her watch. "It's 10:30 in Minnesota. I guess it's not too late."

"Maybe we can do some calculations before you call. From what you said, the rate of absorption of the poison would be proportional to the amount present and inversely proportional to the content of the stomach."

"Daniel, speak English."

"The more poison, the faster the rate of absorption; the greater the content of the stomach, the slower the . . ."

"Got it. Sounds right. So?"

"There's probably a constant of absorbency well known for arsenic and any set of given conditions. It's a simple differential equation."

"You're kidding."

"Never. Well, maybe once in a while. But not this time." I found some paper and said, "If we assume the ratio of arsenic to stomach content was constant, which seems more or less reasonable to me . . ."

"Sounds very unreasonable to me," she said.

"I'm just trying to get a ballpark estimate."

"There's another problem, Daniel. Most of the absorption would take place in the intestine."

"Even so," I said, "it was all liquid and similar numbers should apply." I began writing:

$$\frac{dx}{dt} = c\,x$$

$$\frac{dx}{x} = c\,dt$$

$$\int \frac{dx}{x} = \int c\,dt$$

$$\log x = c\,t + k$$

$$x = a\,e^{ct}$$

Jessie was looking over my shoulder and said, "Looks like gibberish to me."

"It's not. The c is the constant of absorbency. If we assume fifteen minutes for the symptoms to start, we can compute c from the numbers in the medical examiner's report."

"Which you, of course, have."

"Which I, of course, have. Brought the file with me."

We looked at the report, and I said, "Looks like gibberish to me."

"It's not, Daniel."

We managed to come up with some numbers, and she placed the call. MacHenry was in. After a few minutes, Jessie put her hand over the mouthpiece and said, "He says your constant is much too high, but he wants to check something."

"That raises all sorts of questions."

"Do you want him to do the checking?"

"Sure. I want as much information as possible."

She spoke with him a while longer, thanked him, and hung up. "He says he'll call back later."

He did. The conversation was short. Jessie's end of it was, "Really? . . . Interesting . . . Will do . . . Thanks . . . Good-bye."

She looked at me with a smile and said, "My baby brother, the genius."

"To what do I owe such accolades?"

"He said that given that he hadn't eaten, that all he'd consumed was fluids, and that there was a lot of alcohol present, your constant is reasonable."

In a very self-satisfied tone of voice I said, "How many times have I told you, you should have studied more mathematics?"

She eyed me contemptuously. "Daniel, don't push your luck."

"Of course," I said, "this merely means that there's no new information."

Larry, who had mostly been a bystander, said, "Not necessarily. Suppose the killer had done some research and assumed that it would be at least an hour before the arsenic began to take effect?"

"Certainly possible. But I don't see the relevance."

We talked about it further and came up with nothing more. But Jessie's remarks together with Sachlynd's analysis convinced me that Melton was indeed killed with Rat Ravager. When I discussed it with Ralph after returning from New York two weeks later, he didn't trust my mathematics and still had some doubts about the Rat Ravager, suggesting the possibility that a major piece of the puzzle was still missing. I generally concurred, but was nonetheless satisfied that Rat Ravager was the cause of death.

I was still in Brooklyn when Houston met Oakland the following Sunday, and the whole family watched the game, even my mother. Everyone was rooting for the Oilers except for two of Larry's kids and me. The Raiders won 27–7, dominating from the opening gun. Their next stop would be Cleveland.

On Saturday I was on a westbound plane after two delightful weeks in New York. Elaine met me at the airport, and we went to her apartment for dinner. Hypatia, who had been taking care of Elaine for the holidays, greeted me without enthusiasm.

We turned on the tube Sunday morning to watch the Raiders. Oakland was the stronger team, but the game was played in a bitterly cold, windswept Cleveland stadium. Plunkett managed two drives resulting in touchdowns, and the Raiders led 14–12 with two minutes to go. The Browns, however, began marching downfield, and with twenty seconds left, Sipes let fly for the end zone. It was caught—by Mike Davis of the Raiders! Next week it would be in San Diego for the conference championship.

I went home Monday morning, stopping on the way to pick up Herman. Jake had completely rebuilt Herman's engine, put in new brakes and a new clutch, and done a number of minor repairs. He had also taken him to a body shop for a new fender and a paint job. The bill came to eighteen hundred dollars, but Herman looked and drove the way he did in 1952.

It was amazing how fast the fee from Zeke Jones disappeared. Herman and my parents took half, and the expenses involved with finding Peter Jones exceeded a thousand dollars. Then I had to eat and pay the rent and some old bills, not to mention the airfare to New York. After writing the check to Jake, I was left with thirteen hundred. At least I was still in the black. Unusual for me.

It didn't last long. Winter is the rainy season in Northern California, and it had rained during my sojourn East. There was also a leak in the roof of my building. Since my apartment is on the top floor, the leak was not discovered until I got home. When I entered, I was greeted with a hole in the living room ceiling and a steady drip, drip, drip onto my stereo. The carpet was ruined. I was about to call my insurance agent when I realized I had none. In the red again.

∫27

ARWYN FELDNOR

I had a good relationship with my landlord, who had kept the rent down in exchange for my maintaining my own apartment. After a dozen phone calls, I found a contractor who was willing to put on a new roof right away. The estimate, including repairs to the interior, was twenty-five hundred dollars. My share was almost a thousand; the rug and stereo would be another two grand. As if that were not enough, I lost thirty bucks in the poker game that night.

Greg stayed after the game and said, "I've got something for you." He handed me a check from Alice Melton. It would cover the repairs and the carpet, but a new stereo would have to wait. The check was unusual because it had been sent promptly and in full. It normally takes a couple of months for clients to send their remittances, and then they often balk about the time or expenses.

"She seems anxious to have me off the case," I said.

"You've noticed. Is there any beer left?"

"In the fridge. That doesn't make her guilty. She could be the type who pays her bills on time."

"Not likely," he said, sitting down, opening the bottle. "Not in her income bracket. More likely she knows or thinks she knows who killed him and wants to protect the killer."

180

"Either that," I said, "or she may simply be glad he's dead and satisfied that Susan will be acquitted."

"She could also be guilty."

It occurred to me that Susan might be disinclined to pay the bonus if I were to prove her mother guilty. "That could be inconvenient," I said.

He looked at me and smiled. "Have you accomplished anything recently?"

"Not much. I did talk to my sister, and from what she said, I accept the police theory that Rat Ravager killed Melton."

"I never really doubted it, Dan. But we're looking good with the piña colada." He drank some beer and said, "How sure are you that the poison was in the piña colada?"

"Virtually certain. Why?"

"If we go into court with what we've got now, we should be able to blow their case apart. Unless they've already analyzed the piña colada glass and the test came up negative."

"Not likely," I said. "The piña colada glass was a minor point before Sachlynd's analysis. I don't think Ashe held anything out on us. Certainly not that."

"Agreed," he said. "There should be no problem in court. But you can never be sure of what a jury will do."

"What're you getting at?"

"We could go to the D.A. now and have them analyze the piña colada glass. If the test is positive, they'll have to drop all charges against Susan."

"Makes sense to me," I said. "Even if they find no arsenic in the glass, which is unlikely, your case won't be that much weaker. You can argue that they waited too long to perform the analysis."

"Okay," he said. "Let's go see the D.A. tomorrow."

"Why don't we start with Ashe," I said. "He should appreciate it, and I wouldn't mind getting on his good side. You never know what the future will bring."

"Fine."

"Have you spoken with Mayfield?" I said.

"Yeah. He said he'd meet you tomorrow evening at his apartment."

I called Ashe in the morning, and he agreed to meet with us at one o'clock. We arrived on time, but he let us wait half an hour before seeing us.

We were finally ushered into his office, and he said, "Gentlemen. Sit down. What can I do for you?" Before giving us a chance to answer, he went into what sounded like a prepared speech. "I hope you're not planning to ask me to reopen the Melton investigation. I'm satisfied that Susan Melton is guilty, and I'm much too busy to put more time in on it. Speaking candidly, neither the chief of police nor the district attorney would be very pleased if we reopen the investigation. This is the real world, gentlemen, and we must consider the politics involved."

"I'm afraid, Inspector," I said, "that we are going to ask you to reopen the investigation. We can prove that Susan Melton is innocent."

"Horseshit!" he said. "We've got a goddamned good case. If you can prove she's innocent, do it in court." He leaned back in his chair with his hands clasped behind his head.

"We can," Greg said, "but we thought you'd prefer not to lose in public. If you find the real killer now, you could avoid that embarrassment."

"*I* won't be embarrassed if the D.A. blows it."

"Inspector Ashe," I said, "we came to you because we thought uncovering new evidence would be a feather in your cap. We're not interested in having you do a lot more investigating. We simply want you to verify one detail of the case."

He sat forward, reached into his pocket for a cigar, and said, "I'm listening."

I said, "An essential part of your case against Susan Melton is arsenic in her father's wine. The poison was in a drink. A piña colada. You have the glass, and it would be easy to determine if there had been arsenic in it."

He lit the cigar and took a couple of puffs. He pointed it at me and said, "Brodsky, forget it. The arsenic was in the wine. I don't plan to end up with egg on my face, you know. Now get out. I'm busy."

"We could go over your head," Greg said.

"Do that!" he said, pointing the cigar at Greg. "But if you want to function in this city you have to deal with the police. We'll see how much cooperation you get if you start pulling stunts."

"We're not getting much cooperation now," I said.

He pointed to the door with the cigar and said, "Out!"

Downstairs I said, "What a jackass! Who's handling the case in the D.A.'s office?"

"Arwyn Feldnor. A young guy on his way up. Lots of political ambitions. Thinks he'll be governor some day."

"Let's go see him."

We went to the district attorney's offices and found a door marked, Arwyn Feldnor, Ass't District Attorney. We asked to see Feldnor, and his secretary said, "I doubt if he'll see you without an appointment. He's very busy."

Greg picked up a notepad from her desk and wrote, "Future district attorneys are not embarrassed in court," and signed it. "Give this to him and tell him we need fifteen minutes."

She went into his private office and reappeared shortly. "You may go in."

Arwyn Feldnor was in his late thirties, clean shaven with sharp features and close-cropped brown hair. He had a large office and was seated behind a walnut desk.

He stood and shook hands with Greg. "How've you been?" he said with a broad smile. Without waiting for an answer, he shook my hand and said, "You must be Brodsky. Sit down. What can I do for you?"

Greg said, "We can prove Susan Melton is innocent."

"We've got a strong case against her," he said. "You better be sure."

"Sure enough," Greg said. "You have no chance of getting a conviction. We thought you'd be happier if we told you about it now."

"You sound confident," Feldnor said, "but it sounds like a bluff to me." He was getting nervous; Greg was getting warmed up.

"This is a big case," Greg said. "The trial will get a lot of publicity. You can't win. Believe me."

Feldnor shuffled through some papers on his desk and looked through the drawers. He pressed a button on the intercom and said, "Janet, would you get me a pack of cigarettes?"

"You told me not to, sir."

He looked at us and said, "I don't smoke." Then into the intercom, "Just one, Janet."

She said, "But sir. You made me promise not to get you cigarettes under any circumstances."

"That was this morning. Now I'm ordering you to get me a cigarette!"

"Would you like some chewing gum, sir?"

"I don't chew gum."

"I'm sorry, sir."

"Janet, you're fired!"

She remained calm. "Should I leave now, or should I finish the letter I'm typing?"

"Get me a cigarette! Then finish the letter!"

"I'll finish the letter."

Feldnor gave up and composed himself. He said, "I don't smoke. You were saying?"

"You ought to reopen the Melton investigation," Greg said.

"Why? If I were to believe every defendant innocent on his attorney's say-so, I'd never get a conviction."

"Your case," Greg said, "depends on the theory that Susan laced Melton's wine with arsenic. Without that, your case goes out the window."

"So?"

"Did you know that Melton drank whiskey sours and rarely anything else?"

"Yes. He had three of them that night."

"Did you know that he also had a piña colada?" Greg said.

"So what?"

"The poison was in the piña colada."

He smiled and said, "You had me going for a second, but the police lab . . ."

"The lab boys are wrong," I said. "They weren't thorough enough. They found Melton's wineglass in the ice bucket, and they found traces of arsenic in the wineglass. Ergo, the arsenic was in the wine."

"Sounds good to me."

"Not good enough," I said. "There was arsenic in the ice bucket as well."

"Of course. From the wine."

"It was the other way around. The piña colada containing the poison was emptied into the ice bucket. The wineglass, sitting in the ice bucket, picked up traces of the arsenic."

"How did you come to that conclusion?"

"As you know," Greg said, "we had an independent chemist analyze the contents of the ice bucket. He was able to establish the presence of the piña colada."

"Still doesn't prove anything," Feldnor said.

"The piña colada glass was not in the ice bucket," I said. "If there were traces of arsenic on the piña colada glass, that would prove our point."

"Well? Were there?"

"We don't know. The police didn't send our chemist the piña colada glass to analyze."

He sat back with a sigh of relief. "The police probably analyzed the piña colada glass a long time ago and found no arsenic in it."

"I don't think so," I said.

He said into the intercom, "Janet, get John Ashe on the phone." To us he said, "If you're right, we better have that glass analyzed."

Janet's voice came over the intercom. "He's on line one."

Feldnor picked up the receiver and said, "Hello, Jack. Anything new on the Barnwell investigation? . . . I thought so. Listen, I've been talking with Langley and Brodsky. Melton was drinking a piña colada. I think we ought to have the glass analyzed. I assume you still have it . . . I know, but humor me . . . Goddamnit, Jack, just do it! . . . Yeah, they're here now." He looked at me and said, "He wants to talk to you."

He handed me the phone, and I said, "This is Brodsky."

Ashe said, "Brodsky, you'll regret this!" and slammed down the receiver.

I returned the phone to Feldnor, and Greg said, "You'll call me when you get the results?"

"You can count on it."

Outside Feldnor's office, Greg said, "What did Ashe want?"

"To make it clear we shouldn't have gone to see Feldnor."

"There better be arsenic in that glass."

"Keep the faith, Greg. It's there."

I dropped Greg off and went to the Delkin Tower to meet Elaine for dinner. She sat in the car and said excitedly, "I know where Delkin is. He has a ranch in Oregon, near Florence. He'll be there until Friday."

186

28
ROGER MAYFIELD

Roger Mayfield lives in a penthouse halfway up the western slope of Nob Hill. The building has a doorman, who said I was expected and sent me directly to Mayfield's apartment. He admitted me to a large, elegantly furnished living room—his share of the Prince profits was evident. He was average looking: average height, average weight, brown hair and eyes, undistinguished features.

He offered me a drink, and I accepted a beer. He went into the kitchen for the beer and made himself a cocktail. I sat on a brown velvet couch and said, "You're a hard man to find."

"It's been very busy at Fabricon, as you can imagine. Our fiscal year coincides with the calendar year. Between Melton's death and end-of-year accounting, I've been very busy. I hope I haven't held up your investigation."

There were two matters I wanted to discuss with Mayfield: the piña colada and Prince Jeans. The second would require some diplomacy, and I began by reviewing the events leading up to Melton's demise. He was foggy on many of the details, and his account did not reveal anything new.

"Do you remember what Melton was drinking?" I asked.

"No, but he usually had whiskey sours."

"A piña colada was mentioned."

"It's possible," he said. "I'd be surprised, though. He liked whiskey sours."

"Did anyone leave the table during dinner?"

"As I recall," he said, "we all stood to toast Melton. I think it was my toast. Then I made a phone call. My mother had been ill."

"Were you gone long?"

"A few minutes. My mother was asleep, and my father said she was okay."

"You went straight back to the table?"

"Yes, I think so."

"You didn't stop at the bar?"

"No. Certainly not. Though now that you mention it, someone did hand me a drink for Melton. They said it was on the house. It could have been a piña colada." He fidgeted with his drink, took a sip, and said, "Is that important?"

"Probably not. What did you do with the drink?"

He shrugged. "I guess I gave it to Melton."

"You were sitting at opposite ends of the table. Did you walk over to him to give him the drink?"

"It's hard to be sure; it's been quite a while. What difference does it make? Wasn't the poison in his wine?"

"Apparently. But I like to fill in all the details. Especially if two witnesses disagree."

"You mean someone said I didn't give the drink directly to Melton?"

"Yes."

He sat back and sipped his drink. "I'm trying to remember the scene . . . I brought it back with me to the table. I think I said, 'This is on the house.' Then I handed it to Margaret Melton. She gave it to Jason Bealer, and he gave it to Melton. I think that's right."

"Do you remember who gave it to you?"

"No. Someone who worked there, I suppose."

"It wasn't your waiter or waitress?"

"No. I'd remember if it were."

"Are you sure it was someone who worked for Le Petit Chateau?"

"Who else could have given it to me?"

"Almost anyone. That's why I asked."

"I don't really know."

"Can you remember if it was a man or a woman?"

"I'm afraid the answer is no again. It's been too long." He stood and said, "Would you like another beer?"

"Yes. Thank you."

He disappeared into the kitchen and returned with a beer for me and a refill for himself. "Let me ask you a couple of questions," he said. "You're working for Susan Melton?"

"That's right. And I think she's innocent."

"I'm sure you're right. Are you making any progress? It would be a tragedy if she were convicted."

"We're developing a strong defense. There are still a few points to be cleared up."

He picked up his glass and asked, "Do you know who did it?"

"Not yet," I said. "My goal is to clear Susan. That may not involve identifying the real killer."

"I see," he said, putting down his glass. "Is there anything else I can do for you? I'm as anxious as you to see Susan acquitted. The family has suffered enough from Melton's death."

"Do you recall what happened when he collapsed?"

"I could see he was in trouble, and I jumped up to get help. A crowd gathered. An ambulance eventually showed up."

I drank some beer. "Did anyone go near Melton, to help or even just to look?"

"Bealer and Raskin were sitting next to him, and they were trying to help. I got up and didn't see what happened at the table after that."

"Do you know of any problems that may have existed between Melton and others at the table? Maybe someone bore him a grudge?"

"That's a funny question," he said. "Bradford Melton was a hard man. He was ambitious and a tough businessman. He knew what he wanted, and most of the time he got it. Some people had trouble dealing with him. Some members of his family didn't like the way he did business. But I don't think any of them would have wanted him dead."

"I've heard that Jason Bealer was his only real friend," I said. "It's been suggested that his wife and children all hated him."

"He and Bealer were good friends, and I know that he had family problems. But I don't think they all hated him."

"He certainly didn't get along well with them."

"No. But not getting along doesn't normally lead to murder. If it did, half the world would be dead."

"Perhaps," I said. "But Melton was murdered. Someone had sufficient motivation to plan and execute the crime. Why?"

"I certainly don't know."

"Let me put it this way. Do you know of any specific problems that Melton had with anyone?"

"The only thing I can think of," he said, "is that I can remember him and Margaret Melton fighting a couple weeks before he died. I had stopped by to discuss business, and they were in the middle of a terrible argument. I didn't hear much, but it sounded as if she felt her husband was not being treated fairly at Fabricon. She always thought Henry deserved more credit because he was the designer."

"Was she right?"

"I don't think so. Sure, design is important. It's a highly competitive business. But there are many good designers.

190

Bradford Melton's business sense was unique, and Fabricon would never have enjoyed the same success without him. In my opinion, Henry Melton was a fine designer but could have been replaced."

"Some people would claim that without his designs, Fabricon would have been second-rate."

"Not in my opinion," he said. "I'm the company comptroller, and I consider only the business end. Bradford Melton was very sharp. I don't think Henry's designs were that unique."

"Anything unusual between Melton and his wife?"

"They didn't have what you'd call an ideal marriage, but they worked things out. I'd say that Alice Melton does not make a very good suspect."

"Anything with either of his children?"

"No."

"His brother or Jason Bealer?"

"Nothing."

"Billy Raskin."

"I'm afraid I can't help you there either," he said. "Although I'd say he's a good suspect. He wanted to get his hands on the Melton fortune. But there's nothing specific I can think of. I wasn't privy to family matters. I don't think I can help you in that regard."

"You have given me some useful information," I said. He had seemed nervous when I first arrived, but he was now settling down and answering with much greater confidence. It was time to talk about Prince.

"Everyone at the birthday party except Raskin was involved with Fabricon. Could Melton have done anything to anger anyone?"

"Not that I can think of."

"He wasn't trying to squeeze some of his partners out or embezzling funds?"

"Certainly not." He gulped down the rest of his drink.

"If anything funny were going on at Fabricon, I would know about it. After all, I am the company comptroller."

"I know what you were doing with Prince."

"What?"

"I know all about your Prince stock deals."

"You're crazy! How could you? Even Bradford . . . I think I've said enough. Good night."

What did he mean by "even Bradford"? Could it be a motive for murder?

"Look, Mayfield. I haven't spoken with the police yet. We can leave it that way. It's up to you."

"I have nothing further to say."

"If I go to the police, they'll know everything I know, and if there's more to find, they'll find it. If I don't talk with them, they'll probably never look at the books. Even if they do, it's unlikely they'll be as thorough as our accountant. She did a lot of research. If you won't talk to me, I'll give it all to the police."

"What do you think you know?"

"I know you and Melton moved large sums around to buy stock, and I know about the stock options. That's as much as I'll tell you. Should I call the police?"

He paced the floor. "How can I be sure you won't talk to the police anyway?"

"You can't. But I won't. I'm not that fond of them."

"I'll tell you what," he said. "I'll answer your questions and fill in details, but I won't offer any information."

I said, "Okay," recognizing that I might not discover what "even Bradford" didn't know about. "How did the original Prince project get started?"

"Five or six years ago. Melton wanted to get in on the designer jeans fad and decided to go after Prince. He bought up a lot of Prince stock. He used some of his own money and a lot of Fabricon's. It was completely above-board."

"His partners at Fabricon agreed?"

"Sure. They were all for it."

"How did the takeover come about?"

"Melton and Fabricon held enough Prince stock for Melton to be elected to the board of directors. The man who ran Prince, Jones as I recall, was rather naïve. He'd been fairly lucky, and Prince had a respectable share of the market."

"Melton then brought suit for mismanagement?"

"That's right."

"How could he if Prince was doing so well?"

"That's easy," he said. "No company is run that well. You can always find something. Melton planned it out carefully, and Jones's lawyers weren't very good."

"I've heard they were bought off."

"Could be. He changed lawyers in the middle of the case. His new attorneys did salvage something for him."

"When did the stock purchases start?"

"Right after the lawsuit. Jones had sold seventy-five percent of his stock to raise capital when jeans sales took off. Even after the takeover, more than fifty percent was outstanding, and Melton went after it."

"His original intention didn't include special options for himself?"

"That's what I thought at the time. Prince stock was undervalued after the suit. It made sense. But he was shrewd. It's hard to say."

"When did the stock options start?"

"Only a couple of years ago."

"Were you in on it from the beginning?"

"No," he said. "Melton was president and chairman of the board of both corporations. It was simple for him to give himself options as president of the corporation."

"But you had options, too."

"He was selling himself a large number of shares at low prices. It was inevitable I would find out. When I asked him about it, he gave me the impression that he was waiting for me. He immediately suggested I buy stock at similar prices."

It sounded like blackmail to me. But not a motive for murder. If anything, Melton would have wanted to get rid of Mayfield.

"With you as comptroller," I said, "it wasn't difficult to cover up the details of your arrangement."

"No, it wasn't. The other Fabricon investors had agreed to buy up Prince stock, and the stock options were footnotes in fine print."

"None of the other Fabricon investors knew about them?"

"I doubt it."

"When did you begin your own private deal?"

He stared at me and smiled. "What private deal?" It was clear there was something, but he was obviously confident that no evidence remained. He was not about to give me any details.

Ralph and I discussed the interview that evening, and he said that he could explain why Mayfield had been unable to meet with me sooner: He was busy covering his tracks. Ralph considered Mayfield to be our prime suspect, pointing out that he had handled the piña colada and that the interview implied motive. I was less sure and certainly not ready to make any accusations.

$\int$ 29

JACKSON HAYES

I telephoned Greg in the morning and described the interview with Mayfield.

"The plot thickens," he said.

"I assume you haven't heard anything from Feldnor yet."

"No. I'm sure he'll get in touch as soon as he knows anything. I'm a little nervous, Dan. There better be arsenic in that glass."

"If there isn't," I said, "You're in trouble."

"*We're* in trouble."

"It's there."

"What's your next step?"

"I'm heading north."

"North?"

"Yes. As in Oregon. Delkin has a hideaway near Florence."

"You're driving?"

"I'll keep the expenses down."

"Good! While you're at it, how 'bout serving the subpoena?"

"Good-bye, Greg."

I packed a bag and in so doing knocked over the telephone. This would have been totally insignificant except that I discovered a small metallic object taped to the bottom. A bug. Who would be snooping on me? Melton's assassin? It did dawn on me that I was getting close to a solution and might be in danger. After all, the murderer was obviously capable of murder. Private investigating is not ordinarily hazardous to my health, and the thought of potential peril was somewhat unsettling. My reaction to the bug was purely emotional. Had I had a little more class, I would have left it intact and fed the eavesdropper phony information. Instead, I smashed the thing with a hammer, hoping to give someone an earache. A second one attached to the kitchen phone was similarly disposed of. If there were others, I didn't find them.

I drove up Route 1, which winds along the Pacific coast on rugged cliffs above the ocean. I made frequent stops, enjoying the scenic grandeur. The trip was marred by the sense of being followed, which was probably caused by finding the bug, but I did see the same gray Chevy behind me more than once. I found a motel in Coos Bay, Oregon, and in the morning set Herman on a course for Florence. The gray Chevy was not in evidence.

Elaine had not known the exact location of Delkin's ranch, and I pulled into a service station in Florence for gas and information. The attendant was not familiar with Delkin, but he directed me to a nearby saloon, where the bartender, he said, would know everyone in town.

Mike's Bar and Grill was situated north of Florence overlooking the ocean. It was two o'clock when I walked in, and only two tables were occupied. I ordered a beer at the bar and said, "You must be Mike."

"You got it."

"A young fellow at P & R Gas said you know everything and everyone in Florence."

"He exaggerates."

"How about Herbert Delkin? I understand he has a spread around here."

"That's right."

"Can you tell me where it is?"

"He's a very private man. Hard to find."

"But you could help me," I said.

"Could be." I put a ten spot on the bar. He stuffed the bill in his pocket and said, "It's two miles north of town."

I held out a twenty and said, "That's as high as I'll go."

He nodded and grabbed the note. "Look for a dirt road. Vista Way. Make a right and then the second left. You can't miss it."

I thanked him and turned to leave when the gray Chevy pulled up. Two tall men in gray flannel suits strolled in. They looked like oversized accountants and could have been twins, King and Kong. They walked over to me, and Kong said, "Herbert Delkin don't like being bothered."

196

I smiled and said, "Do tell." I went back to the bar and sipped my beer.

"People that follow him tend to be accident prone."

I turned and faced him, leaning against the bar. "Don't worry fellows. I'm just enjoying the scenery. Oregon's a beautiful state."

"It would be a lot safer if you went home, Brodsky. Driving conditions are hazardous around here."

"I'll watch out for wild gorillas."

"I'm warning you, Brodsky," Kong said. "For the last time. Now get out!"

A little voice in my head said, "Shut up! These guys mean business," but my big mouth said, "I go where the spirit of Herman takes me."

King had been quiet. He stepped forward and threw a roundhouse right. I was surprised at the ease with which I ducked out of the way—until the left that followed landed squarely on my jaw, slamming me against the bar. As I went down I concluded that they were not accountants.

An elderly gentleman who had been finishing one of Mike's grilled specialties ambled over. He looked to be sixty, with graying curly hair and a round nose. He was short and stocky and carried a magazine rolled tightly in his left hand. He said, "What seems to be the problem, boys?"

Kong said, "Mind your own business, Pop."

"You're disturbing my lunch. Maybe you gentlemen should leave this poor fellow alone."

King spoke for the first time. "Pop, you could get hurt, too. Now buzz off!"

The old man remained calm and said softly, "I'm afraid I can't do that. Maybe it would be better if the two of you moseyed along."

King reached over and grabbed his shirt collar, apparently intending to toss the man on his ear. Whatever his intention, King doubled over when the magazine struck home in the belly; before Kong could react, the old man's right shot out, connected solidly, and sent him flying across the room. I watched in amazement from my prone position.

My savior extended his hand and helped me to my feet. He smiled and said, "Looks to me like you should pick on someone your own size."

"Next time," I said, "I'll keep that in mind. Can I buy you a beer?"

"Maybe we ought to get out of here. I've got some beer on ice at my place."

"That's fine with me," I said. "Sounds a lot safer, too."

King was beginning to revive, staggering to his feet. I fired as hard a punch as I could muster, and he collapsed in a heap. But it was I who let out the cry of pain: It felt as if I had broken my hand on his jaw.

The old man laughed. "Son, you might do better if there were no next time. Shall we go?" In the safety and comfort provided by Herman, he directed me to his home. "My name's Jackson Hayes," he said. "Most of my friends call me Jack."

"I'm Dan Brodsky."

He lived on a small farm outside Florence. The house was a two-bedroom cottage, tastefully furnished on a limited budget. He introduced me to his wife, Harriet, a heavyset woman in her late fifties with a warm, broad smile. She said to me, "What did you do to yourself? Run into a door?"

Jack said, "More like a fist. See what you can do for him. Take a look at his hand, too. It ran into a jaw."

We went into the kitchen where he obtained beer from the icebox while Harriet tended my wounds. "Nothing seems to be broken," she said, "but that hand may hurt a while. Your jaw should heal in a couple of days."

Jack handed me a beer, saying, "You can trust her judgment. She used to be a nurse."

I took a long swig—it was ice cold and delicious.

"That," I said, "is what I needed." I put the glass down. "Where did you learn to handle a magazine like that?"

"It's an old trick from my union days."

He was a fascinating man. Born in Alabama and reared in the Detroit ghetto, he had little formal education. He was self-educated and articulate, and the three of us spent a pleasant evening talking about politics, history, and Shakespeare. (They were not football fans, and we did not discuss the Raiders.)

His first job was in an auto plant in Flint, Michigan, at the age of seventeen. He had been working three months when a sit-down strike began because General Motors refused to recognize the union. After six weeks of intense struggle, a contract was signed and unions were established in the automobile industry.

He met Harriet after a mêlée with police during a strike. His nose had been broken by a billy club, and Harriet was a nurse in the hospital he had been taken to. They had two children, both grown and living in Portland, and had retired a year earlier and moved to Oregon.

They put me up for the night, and in the morning I had no difficulty finding Delkin's ranch. I drove past and found a vantage point two hundred yards above, which gave me a clear view of the ranch, the highway below, and the ocean to the west. There were two cars parked in the driveway: a limousine, which I assumed to be Delkin's, and the gray Chevy. I sat leaning against a tree and watched the house, trying to determine a way to trap Delkin. After a while, I realized I had no intention of tangling with King and Kong again; I would sit there watching until Delkin was on his way to San Francisco and out of my reach. I did not wait long. Delkin, his chauffeur, and a young woman emerged shortly and drove off in the limousine with King and Kong following in the Chevy. I watched them descend to the highway and head south. I was frustrated and angry—angry with myself because of my cowardice.

I revved up Herman with no particular direction in mind. I drove until I found myself on the beach at Devil's Elbow. It was a beautiful sandy beach, sprinkled with shells and driftwood. I perched myself on a huge boulder jutting fifty feet above the ocean. It was a gray, chilly day, and I sat with the wind in my face, smelling the sea, watching the cormorants and gulls soar across the sky. An occasional ship dotted the horizon, bound for unknown destinations. It was both hypnotic and invigorating.

Sitting there I understood the allure of the sea that had compelled countless mariners to roam the vast oceans; I understood why they could not live without the salt air, the great whales, the exotic ports. I imagined myself standing at the bow of a craft with sails full, headed for distant Pacific islands.

Three hours later I drove south, alive and renewed. I stopped in northern California to walk among the redwoods—no matter how often I see them, the magnificence of those old giants endures. Herbert Delkin had no right to destroy such majesty. I would serve the subpoena, accountants, secretaries, and police notwithstanding.

I crawled into bed at two A.M. and slept soundly until I was awakened by a call from Greg at nine.

"You were right about the piña colada," he said.

"Good."

"They haven't dropped the charges against Susan yet."

"They haven't? Why not?"

"Feldnor won't say," Greg said, "but he wants to meet with us. I imagine he thinks you know a lot more than you told him last week."

"That's no problem," I said. "I'll tell him who killed Melton."

"You know? Are you sure?"

"Reasonably."

"Who?"

"Who what?" I said.

"Who killed him, goddamnit."

"I don't want to mention any names over the phone."

"Danny, don't be a pain."

"You'll have to wait, Greg."

"He expects us Monday morning at nine. Sharp."

"As long as I can be back here by eleven."

"This is an important meeting," he said. "Cancel tennis."

"But Greg . . ."

"Cancel!"

"You're the boss."

"Did you serve the subpoena?"

"No. I . . ."

"Dan. You can't do this to me. The trial's coming up."

"I'll get Delkin. You can count on it."

"Fine. See you Monday."

Elaine came to Berkeley that evening and stayed to watch the Raiders' game Sunday. Oakland built an early lead from which San Diego could not recover. Next stop: the Super Bowl.

∫30

SHERMAN WEATHERSBY

Greg and I arrived at Feldnor's office at 9:00, and his secretary said, "Please be seated. He'll be with you shortly."

After waiting a few minutes I said to Greg, "I thought he wanted us here at nine *sharp*."

"That's what he said. Be patient."

It seemed to me that we were there as a favor to Feldnor, and I said to his secretary, "It is now nine oh five. Tell him I'm leaving at nine oh seven."

She knocked on his door, entered, returned, and said, "He advises against leaving."

"It's nine oh six," I said.

She went in a second time, and Feldnor came storming out. "Brodsky! What the hell do you think you're doing?"

"We're here at your request," I said. "I expect to be treated with courtesy and civility."

He stared at me and calmed down. "Give me a break, will you? Ashe is angry, the chief of police is angry, and the D.A. is angry. Everybody is angry, and I'm caught in the middle."

"Fine. But don't bring me into it."

"Okay. Okay. Would you like to come in now?"

We followed him into his office. There was an ashtray on his desk, filled with cigarette butts. "Please sit down," he said.

"Why haven't you dropped charges against Susan Melton?" I said.

"She's still our best suspect."

"You know she's not guilty, and you can't go to trial with the evidence you have."

"I'm not so sure," he said.

"Yes, you are. You haven't dropped the charges because you want something. What is it?"

"Let's put our cards on the table," he said. "If I had a better suspect than Susan Melton . . ."

"In other words," I said, "you're holding her for ransom, the ransom being the identity of the murderer."

"You know who killed him?"

"Of course. Don't you?"

"Brodsky, I'm being polite." He lit a cigarette and said, "I'll drop charges against Susan Melton and Billy Raskin. Tell me what you know."

"Roger Mayfield did it." (Yes, I had accepted Ralph's analysis.)

"Mayfield?" Feldnor said, obviously surprised. "How could he? He was sitting at the opposite end of the table from Melton."

"It's simple enough. The police weren't very thorough."

"What evidence do you have?"

"It always bothered me that the killer let suspicion fall on Susan Melton. Everyone at the table was a Melton or a close family friend. Everyone, that is, except Roger Mayfield. I was convinced the killer knew Susan had purchased Rat Ravager. Mayfield knew, and he was the one person least likely to be concerned about Susan."

"Possibly," Feldnor said, "but do you have any direct evidence?"

"I should say so. It also bothered me that your case depended on sleight of hand: Susan had to put the poison in the wine in front of witnesses. While a number of people handled the piña colada, the problem of sleight of hand existed with each of them, too. That is, except for Mayfield once again. He left the table, ostensibly to make a phone call, and returned with the piña colada."

"Do you know that for a fact?" Feldnor said.

"Yes. There are several witnesses who can testify that Mayfield brought the piña colada back with him."

"Then he had the opportunity to add the Rat Ravager to the piña colada without being seen."

"That's right," I said. "His story is that the drink was on the house. It seemed to me that if the cocktail were complimentary, it would have been given directly to Melton, not to Mayfield."

Feldnor leaned back, inhaled deeply, and closed his eyes. He sat forward and said, "That's method and opportunity. What about motive?"

"I'm afraid I can't answer that."

"You don't know?"

"I do," I said, "but I'm not at liberty to reveal that information."

"Not at liberty! Brodsky, this is a murder investigation."

"I'm sorry. I promised my source I wouldn't divulge that aspect of the case. You'll have no trouble determining a motive."

"I can't accept that. I insist you tell me what you know. And now."

"No."

"I could hold you for concealing evidence," Feldnor said.

"You could, but you won't."

"What makes you so sure?"

"Because you'd be the laughing stock of San Francisco arresting me for solving a crime that your office and the entire police department couldn't handle. I've given you the key physical evidence. It's up to you to find the motive."

He stroked his chin and stubbed out his cigarette. "All right. You have been cooperative."

We left and I said to Greg, "Satisfied?"

"Not entirely. Are you sure Mayfield is guilty?"

"Reasonably. He was the only one with the opportunity to put the arsenic in Melton's drink."

"Maybe, Dan. I'm not convinced, but it's no longer our problem."

"At last," I said. "Greg. When you talk to Susan, you might suggest she show her appreciation by sending me a check."

"I'll do that," he said.

* * *

Mayfield was arrested Tuesday afternoon.

Tuesday evening Jason Bealer telephoned. "Brodsky," he said, "I was very impressed with the way you handled the investigation, not to mention pleased with the results."

"Thank you."

"You might be interested to know the police are turning Fabricon upside down."

"I guess they want to be more thorough this time."

"Very likely," he said. "Let me say again I appreciate the job you did. If there's ever anything I can do for you, don't be afraid to ask."

"Now that you mention it," I said, "there is a favor you . . ."

"Shoot."

"Could you get me a couple tickets to the Super Bowl?"

"I had in mind a professional favor, but sure. No problem."

"It is a professional favor," I said.

"How do seats on the forty-yard line sound?"

"Great."

I called Elaine and said, "How would you like to go to New Orleans in two weeks?"

"New Orleans?"

"Yes. The Super Bowl."

"You're crazy."

"I'm serious," I said. "Delkin will be there, and I'm going to get him."

There were two phone calls the following Monday morning. The first was from Reed College asking me to come to Portland for an interview. I agreed to fly up Thursday, January 29.

The second call was made by the secretary of an attorney named Sherman Weathersby. She said, "Mr.

Weathersby would very much appreciate your meeting with him this afternoon."

"In connection with what?" I said.

"He's Roger Mayfield's attorney and would like to talk with you."

"It will have to be tomorrow," I said.

"Will two o'clock be acceptable?"

"I'll be there."

Sherman Weathersby was a high-class criminal attorney, and his suite of offices in downtown San Francisco reflected his success. I was ushered directly into his private office and was greeted by Weathersby and Roger Mayfield. Weathersby was a tall, very thin man in his fifties.

Mayfield said, "You agreed not to talk to the police."

"I said I wouldn't tell them anything you told me, and I didn't."

"Then why did they spend so much time with Fabricon's books?"

"It was the obvious place to look," I said. "I did tell them you were the culprit."

"Gentlemen, gentlemen," Weathersby said. "This will get us no place."

"I presume you want me tell you what I know," I said.

"Well, yes," he said. "But that's not primarily why I asked you here."

"What then?"

"I'd like to hire you."

"Hire me?"

"This is crazy, Weathersby," Mayfield said. "He's the one who got me into this in the first place."

"I think Mayfield's right," I said.

"Hear me out," Weathersby said. "In the first place, you know more about the case than anyone. Secondly, you did do a much better job than the police, albeit you, too, came to the wrong conclusion."

"I think he's guilty."

"I know you do. But he's not."

"It doesn't make sense to hire me. I think he's guilty."

"You needn't repeat yourself, Mr. Brodsky. I've spoken with Gregory Langley, and he . . ."

"Greg put you up to this?"

"No. He did say you were reliable and would pursue the matter even if you thought Roger were guilty. After all, you did originally think Susan Melton was guilty."

"That's true," I said. "Nonetheless, I wouldn't hire me if I were in your place."

"At least we agree on something," Mayfield said.

"I'm the one who will defend you, Roger," Weathersby said. "You'll have to trust me in this matter."

"I'm not at all sure I care to spend any more time on this case," I said.

"Mr. Brodsky," Weathersby said, "if we were to hire another investigator now, it would cost thousands of dollars to have him learn what you already know."

"I can give you or your investigator what I know for considerably less," I said. "I won't charge you anything."

"It's not the same as getting it firsthand," he said. "No, Mr. Brodsky, you're the man for the job. We'll make it worth your while."

"I'm not going to pay him to get me out of the trouble he got me into," Mayfield said.

"You will," Weathersby said. "Time and expenses plus a five-thousand-dollar bonus if he uncovers evidence to clear you."

"How will I collect from him?" I said.

"I will guarantee your fee," Weathersby said.

"In writing?"

"Yes."

"The bonus will have to be ten thousand," I said.

"Five."

"You have been talking to Greg," I said.

He shuffled through a file on his desk. He said, "I've taken the liberty of drawing up a contract. You can have this copy."

There I was, on the job again. Bizarre. Now that Mayfield was my client, I of course assumed he was innocent. I needed that bonus.

∫31

∫ FRANÇOISE JOURNET

I went to Le Petit Chateau from Weathersby's office. Ashe was there with two uniformed officers when I arrived. He was talking with Jean Martinot, the maître d'.

"You!" Ashe said when he saw me.

"Hello, Inspector," I said.

"What are you doin' here, Brodsky?"

"I'm hungry."

"You're not wanted. Get out."

"You don't have that authority," I said.

"Wanna bet? There's always interfering with an official investigation. You I could bust for being a pain in the ass. Do you know how much trouble you've caused me?"

"You should have listened to me two weeks ago."

"Brodsky, I don't want to see your face." He saw Herman through the window and said, "Is that your jalopy? Jasper!"

"Yessir?" one of the patrolman said.

"You see that old heap in front? Make sure it can pass inspection."

"Yessir."

"And be sure," Ashe said, "there's time on the meter."

I followed the patrolman outside. He went over Herman carefully, checking everything he could think of. Jake had done his job, and he found nothing wrong. I drove off before Ashe came up with any more bright ideas.

I called Weathersby's office and Mayfield was still there. I wanted to talk to him alone and said, "Mayfield, I'd like to ask you a few more questions. Will you be in your apartment later?"

"I'm leaving here soon. I'll be home in half an hour."

"See you then."

He was considerably less cordial when I arrived than he had been the first time I was there.

He said, "I can't believe I'm paying you after all you've done."

"I'm sorry. It was my job. The only thing I can say is I'll do my best to prove you're innocent."

"So now you think I'm innocent?"

"As soon as you became my client. Let me ask you a couple of questions."

"What do you want to know?"

"May I sit down?" He nodded and I sat on the sofa. "The key is the piña colada: How did the poison find its way into the drink?"

"I'm sure I don't know," he said.

"That wasn't the question." I looked at him and said, "You have every right to dislike me, and if you insist, I'll quit, regardless of what Weathersby thinks. But he's right. I do know more about this case than anyone, and that includes the police."

"I haven't asked you to quit."

"Will you cooperate?"

He sighed and said, "What do you want to know?"

"Everything there is to know about the piña colada.

You gave it to Margaret Melton, she gave it to Bealer, and he gave it to Melton. Is that correct?"

"Yes. I'm a lot clearer than I was two weeks ago. I've thought about that piña colada ever since I was arrested."

"Good. Did either Bealer or Margaret Melton hold the drink for any length of time?"

"I doubt it. They would have passed it on to Melton."

"Did anyone go over to Melton after the piña colada was in front of him?"

"No."

"You're sure?"

"Yes," he said.

"Did anything happen that could have had the effect of creating a diversion?"

"A diversion?"

"Yes," I said. "Perhaps someone dropped a fork or broke a glass. Anything that might draw attention away from the piña colada and give the killer a chance to spike it."

"I see what you mean. As a matter of fact, Susan spilled some wine on Raskin. But I think that was before I made the telephone call."

"You're sure it was before?"

"No."

"Can you think of anything at all out of the ordinary? Something that probably seems minor."

"Not really. It was an ordinary dinner party until Melton collapsed."

"Now. Assuming you're innocent . . ."

"I am."

I nodded. "Someone put the arsenic in the drink. Who gave you the drink?"

"Someone in the restaurant. They said it was for Melton. On the house."

"Do you know it was an employee?"

"No. It's just what they said."

"It was not the waiter or waitress who served your table?"

"No. I'm sure it wasn't," he said.

"And not the maître d'?"

"Definitely not."

"Could it have been the bartender?"

"Possibly, but I doubt it."

"Was it a man or a woman?"

"I'm sorry," he said, "I can't remember."

"We're not getting very far," I said. "Keep thinking about that piña colada, and call me if you remember anything. Anything at all."

"I will."

"One last question. The telephone call. What time did you make it?"

"Eight o'clock. I called around then every evening."

"Because your mother was ill?"

"That's right."

"Who knew you made those calls?"

"Certainly Bradford and Alice."

"Anyone else?"

"I don't know. Maybe."

I stood to leave and said, "May I use your phone?"

"Sure. It's in the kitchen."

I called Le Petit Chateau and asked to speak to Jean Martinot.

"This is Dan Brodsky."

"Ah. Monsieur Brodsky. The police, they are not very friendly toward you."

"No," I said. "Ashe is mad at me for proving Susan Melton innocent."

"Mais oui. That explains it. They have been here three times, disrupting everything."

"I'm sorry," I said.

"It is not your fault, Monsieur. How may I be of assistance?"

"I have a few more questions to ask, but I don't want to interfere with the operation of the restaurant."

"Come here at eleven. It will be quiet."

"Fine. I'll be there."

I was punctual and Martinot greeted me with a smile. "Please be seated," he said. "Would you like some coffee?"

"Yes, I would. Let me ask you a question first. You have treated me graciously, and I appreciate it. But why?"

"You have been courteous and considerate. Unlike the police. When you came here the first time, you could have threatened me because the Meltons are, shall we say, influential. You did not." I shrugged. He said, "I will get your coffee. Françoise and Peter will . . ."

"Peter?"

"Oui. He described to me what happened. He is a good boy."

He went into the kitchen and returned shortly with coffee and a pastry. Françoise and Peter joined us, and Peter said, "Hi, Dan."

"Hello, Peter."

"I talked to Ray Boulanger at State. He wants me to go back to school."

"Will you?"

"Maybe," he said. "Are you still working on the Melton case? I thought Susan Melton was cleared."

"She was. I'm working for Roger Mayfield."

"He's not guilty?"

"No."

"How can we help?"

"I'd like to clarify a couple of points. Did anyone spill some wine?"

"Oui, Monsieur," Françoise said. "Mademoiselle Melton. She knocked over a glass. I cleaned up after her."

"Was that before or after Melton got the piña colada?"

"I do not know."

"You had not served any hors d'oeuvres, but Peter had. Is that correct?"

"I had not served the hors d'oeuvres," she said.

"I did," Peter said.

"When the wine was spilled, Françoise, were there hors d'oeuvres on the table?"

"Non."

"You're certain?"

"Oui."

"Roger Mayfield said someone handed him the piña colada saying it was on the house. Did any of you give it to him?"

"No," Françoise said. "If we had a cocktail for Monsieur Melton, we would give it directly to him."

"Who on your staff might have given Mayfield the piña colada?"

"No one," Martinot said. "If he were given a complimentary cocktail, it would never be given to a customer to bring to the table."

"That's what I thought," I said, standing. "Thank you for your patience."

I was at an impasse. Mayfield certainly seemed to be the only one with the opportunity to put the Rat Ravager in the drink. Ralph suggested that Raskin could have done it when the wine was spilled. Possibly, except the evidence indicated that the piña colada was not yet on the table. I was satisfied that Mayfield was innocent. Some detail was missing or overlooked.

It all seems so simple now, but I was baffled then.

∫32
NANCY CHOU

The next day I pored over my notes and Ashe's file, looking for that small detail that would unravel the mystery. The obvious direction to go was to interview the other witnesses from Le Petit Chateau. But there were a hundred people—a monumental task. Two additional avenues of investigation suggested themselves, and I began with a phone call to Eddie Washington, a friend of mine from my days in SDS.

"Eddie, do you remember the Fabricon strike last spring?"

"Sure. I walked the picket lines often enough."

"Do you know a woman named Nancy Chou?"

"Yes. She was one of the strike leaders. A good woman."

"Can you put me in touch with her?" I said.

"If you like. What should I tell her?"

"I'm investigating the Melton murder. I'd like to ask her a few questions."

"I'll call her now." He called back a while later and said she would meet me the next evening.

She lived in Berkeley and admitted me to a one-room studio apartment. She was five-feet-five-inches tall with long, flowing black hair. She spoke perfect English.

"Sit down," she said. "Would you like some coffee?"

"Yes. Thank you." Her kitchen consisted of a sink, a stove, and a refrigerator built into the wall, hidden by sliding doors. Her coffee was acceptable.

"Eddie said you were investigating the Melton murder," she said.

"That's right."

"I almost refused to talk to you."

"Why?"

"Melton wasn't one of my favorite people," she said.

"Then why are you talking with me?"

"Eddie said you were all right, that you've spent a lot of time supporting strikes."

"That's true," I said. "Especially in my student days."

"Why are you investigating?"

"I was hired by the defendant's attorney," I said. "You didn't like Melton very much . . ."

She snickered, then laughed, an almost hysterical laugh. "Words to express the depth of my hatred do not exist," she said. "He was horrible, depraved, cruel . . ."

"Why do you have such strong feelings about Melton? There are lots of rotten bosses—was he that different?"

"Yes. You can't know how evil he was."

"Tell me about him," I said.

"My family left Taiwan in 1957. My sister was three years old, and they ended up in San Francisco, not entirely legally. My father got a job in a restaurant in Chinatown, and my mother worked for Fabricon as a seamstress."

"You were born here?"

"Yes. In 1958. My mother may have been pregnant when they arrived in San Francisco."

"Being classified as 'illegal aliens' must have made it difficult," I said.

"Certainly. Both of my parents worked twelve hours a day, six days a week for rotten wages, afraid to complain for fear of being deported. We lived in a one-room flat smaller than my apartment. My parents saved nickels and dimes to insure that my sister and I would get educated. Somehow, we got by."

"What happened?"

"My father died when I was thirteen. Patty was about to start at San Francisco State."

"Patty's your sister?"

"Yes. My father's death prevented her from going to school."

"Why? There are scholarships. You could have . . ."

"They were afraid to apply for financial aid because Patty was born in Taiwan. She was still illegal."

"What did she do?" I said.

"She went to work for Fabricon."

"I assume we're getting close to the reason for your particular animosity for Melton."

"Yes," she said. "Patty was less passive than many of the other seamstresses. She quietly spoke about organizing a union and tried to bring in the ILGWU."

"Did she have any success?"

"She was beginning to. One day Melton showed up at the plant and asked her to speak with him privately. He took her into a small office where he raped and beat her. She was in a coma for four months and died."

"I see," I said. "I think I remember something about Melton being accused of rape."

"It did get some publicity," she said. "Not much. Melton was never tried. My mother still hasn't recovered." She looked off into space. "Neither have I." Then she said, "They fired my mother. Supposedly for not coming to work after my sister . . ." She put her face in her hands and cried.

I put my arm around her and said softly, "He did get what he deserved."

"Yes. I only wish he had been made to suffer the way my sister did."

She composed herself, and I said, "How did you end up working for Fabricon?"

"I wanted to get Melton. The only thing I could think of was organizing a union."

"They hired you after all that happened?"

"They didn't know I was Patty's sister. They're not that smart."

"You were more successful than your sister."

"Not really," she said. "There was a strike. It lasted three weeks. But Melton won. He used every trick in the book. Injunctions, arrests, police brutality."

"I remember. You had a lot of support, too."

"We did. That's how we maintained the strike as long as we did. Then he got Immigration to help him. They deported several women, and that broke the strike."

"What did you do next?"

216

"Nothing. I went back to school."

"Berkeley?"

"Yes," she said.

There were a number of questions I would have liked to ask her. Did she know anything about threats against Melton's life? Had she ever been to Le Petit Chateau? Did she know anyone who might have acted against Melton? But I refrained. I would implicate Bealer before Nancy Chou, and if I were to determine the murderer, it would not be with information from her. I thanked her and left, wondering if I really wanted to find the killer.

∫33

∫ HERBERT DELKIN

Super Bowl Sunday was approaching, and further investigation into the Melton murder was postponed. Elaine and I flew to New Orleans Friday evening and spent Saturday in the role of tourists.

We went to the Superdome Sunday afternoon with two goals in mind: a Raider victory and a served subpoena. Determining where Delkin would be was easy: His seat location appeared in the *Chronicle*. Reaching him was another matter, and I decided to wait until the game was in progress.

Oakland kicked off, and after one first down, the Raiders' Rod Martin intercepted a Jaworski pass. A few plays later it was Oakland 7, Philadelphia 0. A few minutes later a fifteen-yard Plunkett-to-King pass became an eighty-yard touchdown.

It was time to make my move. The game wasn't over, but the outcome was no longer in doubt. There was also no doubt that I would get Delkin this time. I proceeded to the appropriate section of the stadium and watched him from a vantage point twenty rows above his seat. He was accompanied by a dozen youngsters. The only difficulty was his two accountants: King and Kong were by his side. I did not see his secretary, Joan Chakeley.

I went to New Orleans prepared for as many different circumstances as I could foresee. This included bringing a telephone message memo pad. I jotted down, "The private eye with the papers is seated in section E-11," and indicated the phone call had come from Joan Chakeley. Section E-11 was across the stadium, and the pad I used would make the note appear legitimate.

I approached a nearby stadium guard and flashed my investigator's license. It looked official, at least as long as the guard didn't have the opportunity to examine it carefully. I said to him, "You know Herbert Delkin's here?"

"Yessir," he said, pointing in Delkin's direction. "I've been keeping my eye on him."

"Good. He received an important telephone message. Would you give it to him?"

"Certainly, sir."

I watched him descend to Delkin's seat and dispatch the message. Delkin read it and whispered something to King (or was it Kong?), who jumped up and looked around. He tapped Kong on the shoulder, and they marched off intending to finish the job they had begun in Oregon. I waited five minutes and made my way for Delkin. Would he remember me or my name? Probably not, and it wouldn't matter if he did. I sat next to him as Philadelphia put three points on the board. "My name is Brodsky, Mr. Delkin. Dan Brodsky." I showed him my press pass. "I'm with the *Orinda Weekly News*."

"Yes?" he said.

"We're not really interested in the game itself—we

don't even have a sports section. But we do care about the human interest angle."

"Of course," he said. "We take a dozen underprivileged youngsters to the Super Bowl every year . . ." He described the program and answered my questions. This was perfect. It would provide me with an article for the *News,* and I owed them one. We sat there chatting pleasantly, watching the game. I even got hot dogs for two of his young guests. The Raiders tried and missed a field goal and then blocked a Philadelphia attempt.

Toward the end of the quarter, I caught sight of King and Kong returning. They looked frustrated, and I had no intention of becoming the object of their frustration. I quickly said to Delkin, "Thank you for the interview. It will appear in next week's paper." I stood and said, "Oh, by the way. I have something for you." I handed him the subpoena and moved to the aisle. King and Kong approached, and I said, "You're a little late fellows." I walked off and returned to my seat to enjoy the second half.

The Raiders continued their domination and the final score was 27–10. It was a most satisfying afternoon.

We caught a plane that evening, and half the passengers had been to the game. They were loyal Raider fans; the ride home was jovial.

∫34
CALVIN AMES

The Raiders were the Super Bowl champs; Delkin had been served; it was time to wrap up the Melton case. Unfortunately, it was not at all clear how to proceed. There was another problem: The trip to New Orleans cleaned me out. I called Susan Melton.

"Susan. You recall that you promised a bonus for finding your father's killer?"

"Yes. Do you know who did it?"

"Roger Mayfield was arrested with information I supplied."

"I heard," she said, "but I thought you were now working for him."

"I am, but . . ."

"Do you still think he's guilty?"

"Well, no. But . . ."

"Dan, when you really solve the case, I'll be happy to pay the bonus. Not before."

I called Greg. "Can you get PURE to pay me soon? I'm kind of tapped out."

"Probably. They were happy when I spoke to them. But they're not that rich, and I'm not sure how they'll feel about footing the bill for a trip to the Super Bowl."

"I did it for their damn subpoena."

"Sure. I guess it was just a coincidence that the Raiders were playing."

"What d'ya' want from my poor life?"

"Dan, I can loan you a few hundred."

"I'll need it."

Desperate for the bonus from Mayfield, I went to the Berkeley House and Garden Shop, vaguely hoping that something would turn up. There was a young man behind the counter, and I said, "Are you Calvin Ames?"

"No," he said. "May I be of assistance?"

"I'd like to speak with Mr. Ames. Do you know when he'll be available?"

"He's in the office. I'll see if he can talk to you."

Calvin Ames, a short, middle-aged man with curly hair, graying at the temples, had sold the Rat Ravager to Susan. When the young man returned with Ames, I introduced myself and showed him a copy of his sworn statement from the police file.

"This is your statement?" I said.

He examined it and said, "Yes."

"Do you remember the customer you were serving?"

"No. It's been a long time, and I serve a lot of people."

"Do you remember anything at all about him?"

"No."

"Man or woman?"

"No. Nothing."

"Do you have any records that might identify him?"

"If it was a 'him'," he said. "As a matter of fact, we might. We normally put the customer's name on the receipt."

"Do you keep the receipts here?"

"What was the date?"

"November eighth of last year," I said.

"It could be in the back. Would you like me to check?"

"Yes. Please do."

"Come with me."

I followed him into a small office. He looked through a filing cabinet and withdrew a folder marked November 1980 containing yellow sheets of paper. He removed a batch and said, "This is the day's receipts."

"There must be over a hundred," I said.

"It was a Saturday."

"Is there any way to cull it down?"

"I don't think so," he said.

"Did you personally make all these sales?"

"No."

"But you did make the sale to the customer in your statement?"

"Yes."

"Could we pull out the ones in your handwriting?" I said.

"I suppose. Sounds like a lot of work."

"Mr. Ames, a man's life is at stake."

He agreed and found twenty-eight receipts representing sales he had made that day.

"Is there any way we can eliminate some of these?" I said. "Perhaps there are regular customers among them?"

He did recognize four names and was certain none was the name of the customer in question. Half the remaining names were almost illegible, but he was able to decipher most of them. There were three names he could not determine, although some of the letters were identifiable. I wrote down the other twenty-one.

"May I take these three receipts?" I said. "I'll return them in a few days."

He began to say something, and I said, "Remember. A man's life is at stake."

He smiled and said, "Okay. Be sure to return them."

"By the way, did you know Susan Melton before she came in here?"

"No. Never saw her before."

"Any other Meltons?"

"Certainly not."

I thanked him and went to Ralph's place. Our first task was to compare the list of twenty-one names from Ames with the police list of witnesses from Le Petit Chateau. None matched nor had Ames himself been there. Of course, one of the illegible three might have been.

The next three days were spent tracking down the twenty-one people on the list. Fourteen lived in or near Berkeley, and after speaking with them, I was satisfied none could assist with the investigation. Three lived in San Francisco and were similarly eliminated. Two were out of town, but based on statements of spouses, it was clear that neither had useful information. There were two not listed in any Bay Area phone book, and I was unable to locate them. For practical reasons, I assumed they were not related to the case. Ralph thought that that was sloppy on my part, but I saw no alternative. The three illegible names remained. One was likely to be the customer in Ames' statement, although it was hardly clear that finding that person would further the investigation.

I flew to Portland Thursday morning for the interview at Reed College. I had been puzzling over the Melton case instead of preparing for the interview, and it went badly; Reed would not offer me a position.

I was depressed on the plane ride home because of the interview and because of my inability to solve the Melton murder. Accusing Mayfield had been convenient, but Greg had raised questions that led me to doubt his guilt. Now that Mayfield was a client, I had no difficulty convincing myself of his innocence.

The basic sequence of events leading to Melton's demise seemed clear. The only problem was that, as I saw it, no one could have killed him.

I had come to a number of conclusions before the trip to Portland. First, I had rejected coincidences that could not be accounted for. Coincidences do occur; Elliot Fielder/Peter Jones is an obvious example. But coincidences of that sort are rare, and I could not accept the notion that the murderer would have chosen the same poison that Susan had purchased *purely by coincidence*, although it was possible that the culprit was an employee of Le Petit Chateau since the poison was stored there in the cellar. Otherwise, the killer must have known that Susan Melton had bought the Rat Ravager.

I also rejected sleight of hand as a means of administering the poison. Jason Bealer and Margaret Melton both handled the piña colada, but only in full view of the other participants at the dinner. The spilled wine might have been used as a diversion, but the evidence was that the spill occurred before the piña colada was served.

Greg was skeptical about Mayfield's guilt because Mayfield did not have the opportunity to dump the piña colada into the ice bucket. That was clear since he was at the opposite end of the table from Melton, and he left the table immediately after Melton collapsed. It is possible Melton himself knocked over the piña colada when he fell. But if he did, it was *very* convenient for the murderer, and once again we're left with a coincidence. Much more likely, the killer emptied the remains of the cocktail into the ice bucket during the commotion. No sleight of hand was required: All eyes were upon the stricken victim.

In sum, I had concluded that the murderer had to satisfy three conditions: First, he or she must have known Susan had purchased Rat Ravager; second, he or she must have had the opportunity to administer the poison without being seen; and third, the killer must have been near Melton after he collapsed.

The difficulty with these conditions was that none of the suspects could have satisfied all three. Jason Bealer, Margaret Melton, and Rachel Janeway, for example, were near the body, but none knew Susan had purchased Rat Ravager. Ralph, Raskin, and Alice Melton did not have the opportunity to add the poison to the piña colada. The remaining suspects could be similarly eliminated.

When Ralph and I talked before the trip to Portland, he was confused, too. We discussed the question of motive. Melton was an odious, abomination of a man; virtually anyone might have wanted to kill him. As a result, we decided to ignore motive and to concentrate on finding an individual who knew that Susan had purchased Rat Ravager, who had the opportunity to mix it with the piña colada, and who was near the body when Melton collapsed. We concluded that no one could have done it.

On the plane home from Portland, I stared at the three receipts and carefully examined my notes and the file that Ashe had given me, searching for some key overlooked detail. Unable to decipher them, I crumpled up the receipts in disgust.

It occurred to me that an important piece of evidence could still be missing, reminding me of *undecidability* in mathematics. A half century ago, a mathematician named Kurt Gödel showed that there exist mathematical propositions that can be neither proven nor disproven within a given axiom system. Proofs may exist with additional axioms, but then some other statements would be undecidable. For example, several mathematicians spent many years trying to prove a conjecture known as the *continuum hypothesis* until Paul Cohen showed that it was undecidable. Nevertheless, we generally assume that the problems on which we work are solvable.

Regarding the evidence in the Melton case as axioms, it was possible that the "axioms" were not strong enough to solve the crime. If that were true, it was likely the killer would never be revealed. I have never accepted that possibility while doing research, and I therefore assumed that all the evidence was in, that the solution lay before me. Reviewing the interviews with the various witnesses, I remembered a chance remark and Larry's comment about the timing. Suddenly the pieces fit.

I decided to discuss my solution with Ralph before going to the police or to Sherman Weathersby. When the plane landed in San Francisco I drove straight to his apartment.

∫35

∫ BRADFORD MELTON

Ralph and Mary were both home, and I got right to the point. "I have two questions: Why did you do it, and why did you frame Susan?"

"That's not a very funny joke," he said.

"It's no joke. I know the two of you did it."

"That's ridiculous."

"No. In fact, the answer to those two questions is all that's missing."

"Tell me about it."

"You recall that we concluded that there were three conditions the murderer had to satisfy?"

"Yes."

"And that no one suspect could satisfy all three?"

He nodded.

"What brought it together for me was realizing that while no one person could have killed him, two working in consort could."

"There are lots of ways you can pair up people to satisfy your three conditions."

"Not that many if we assume the piña colada was not spiked in full view of witnesses."

"Suppose Mayfield did it, and someone was working with him?"

"That did occur to me. But who? Certainly not Bealer; I knew of no connection between Mayfield and Rachel Janeway. I considered everyone who was near the body, and none made a good partner for him."

"What about Raskin?"

"I thought of that, too. But it just didn't feel right. And you, or rather Mary, made one slip. The first time we met, she admitted being at the restaurant."

"That was a slip?" she said.

"No. In fact, you didn't have much choice since the police had your name. But you also told me that you were there because you wanted a chance to speak with Ralph."

"That's right. He had refused to see me."

"That was your mistake: If you hadn't seen him, how did you know he'd be at Le Petit Chateau that night?"

"Ralph could've told me over the phone."

"No. You said that he'd refused to answer your calls."

"Anyone could've told me."

"Who? It would be easy to check. We could call right now."

She didn't answer, and I continued. "I'm sure you were surprised when a policeman wouldn't let anyone leave the restaurant. Had you been able to leave quietly, it would've been impossible to prove your guilt. But they did have your name, and you needed to explain why you were there."

Neither spoke, so I said, "Mary, you should have left the restaurant as soon as you gave Mayfield the drink. Why did you wait?"

Ralph laughed. "You don't have much of a case."

"I think I do. Melton, his wife, and Mayfield visited Susan that afternoon and saw the Rat Ravager. You were there, too, and so you knew about the poison. I suspect you'd been planning it for a while, and the Rat Ravager was just a convenience." They sat quietly, saying nothing. "It was a simple matter for you to call Mary and have her buy the poison. All she had to do was order the piña colada, spike it, and hand it to Mayfield saying it was on the house. You did the rest, *accidently* knocking over the piña colada and the wineglass when you rushed to Melton's aid."

"There are two problems with your theory. First, how could we be sure Mary wouldn't be recognized, and . . ."

"That's easy. The only ones at the dinner party who knew her were Melton himself and Alice and Susan. You knew they'd be there early, so all Mary had to do was be sure to arrive around seven. Even if one of them got up to use the john, the restaurant was crowded, and she'd've had no difficulty avoiding being seen. The second problem?"

"How could we be sure someone would leave the table?

It had to be someone who Mary would know but would not know her."

"That, too, is easy," I said. "Mayfield called his mother every evening. You knew he wouldn't recognize Mary. And she didn't have to recognize him—she merely needed to see a man from the back room use the telephone."

"How could I have known Mayfield called his mother every night?"

"Several Meltons knew, so you must have, too. You were the discreet bodyguard, quiet and unobtrusive, hardly noticed. But you were aware of everybody's activities."

"You're reaching. Wouldn't Mayfield have remembered that Mary had given him the piña colada?"

"Why would he? Her giving him the drink didn't become significant until long after it happened."

"You'll never get a conviction," he said.

"That's not my job, and I have no interest in a conviction anyway. But I suspect the police will be able to put it together once they know the exact chain of events."

He sat back and sighed. He looked at Mary, and she nodded.

"Will you answer my two questions?"

"It doesn't matter now, does it?"

"No."

"We weren't trying to frame Susan. We thought the wine, the piña colada, and the Rat Ravager would confuse the issue. When we first planned it, we were afraid Mayfield would be accused. We hoped the Rat Ravager would prevent that."

"And the motive?"

"When I first went to work for Melton, I was still a cop. He ran a check on me and met my ex-partner, who had become a drug addict. We had been in the narcotics squad, and he'd been dealing in drugs. He resigned when

I found out, and I never reported him. Melton must have paid him off because he showed me a statement implicating me in dealing."

"Melton was blackmailing you?"

"Not at first. He didn't say anything to me when he got the information. But about a year ago, he asked me to move onto his estate."

"And you didn't want to?"

"It was more than that," Mary said. "Ralph had been putting in very long hours. That's what started our marital problems. We'd been fighting about his job for a couple of months."

Ralph said, "I told Melton that it would be difficult for Mary. He said he'd talk to her. He did a lot more than talk."

He looked at Mary, and she said, "Melton could be a charming man when he wanted to be, and I was very angry at Ralph."

"Ralph found out about your affair with him?"

"It wasn't an affair. It only happened once. And Ralph didn't *find out*. I told him."

"I was seething," Ralph said. "I told Melton I quit. That was when he threatened to expose what he knew."

"Would that have been so bad?"

"Yes. He could've made it almost impossible for me to find another job. He claimed he had enough on me to get me sentenced to prison."

"So you broke up with Mary and stayed on with Melton?"

"Right. He was an arrogant, horrible man. I hated him more and more every day."

"That's when you began developing your plan to kill him."

"Not exactly. I was biding my time, trying to figure out what to do. Mary and I met to discuss the divorce. We ended up deciding to try to work things out but didn't know how to do it because of Melton. I couldn't quit, and it was impossible for Mary and me to live together on the estate."

"So you decided that murder was your only way out."

"Yes." He looked at me. "Bradford Melton was an evil man."

"Mary, I'm still confused about why you didn't leave the restaurant as soon as you gave Mayfield the piña colada. I assume you expected to have at least an hour before the poison took effect, but wouldn't it have been safer to leave right away?"

"Ralph cautioned me against doing anything that would make anyone remember me. Once I was seated, I had to order. I was in the middle of my dinner when Mayfield made the telephone call. It was easy enough to order the drink from the bar and give it to him. But if I left without paying, I might be remembered."

"Then why not ask for your check right away?"

"Because asking for a check without finishing the meal might be remembered."

"That was my fault," Ralph said. "I was sure she'd have no difficulty leaving inconspicuously if she had dinner normally. First of all, it should have been at least an hour before Melton showed any symptoms."

"Yeah, that fits. In fact, realizing that the killer might've been depending on having that much time helped me determine what happened."

"Why should that be important?"

"Because the time would matter only to someone who was not in the Melton party. On the other hand, it seemed that the murderer had to be in the back room. The only explanation was two people."

Ralph shook his head in despair. "I was so sure that even if something happened before Mary left, the police wouldn't act until at least the next day."

"And by then no one would remember her."

230

"Exactly."

"When we first met, Mary, why did you tell me your name?"

"It would've been worse to lie. You'd have eventually found out who I was, and the lie would give us away."

"That's right," Ralph said. "Once the police had her name, I told her to be honest about everything. Except of course about the piña colada. Once you get caught lying, you've had it."

"One last question. You decided to get back together. But then you were divorced anyway, and Mary went back to her maiden name."

"We felt so trapped," he said. "Once we decided to, well, to do it, it seemed safer to go through with the divorce and not be seen together."

"Dan," Mary said, "try to understand. We had very few options."

The case was solved, but I wasn't very happy about it. Ralph and Mary were caught up in circumstances created by a malevolent man; they were not my image of murderers. I said, "It's a long weekend, and I have lots of work to do. I doubt if I'll get a chance to contact the police before Tuesday. By the way, I understand it's nice in Brazil this time of year."

I, in fact, spent the weekend relaxing with Elaine. After a good tennis match with Jim on Monday, I stopped at several electronics stores, planning the new stereo I would buy with the bonus from Mayfield. I picked out a $2,500 system that was far superior to the one that had been destroyed by the leaky roof.

I was in a good mood when I called Sherman Weathersby Tuesday morning to tell him the good news. His secretary put me through right away.

"Brodsky," he said, "I wasn't expecting to hear from you."

"I've solved the Melton murder, and Mayfield's in the clear."

"What are you trying to pull?"

"Nothing. I know who did it."

"So do I. Ralph Cordova and Mary Clark confessed yesterday. They made some kind of deal and probably won't serve more than a couple of years."

"But I figured out . . ."

"Even if you did, it doesn't matter."

"But what about my bonus?"

"The bonus was for getting Roger off. You didn't do that."

"But . . ."

"No buts, Brodsky, and no bonus. Good-bye!"

So much for my new stereo.